# ROBERT RUSSELL

# *Go On, I'm Listening*

PAN BOOKS LONDON AND SYDNEY

First published 1983 by Souvenir Press Ltd
This edition published 1985 by Pan Books Ltd,
Cavaye Place, London SW10 9PG

9 8 7 6 5 4 3 2 1

© Robert Russell 1983

ISBN 0 330 28546 7

Printed and bound in Great Britain by
Hunt Barnard Printing Ltd, Aylesbury, Bucks

*All the characters in this book are imaginary.
Any resemblance to actual persons, whether living or dead,
is purely coincidental and completely unintentional.*

TO DOROTHY

# 1

On a cold Monday morning in early January I drove up the main Mottley road from Wishton General Hospital. The hospital canteen breakfast lurked around like a restless predator underneath my diaphragm. I glanced anxiously at the sketch of the surgery's whereabouts which I had taped to the dashboard in such a way as to hide the oil-pressure and temperature gauges: both instruments were giving me information which I preferred not to know, for the sixteen-year-old Austin Somerset was terminally sick. I was relieved when the steep winding road levelled out and I passed a sign which read: "Mottley welcomes new industry. Please drive carefully – sheep".

I had been married for twelve months, qualified for eighteen months and been broke for as long as I could remember. At the time I was working each night in the Casualty Department of Wishton General as a Casualty Officer, so that Tanya and I saw little of one another. But the offer of fifty pounds a week for a month as locum for Dr. Lilian Atherton in Mottley was an opportunity too good to miss. Even so, a twelve-hour stint in Casualty was not the ideal aperitif for what was to be my first taste of general practice.

The road twisted round to the right, then plunged abruptly down a steep incline. I could see the town below through a faint pall of smoke from the chimneys of the dense huddle of terraced stone cottages which seemed to lurch up and down the steep narrow streets of the centre. Mottley lay on the border between Lancashire and Yorkshire, and was hidden from view until this bend in the road was reached. It was separated from Wishton by soft, round, sheep-nibbled hills on one side, and on the other side was separated from

7

Yorkshire by the cold, wet high moors of the Pennines. It seemed as alien as another planet.

I drove down the main street, stopping at the traffic lights. A butcher in a blue and white striped apron stepped out of his shop doorway and gave me a blank stare as he wiped his hands on a cloth which steamed in the cold morning air.

I turned off the main road into a narrow street lined with small stone cottages and one or two shops which, through their dark dusty windows, I could see contained very little apart from dummy soap packets and Player's advertisements. At the end of the street was the surgery, and I had to drive the car round the unruly front garden via a cobbled cul-de-sac to the rear. A rusty wrought-iron gate led into the back garden which was waist high in couch grass and rose bay willow herb, and as I fought my way to the rear door I caught sight of a very old Daimler limousine up to its axles in the soft earth. The broken running boards were covered with moss, and sparrows were flying in and out through the open rear windows.

The back door was open and I went into the cluttered kitchen. A grey cat with eyes like an owl stared from the top of the kitchen range and I stared back. Suddenly a voice behind me made me jump.

"My word, you're here early. What's up – did you wet the bed this morning?"

I turned and saw that the voice belonged to a small, grey-haired woman in her late sixties. She had a deeply lined face which creased into a mosaic when she smiled. She was made to look bulkier than she actually was by the thick woollen sweater she wore over her tweed skirt and she had a long coarsely-knitted scarf around her neck.

"The last locum we had never got here before half past ten in the morning, then used to spend the next half-hour sobering up and blowing his nose in the sink. I'm Annie Lewis, Dr. Atherton's housekeeper and receptionist. You're Dr. Rushton, I heard you were coming." We shook hands and she stood back, smiling.

"You don't look long out of medical school, really. Well,

8

if you get stuck or can't find anything, just ask me. Dr. Atherton had her own way of doing things round here, but I expect you'll settle in soon enough. I'll show you the surgery, then you can get on. There's a few waiting to see you."

I followed her into the consulting room and looked round in dismay. Through the single grimy window there was just enough light to see that it was a mess. I switched on the main light — a sixty watt bulb on the end of a knotted flex which snaked from the flaky ceiling. The desk was covered with mounds of unopened letters, drug samples, pamphlets, cotton wool buds and tongue-depressors. Behind was an ancient swivel chair which, judging by the angle of the seat, was going to fall apart any minute. Heaped in every direction were dusty record-cards, and a bank of filing cabinets by the back wall had not been touched in years. I stumbled across to a door on one wall and opened it with difficulty. Inside was an examination couch covered with brown paper; it was impossible to go into the room for the floor was covered with piles of out-of-date drug samples. By a tiny window over the couch was a portrait of the young king George VI.

I carefully sat down on the swivel chair, feeling very vulnerable. With no diagnostic aids apart from my own five senses and with no knowledge or experience of the sort of problems that would present themselves over the next four weeks, I began to wish that I was back in the safe womb of the hospital. Annie Lewis could see the expression on my face. She laughed quietly.

"I told you Dr. Atherton had her own way of doing things. You'll be all right. Just remember that folk round here want you to look as if you know what you're doing but don't want you to look *too* clever, if you see what I mean. Just ring the bell on the desk to call the patients in and if it doesn't work, just shout 'next.' You needn't shout too loud because the waiting room is only through that door and they can hear every word you say in here anyway." She turned and went back into the kitchen.

My first consultation was a complete mess and even now I break into a sweat at the memory of it. The patient who came

9

in from the waiting room was a large middle-aged man in a boiler suit. When he sat down heavily in the chair at the other side of the desk, I had to move a stack of medical journals to one side to get a proper look at him.

"By 'eck, another new face again this week," grunted the patient. He looked across at me and tutted loudly. "Don't know where we're bloody up to with this lot. Any road – I've had this bad chest ferra fortneet and nowt's shiftin' yon. Can yer give us some stuff fer it?"

"Yes, I'm sure we can," I said as briskly as possible, hoping to sound efficient. I had noticed old wise doctors say "we" instead of "I" – it seemed to reflect wisdom *and* humility. The patient was not impressed.

"What d'yer mean, 'we'? 'Ave you got some bugger else under t'desk?" he asked impatiently. I ignored him and rattled my stethoscope on the desk top.

"Well, erm, I'd like to listen to your chest first, if you don't mind," I said. I began to regain my composure, knowing that the little ritual with the stethoscope on his chest would settle him down a bit. Never had this trouble with hospital patients.

"Yer what?" said the patient incredulously, leaning forward in his chair. "Dr. Atherton never had my shirt off in twenty years with my chest. Could tell as soon as I walked through that door what were up with me. Had the prescription made out 'fore I sat down. None of that there bloody nonsense." He jiggled his finger at the stethoscope.

"Twenty years!" I gasped. I sat down heavily in the chair. Trying not to look the fool and novice that I was, I began to improvise. Very badly.

"Let's see now ... you've had chest trouble for twenty years ... Hmmm ..." I took my glasses off slowly and leaned back in the sagging chair, rather in the manner of a professor of psychiatry I once knew. The back of the chair broke, the base tipped over and I did a violent back somersault into a dusty pile of *British Medical Journals* and old reagent bottles. The dust caught in my throat and made me cough. I got up and dusted my jacket just in time to see the patient cast a single disgusted glance over his shoulder as he disappeared into the waiting room. He slammed the door shut but I could hear his voice clearly on the other side, addressing the other waiting patients.

"Shouldn't bother with yon bugger in there. 'Ee's a bloody piss-artist same as t'other as were 'ere last week!"

He left, slamming the outer door. I heard feet shuffling about and the outer door opened and shut three more times. My God, what a start. I shifted the remains of the swivel chair into a corner and Annie Lewis came in carrying a kitchen chair, chuckling to herself.

"Had a bit of trouble with that chair by the sound of it. Well, it was bound to happen some time. Would you like a cup of tea, doctor?" She was so matter of fact and pleasant that I couldn't help smiling as well.

"Yes, sure, that would be great. Put a drop of Scotch in it, too. I'll need it."

She laughed and went through into the kitchen, while I summoned the next patient. He was a man of about twenty-three who shuffled in without looking up from the floor. He wore a surly expression on his face and mumbled down his open shirt-front.

"Wife says, can you give her summat to stop t'milk and also she can't get a road through."

I swallowed, my mind racing. What in God's name was this man talking about?

"I'm sorry, I didn't quite...?"

"Wife says, can you stop t'milk and also she can't get a road through," he said in a very loud voice, looking up and scowling. There were a few loud sniggers in the waiting room and I began to sweat. Did he want the dairy or the Highways Department, or what?

"Is your wife at home?" I asked, praying for a clue.

"Course she is. She's in bed. Just had the baby yesterday. And all those iron tablets made her so as she can't get a road through."

I breathed a sigh of relief as the penny dropped.

"She wants the breast milk stopping because she's going to bottle feed – and she's constipated, too!" I said, as though I

11

had deciphered the Dead Sea Scrolls.

"That's worra said i'n't it?" he said scornfully.

I hurriedly wrote out a prescription for some oestrogens and liquid paraffin, and in my relief at making some form of communication with the man I began to babble inanely.

"I suppose you, er, as the er, proud father will be showing the baby off now, eh?"

I was met with a snort of fury.

"Some hope. If I ever get my hands on the father I'll crack his bleedin' skull open!" He snatched the prescription off the desk and stormed out. I was so taken aback that I didn't notice Annie Lewis come in with the tea. I thanked her and drank it gratefully before I rang for the next patient who was a nervous-looking spinster in her early fifties. She smiled briefly and described her symptoms, nodding her head slowly and saying "Mmmm" at the end of each stage as if agreeing with herself.

"I get this pain, doctor, like I told the doctor last week, mmm, it starts between my eyes and then travels right down the left side, mmm, then this rushing feeling starts in my legs, mmm, and it goes right up to my throat and then I break wind and it goes just as quick as it came, mmm."

And so it went on. And on. And on. Eventually I managed to stop her by handing her a prescription for a foul-tasting but innocuous tonic.

"What do you think it is, doctor?" she asked nervously, not in the least exhausted after her outpourings.

"I really have no idea, but this should help," I replied. I was as bewildered as she was but to my amazement she thanked me warmly and left.

The whole surgery went like this. It was a succession of bizarre symptomatology the like of which I had never read in any medical textbook. What I needed was a textbook of Martian diseases, for surely these ailments did not exist on this planet. I realised there and then that my medical education so far had been largely irrelevant or unhelpful and that my knowledge of human behaviour and sick people, as opposed to disease, was sadly lacking. It seemed incredible that it had taken nearly six years of my life at the University of Edinburgh, at a cost of many thousands of pounds to the taxpayer, to reach this stage of knowledge – and yet I had sat for over an hour in almost mute ignorance listening to people who had presumably come for help. If ever I became a general practitioner, it would take another seven years before I would be able to offer anything other than the most rudimentary kind of help if that morning's episode was anything to go by. These were uncharted waters.

The last patient of the day brought a temporary boost to my badly shaken confidence, but it illustrated nicely that, for the vast majority of cases, a purely standardised scientific approach was not going to be much help if I was to get through the next four weeks. As the patient described the classic symptoms of acute appendicitis my spirits rose. At last – something made sense! I eagerly palpated the man's abdomen and confirmed the diagnosis. My relief, that out of the whole morning I had at last come face to face with a problem I understood, was so overwhelming that I shook the patient's hand and grinned with gratitude and pleasure as if he had just given me an expensive gift.

"I'm very pleased to be able to tell you that you've got acute appendicitis," I cried enthusiastically. The patient sat up slowly, winced, and looked me straight in the eye.

"Acute appendicitis, eh? The way you were goin' on I thought I'd just won the bloody pools. You've a funny bloody way of tellin' a feller his guts are rotten." He put his jacket on and looked at me as if I were mad.

"If you hang on I'll order an ambulance – " I began, trying to find the telephone amongst the heap of rubbish on the desk. The patient shook his head.

"Not bloody likely. I'll mek my own way to hospital. If I leave it to you you'll probably order a brass band and bloody floral dancers as well. Funny bloody doctor you are..." He put his hat on and went out, leaving me standing limp in the middle of the room.

Before I could gather myself together, the door opened and in walked a lanky, stooping figure in a long crumpled raincoat

13

which looked like a well-used paper bag. He put down a small worn suitcase he was carrying, smiled and introduced himself.

"Last case today, doctor. Joe Smedley's the name, chief rep at Pollitt's Pharmaceuticals – well, actually, I'm the only rep, to tell you the truth." He smiled even more, revealing an appalling set of teeth which stuck up at all angles from the shrunken gums, in the same way that the masts of wrecked ships are exposed by the receding tide.

"Just to tell you about our new tonic. It tastes nice and..." he yanked a bottle containing a greenish fluid out of his case, "it looks all right, costs the same as all the other tonics and frankly isn't any better. Anyway, doctor, here's your bribe, I hope you'll prescribe it." He handed over a plastic wallet and a few ball-point pens. I liked his direct approach.

"We're a local firm. In fact I'm a local man myself, and I know the people round here will like this stuff," he concluded.

"Is it any good for women who have a pain between their eyes which travels down the left side and is only relieved by breaking wind?" I asked wearily.

"Oh, doctor! Don't tell me my sister's been in to see you this morning as well?" Smedley began to laugh, shaking his head and curling one leg round the other, his raincoat flapping around his knees.

"Was that – your sister?" I couldn't help giggling. Smedley shook his head then suddenly looked very serious.

"I think you can take it from me – joking apart, doctor – that our tonic will work a treat on my sister and for any other case of a similar nature for that matter..."

For a moment I just stared at him in disbelief. Then I threw back my head and roared with uncontrollable laughter at Smedley's outrageous claim. He was, in fact, advocating a kind of therapeutic nihilism in the face of the infinitely complex and devious ways in which people reacted when ill or under stress. The absurd simplicity of it seemed so comical that I laughed until the tears rolled down my face.

# 2

The next few years following the Mottley episode were, for me, a voyage of discovery. Amongst other things, Tanya and I returned to Edinburgh where I made an abortive attempt at scaling the first few rungs of the surgical ladder. The first thing I discovered was that ambition alone did not pay the rent; and the second thing I discovered was that I was clearly not cut out to be a surgeon. But I should have known that anyway: a year earlier, whilst I was a house-surgeon at Wishton, I had set fire to a patient's backside by accidentally applying cautery to the surgical spirit with which he had just been painted. Whilst no harm was done I shall never forget the sound of dry grass burning and the breathtaking sight which, in the words of the surgeon in charge, was like "a monstrous Christmas pudding". It was, I suppose, the funeral pyre of my surgical career.

In Edinburgh, a year later, I saw some of my more able contemporaries tip-toeing around the corridors of the Royal Infirmary as if they were walking on egg-shells, ever poised to sprint through the right opening. The writing was on the wall: it would have been futile to continue to flog the dead horse of my ability in the face of such unhealthy competition. In addition to this, Tanya was expecting our first child and neither of us relished the thought of moving from one post to another every six months or whenever each hospital contract expired. I saw the advertisement in the *British Medical Journal* for a partnership in Overton, Lancashire. It seemed the obvious decision to make – and as it has turned out up until now, it was one of the best decisions I ever made. So that, more or less, is how I came to be a general practitioner working in the town in which I was born and bred – two things which I had vowed I would *never* do!

On a bright November morning I sat at my desk signing a pile of repeat prescriptions which lay in front of me. God, what a catalogue of pharmacological futility it was: sleeping pills for Mrs. Edgely who, aged seventy-nine, lived alone and longed in vain for a visit from her relatives; anti-depressants for Mrs. Whitelaw whose slob of a husband boozed himself stupid every night and belted the kids whenever they came within range; tranquillizers for Mr. Milden the company secretary who was unwilling to recognize that the job was beyond his capabilities; laxatives for Mrs. Oaks whose torpid descending colon reflected a lifetime of her own sphinx-like physical inactivity. The mounting tons of this rubbish we prescribed each year represented our efforts at keeping a tidal wave of impossible problems at bay: a symbol of our recognition of such problems. There was no evidence that most of these preparations made the slightest difference to a lifetime of inappropriate behaviour, and yet pills and medicines were demanded by an increasing number of patients for every conceivable unpleasant situation. We were becoming the entreatied pursued by the untreatable.

The consulting room door opened and Miss Cope, our receptionist, walked in with a cup of tea in her hand and a grim smile on her face. She was nearing retiring age, a woman of faultless integrity and enormous efficiency.

"There's a Mr. Tasker from Boreham's Pharmaceuticals waiting to see you. And Mr. Meade's daughter rang to ask you to visit. Mr. Meade has abdominal pain. He's in bed. Shall I ask this Mr. Tasker to come in now?"

I nodded. Ian didn't much like seeing the drug reps so it was left to me to sit through the company sales patter. Still, the reps nearly always brought ball-point pens, calendars, scribbling pads and so on, so I didn't mind.

Miss Cope left silently. I stared at my tea and thought about Thorley Meade. He never ailed much and if he was in his bed it meant that he needed attention. Miss Cope knew it and she knew that I knew it. As she never wasted words, she felt it unnecessary to elaborate any further on the message.

There was a purposeful knock on the door and Tasker came in. He took three mighty strides into the room and as he did so he held out his right arm as if there were a broom-handle down the sleeve of his immaculately tailored jacket.

"*Good* morning, doctor," he boomed, bristling with positive thinking, for he was a superb specimen of corporate man. He appeared to have recently attended a Ministry of Defence course on psychological warfare, for he literally got the upper hand in the confrontation right away. He crossed the room and stuck his outstretched arm not twelve inches from my face, which meant that I could not get out of my chair without getting his hand in my mouth. Tasker offered his hand with the palm facing down and deviating away from him at the wrist joint. As a result, I had to shake his hand whilst half-standing, half-crouching, with bent knees and bowed head, offering my own palm face upwards. I could only achieve this by contorting my forearm and tucking my elbow into my ribs. I must have looked like a geriatric serf receiving a groat from a rich baron. I had noticed Tasker's sort of handshake before in sexually aggressive types who used it as a symbol of dominance. I fell back into my chair, the victim of psychological rape.

Tasker sat down and opened his black Samsonite case. He took out a large folder and looked up thoughtfully.

"Now, as I am sure you are aware, doctor," he began, using the well-worn gambit to get me on his side, "Boreham Pharmaceuticals have introduced a new tranquillizer which we have called Oblivium. I would like to show you some data..."

Jesus — another tranquillizer. I stifled a yawn and crossed my legs uncomfortably. I was dying for a pee. Tasker flicked over a page to show a multitude of benzene rings, carbon atoms, methyl groups and God knows what else: a hypnotic mess of chemical symbols which threatened to turn my brain into gelatin. As he flicked through the folder a series of multi-coloured graphs and diagrams danced in front of my glazed eyes and I could hear his voice droning on from far off. Eventually he turned to the last page which showed nice

17

photographs of anxious housewives and harassed businessmen, and it was at this point that I was supposed to feel comfortable again: on familiar ground after all that biochemistry.

"... and of course, doctor," I heard him say, "these are the cases with which you must be terribly familiar in your day-to-day practice. I think you will agree that this is where Oblivium can really help you in this sort of patient situation."

I had heard it all a hundred times before. I took a last look at the photographs and one of them made me catch my breath. It showed a middle-aged woman talking to a wise looking grey-haired GP. The patient looked exactly like Joe Smedley's sister in Mottley. I began to laugh.

"Is this Oblivium any good for ladies who get a pain which starts between their eyes, rushes down to their feet and is only relieved by breaking wind?"

Tasker twitched his Zapata moustache and pushed his horn-rimmed spectacles up the bridge of his nose with his index finger. He put the folder away carefully and gave me a cold stare.

"I don't see why not, doctor – depending on the underlying cause, of course. But if the symptoms were associated with depression or anxiety then I see no reason..."

I grunted. The product was different but the claim was the same. I thanked him and began to shuffle papers around my desk, impatient to get out of the surgery and into the fresh air. He left, and I gathered my things together and put my coat on. I decided to see Thorley Meade first and then come back to sort out the rest of the visits with Ian.

# 3

The surgery, which occupied the back of a large building housing a gents' tailors, was about half a mile from the centre of Overton, a town which was divided into four segments by the meeting of four major roads in its centre, the whole area being part of a large suburban sprawl east of Manchester. Overton itself was situated on the edge of this dense conurbation and Thorley Meade lived at the rural end known as Overdale, on the edge of a large green belt which began with the thickly wooded Dane Valley, separating this part of Lancashire from Cheshire. Across the valley rose the foot of the Pennines, with Derbyshire beyond that. Much of the area owed its previous prosperity to the cotton industry, but now many of these mills were empty or were occupied by small firms making machine tools or plastics. Over the last thirty years the town had seen an explosion of new industry which had brought new wealth to the district and at the same time had nearly doubled the population to its present level of thirty thousand. Many of the older terraced properties had been pulled down on the Manchester side to make way for a new ring road, the occupants having been lifted out and placed in a large draughty housing estate about a mile away. Much of the development of industry and housing had been a piecemeal affair, making the whole town a place of untidy contrasts from street to street. Glass and steel supermarkets in the town centre squatted low and clean next to huge Victorian pubs and banks. The old pubs, smelling of stale beer and pipe-smoke, were friendly and accommodating like old shoes, compared to the new ones which smelled faintly of Dettol and whose interiors were about as cosy as a hospital out-patient department.

As I approached the traffic signals at the town centre where the four roads met, I had to screw my eyes up against the reflected sunlight. The roads were still wet from early morning rain and the harsh cold sun had turned them into glaring strips of stainless steel against which the car's sun visor was useless. The lights were on red and as I stopped, throngs of shoppers jostled past my line of vision. I gazed over their heads across to the other side where two corners of the junction were formed by the Boar's Head and the Old Crown Inn respectively. Each pub was a beery mausoleum with enough room inside to hold a light aircraft rally. A large brown Whitbread tanker stood outside the Boar's Head, a long hose pumping its scientifically produced contents into the cellar through wooden trap doors set in the flagged pavement, over which at one time had rumbled real wooden barrels. Outside the Crown Inn, not yet open, a woman mopped the tiled vestibule at the main door. She wore a large headscarf under which bulged a score of plastic curlers. On the other corner was the Trustee Savings Bank, and an electrical retailers made up the fourth. Having been born and brought up in Overton, I could vividly remember this shop before its present owners took over. Then, it was a schoolboy's dream: a chaotic, filthy treasure trove of games, toys and trinkets of every description. It was run by two old sisters who were at least eighty apiece, short sighted to the point of being a hazard to themselves, but who had infinite patience and courtesy as they stumbled knee-deep amongst piles of pea-shooters, magician sets, fishing nets and books.

The lights changed and I moved across, past the market square on the right, where Overton's magnificent public lavatory, looking like a green-tiled Parthenon, cast a long shadow over the empty market stalls. The houses thinned out and the road swung to the right into Overdale. The houses here were in small terraces, clean and neat, whose front doors with their brass latches opened directly onto the pavement. They had no front garden and at the rear of each was a small flagged back yard. There was once a real village green in the centre of this little community where townspeople came to picnic and where the local children played cricket. In those days, Overdale consisted of a few dozen houses, a couple of pubs, and was joined to Overton only by a single slender tentacle of road sparsely lined with a few small cottages. The locals at that time considered themselves to be quite separate from the main town, but in recent years massive development had taken place, so that Overton and Overdale were now welded together by a broad isthmus of semi-detached dwellings whose clean, sharp lines squatted uneasily on those gently-rolling fields which once separated the two communities. All that was left of the green was an untidy triangle of grass between the bus terminal and the small asphalt car-park at the Top Dale, one of Overdale's oldest public houses. The landlord of the Top Dale grudgingly acknowledged the increase in trade in his pub by putting a forty watt bulb in the outside toilets which, although it did nothing to improve the quality of the graffiti or the stench of urine and Jeyes' Fluid, did at least reduce the chances of some of its regulars urinating over each other towards the end of an evening of heavy beer-drinking. Like many of the older inhabitants of Overdale, the landlord never referred to Overdale as "the village" – even though that is what it was. The expression was only used by the newer middle-class arrivals who populated a very picturesque estate of privately owned houses at the end of Overdale before it sloped down to the river Dane. It had come as quite a shock when a huge overspill estate sprawled its way from one end of Overton on to their front door-step some ten years before.

The main road stopped abruptly at the end of the village, facing a beautiful lath and plaster church built in the seventeenth century, whose soft irregular lines looked pathetically vulnerable against the stark, geometrical blocks of the new overspill estate which stood with the hunched shoulders of its high-rises not more than a few hundred yards away. By the church a dirt track turned off, winding down steeply in the direction of the river. The track was lined on either side with beech and poplar and the low sun caused an uncomfortable flicker through the branches as I drove along. Two thirds of the way down the trees cleared and I stopped

21

outside the house of Thorley Meade. It was remarkably quiet and peaceful considering that it was only a mile and a half from Overton town centre with all its commercial bustle. On the whole, although it wasn't exactly the garden of England, Overton wasn't a bad place at all, neither were the people. I could have done a lot worse coming back here.

I got out of the car slowly and saw Mr. Meade's daughter coming down from the house which stood on a rise thirty yards back from the road. She smiled and turned back, and I followed her up the sloping garden path to the house. As we went through the side door and into the kitchen she turned and with exaggerated lip movements whispered, "He's not good, doctor. Not good at all. His tummy's all swollen up and, like I told Miss Cope on the telephone this morning, he's not been to the toilet for five days. I've given him some magnesia this morning. I hope that was all right."

I nodded and she led the way into the bedroom. The room itself was drab and functional but quite clean. There was an old tallboy in one corner, a small upright chair with a wicker back and a mahogany dressing table on top of which was a very large pre-war wireless set with tuning knobs as big as tea-cups. It was straight out of a British World War II film ("... I have to tell you that a state of war therefore now exists between Great Britain and Germany...").

Mr. Meade lay in a large neat bed which was adjacent to the far window with its faded linen curtains. The window looked onto the edge of the garden, then to the valley and the hills beyond. It was a wonderful view, and shed a good diffuse light into the room. He looked very small as he lay dozing in that double bed – indeed he looked as if he had shrunk since I had last seen him. He was nearly bald now, and his broad dome-like head narrowed down to the thin pinched face which accentuated his long ears. I put my bag down on the chair. The old man opened his eyes, looked across at me, nodded, then shut his eyes again immediately.

"How are you today?" I asked.

"Same as yesterday. And t'day afore. Middlin'," he muttered.

"What does that mean?" I knew well enough what he meant but could tell right away that this particular conversation was going to limp to a standstill without a push.

"Nowt much. Just middlin'. Has my daughter sent for you?"

"Yes, she did ring me..."

"Y'aren't going to send me in hospital are you?"

"Well, let's see..."

"Not with all them owd buggers lined up for t'knacker's yard."

All the while he kept his eyes closed, but I could see that he was afraid. He kept swallowing and compressing his lips, and even before the covers were pulled back to reveal his abdomen I was pretty sure what I was going to find. When I looked, it was just as I thought it would be. The old man's abdomen was distended, tight as a drum, gurgling with trapped gas. The rectum was empty. I figured that there was an obstruction about two thirds up along the large bowel, and I leaned over and prodded about, feeling for a growth. I couldn't find one, but carried on for a few moments while I thought about what to say next and how Thorley and his daughter were going to react. His daughter stood back, fiddling with a brooch she was holding, clicking the catch-pin in and out and looking anxiously across at her father.

"He said he mentioned he was a bit caustic when he came to see you in September with his chest," she said. It was unusual for someone in their forties to use that word which meant "constipated", but frequent contact with Thorley would account for that. I thought about what she had just said, and although there was not a hint of reproach in her voice, my heart sank. She was right. Her father had come to see me two months ago with bronchitis and in passing had mentioned his stubborn bowels. I had not taken a great deal of notice – in fact I had joked about Thorley's eating habits but had not thought it important at the time. I hoped that the patient wasn't now going to pay the price for my oversight. I sat on the bed and explained to him that it was necessary to go into hospital right away for an X-ray and possibly an

23

operation to sort the blockage out. The old man nodded. "If you think it's for t'best," he said in a resigned voice.

I went through to the sitting room to make the arrangements for admission to Wishton General. Thorley's daughter followed, still clicking the brooch. When I put the phone down I could see she had tears in her eyes and she was sucking her bottom lip.

"I hope he doesn't have to have one of those bags on the outside. He'd die before he'd put up with that," she said quietly.

I explained to her that a colostomy was the least of the problems at the moment: that if left like this he would certainly die within a few days, especially if he began to vomit. If the growth was confined to the bowel he stood a good chance of a complete recovery. If that reassured her she did not show it. I had tried to tell her as gently as I could but the facts were brutal and unpleasant no matter how they were presented.

Having made all the arrangements with the surgical registrar at Wishton General, there was little else I could do. The ambulance was on its way. I wrote a note for the registrar, said a few encouraging words to Thorley, then left the house and set off back to the surgery to sort out the rest of the morning's visits. The sun had disappeared behind thin cloud and the earlier crispness had gone. The day was beginning to feel as appetising as old cornflakes left out in a damp kitchen.

# 4

I got back to the surgery and walked through the small crumbling back yard into the gloomy waiting room with its fizzing two-bar electric fire and disintegrating linoleum. In common with all the GPs' surgeries in Overton, it was not an attractive place. But at least it was not expensive and it was conveniently situated in the centre of the town. It was not our intention to spend any money on it since the lease had only a couple of years to run. We had looked round for alternative accommodation, but because of the ring road much of the available land and property round about was needed by the Ministry of Transport — a fact which had restricted our options and had made us decide to go into a health centre. The old welfare clinic, smelling of cod liver oil and orange juice, was due to be demolished as it lay in the path of the proposed new road, and the idea of working in a new, purpose-built surgery incorporated into a new clinic was quite an exciting one. Over the last few months we had met the county architect and various administrators to discuss designs and sites, but progress was slow and a site had so far not been found. Still, it was something to look forward to and at the moment there was no urgency about it: the surgery had, after all, been there for sixty years and the owners, who occupied the front of the property, would not be in a hurry to throw us out even if our lease did expire before the new centre had been built.

I walked through to the other consulting room which, with its high ceiling, heavy curtain over the door and dim light filtering from its yellowing windows, looked as if it was part of a set from Hammer film studios. My senior partner sat behind his desk scowling at a medical report he was writing. All the relevant documents from the patient's records were spread out in front of him. Ian Murray McDonald was a hard-working, conscientious and careful man who would not put pen to paper without great deliberation. Today, however, he was showing signs of impatience for it was his half-day and that meant an early retreat on to the golf course. He gruffly muttered a greeting and glanced at the clock.

"Oh hell," he said, flattening the "e" to make the word sound like "hayell". "Is that the time? Is it *really* that time?" He jumped up and hurriedly shuffled all his papers into an untidy pile, pushing them into his desk drawer. He put his pen away in one pocket, at the same time dragging a bunch of keys out of another pocket with his free hand. He couldn't lock the drawer for some reason and his bristly moustache twitched with impatience.

"All those hospital reports refer to a single young man. It's amazing. How is it possible even to find the time to get all those illnesses and see all those specialists, eh? Can you answer me that?" He managed to lock the drawer and began putting his coat on.

"Look at the time! Is that clock right? Good God, it can't be that time, surely. Never enough hours in the day. Have to leave that report until tomorrow."

I told him about Thorley Meade, and he stopped with both arms half way in the sleeves of his coat. The coat bunched up behind his back like a parachute about to open.

"No, really? Old Thorley, eh? Well, I'm damn sorry to hear that, I certainly am."

And I knew that he was, for Ian had pretty well as deep an affection for his patients as they had for him. He unravelled his coat, then stopped by the door, twitching his moustache thoughtfully.

"I just remembered, by the way. We've had an invitation to the town hall next week to meet the mayor and a few other local dignitaries. Might be a good opportunity to try and push the health centre plans along a bit."

"You must have been reading my thoughts a few minutes ago," I replied. "What's the idea?"

"Oh well, the mayor usually gives a buffet lunch and sherry

26

to the local business community once a year and we've been invited. The way these last few meetings have been going with the centre it might be a good idea, that's all. We're in no rush, of course."

"That's true. All the same, we could let it drag on for years if we left it to the planners. This so-called consensus management seems to give the kiss of death to decision-making – I mean they haven't even made up their minds on a site yet."

Ian smiled, then looked serious again. "Oh, it'll be all right. We can stay here pretty well as long as we like until the centre is built. Anyway, Steven – there's just one visit today. It's a case I normally deal with but it's so interesting I thought you'd like to see to it today. Miss Cope's got the records through in her room. See you tomorrow!"

I couldn't help smiling. He had a way of putting these things. I heard him start his car and crunch first gear impatiently as he took off down the drive outside.

I went into Miss Cope's small but tidy office and she handed me the notes of Norman Young.

"The doctor got away in good time, I see," she said with an approving smile on her face. "You'll want to see these, I expect. They'll be worth reading. A very unusual family, that."

I glanced at her as she turned away. I had learned not to question these cryptic remarks of hers – it only led to further observations even more mysterious than the last.

I looked through the medical records. I could read very little of what Ian had written but there was a stack of letters from David Neale, one of the psychiatrists at Wishton General. It looked as if Miss Cope was right. Norman was a schizophrenic who, between bouts of relatively normal behaviour, had episodes of severe paranoia and delusions during which he invariably became violent. He had been an in-patient on and off many times as a result of these episodes. He had three sisters, two of whom were hopelessly psychotic and had been institutionalised for ages. A third sister, a severe depressive, lived a few streets away with Norman's brother,

Eddie. Eddie himself was also schizophrenic and prone to bizarre but mainly non-violent flights of fancy. He had lost a leg a year or so ago in the middle of Overton. He had imagined that he was a policeman directing traffic, leaping in and out of the stream of fast-moving vehicles, his arms windmilling round wildly in a sort of maniacal semaphore which snarled up the rush-hour traffic completely. When Eddie was finally knocked down by a truck the police arrived to sort out the mess. One of the officers, better known for his wit than his sensibility, had taken one look at the unfortunate man and remarked grimly: "If this bugger snuffs it, it'll be justifiable homicide if you ask me."

Norman's house was one of a long row of two-up and two-down terraces which had gone to seed because they were at the end of the town blighted by the muck and filth of the new by-pass. Over the old irregular slate roofs I could see the tall spidery cranes of the construction unit and the clean grey concrete uprights of a bridge which was being built over a small valley formed by the ox-bow curl of the River Dane as it lapped close to this particular edge of the town.

As I turned into the street, mud and stones thudded under the wheel-arches. I slowed down, finally stopping at Norman's house, number fourteen, Broom Street. When I got out of the car I could hear the drone of earth-moving machinery down the slope at the other side of the houses, and the rhythmic boom of a pile-driver. The street itself was deserted.

The door to number fourteen was open so I walked straight in, automatically calling "Hello – anybody in?" as I did so. I reeled back as soon as I stepped through the small vestibule. The place was full of steam and as hot as hell. My glasses fogged up immediately and for a moment I couldn't see a thing. There was a fierce hissing and bubbling from the kitchen and when the lenses cleared themselves I could see through the open door to the back kitchen that the gas stove was blazing on all four rings. The heat was scorching the wooden pan-rack above, while the paintwork on the ceiling directly over the stove was blistering and bubbling like porridge on the boil.

I went over and turned off all the gas taps, then looked round. There didn't appear to be anyone in the house, but the owner wasn't far away because I noticed that on the small folding kitchen table was a mug of tea which was still hot. I turned and slipped on a rasher of uncooked bacon which was lying on the floor by the table, banging my head on the kitchen door. As I cursed, the back door burst open and Norman Young came in. He was quite short and wiry in stature, his bullet-shaped head accentuated by his hair which was closely shaved at the side but stood up vertically about three inches on top. This, together with his raised eyebrows and widely opened eyes, gave the impression that about three thousand volts were coursing through his whole body. He was filthy from head to foot. In his left hand he held a hacksaw and under his right arm he was holding the entire exhaust system of a motor car.

"Who the bleeding 'ell might you be?" he bellowed.

"I'm the..."

"Who told you to bleedin' well come in?"

"I'm the doctor."

"No bleedin' excuse. Bleedin' knock before you come into my bleedin' house, cock. Now – out!"

He shoved the exhaust pipe into my chest which made me stumble back through the sitting room and out through the front door which he then kicked shut. I stood in the street and stared at the closed door for a few seconds, then I heard Norman shout from within.

"*Now* bleedin' knock!"

After a fleeting hesitation, I knocked. There was a crash from inside as he flung the stuff he was carrying onto the floor, and the door opened. He stood to one side, grinning maniacally.

"Morning, doctor. Just like people to knock, you know. Can't be too bleedin' careful. Some peculiar buggers round here." He turned his head swiftly to one side and spat into the fireplace, then spun his head back again.

"Come in, come in, don't stand there! Just caught me in the

middle of a job. There's always summat needs tending to, that's what I say. Always summat."

He turned and walked through to the kitchen, babbling as he went. I followed, taking care not to fall over the exhaust system which was strewn all over the floor. Norman never stopped to glance at the stove but went straight over to the enamel sink which sagged with unwashed pots and was held to the wall with a single rusted bracket and two lead pipes curling backwards to bury themselves in the wall like umbilical cords. He grabbed each side of the sink and shook it violently. The whole thing was in danger of falling to the floor. His eyes darted wildly all over the kitchen like a nervous ferret.

"See? That's the next job. Rip the lot out. New units, formica tops, cupboards straight to the bleedin' ceiling. Then new lino, black and white squares, look like bleedin' whatsisname, Ideal Home."

I stood and watched Norman's bobbing head and waving arms as he outlined his plans. There was a jerky, restless quality to the man's movements which I found disturbing. Then, for no reason at all, hardly before the last words were out of his mouth, he lunged up to one of the shelves and took down a large pack of Shredded Wheat. He put it down on the kitchen table, took a bowl from the cupboard and wiped it with his hands, tore four cobs out of the packet and put them in the bowl. He poured half a pint of milk from a bottle on the table and proceeded to eat them with a greasy-looking spoon which he had taken out of his pocket. I stared, fascinated. He pushed the packet of cereal towards me.

"Help yourself, cock," he blurted in a gurgling, choking voice.

I blanched. "Not right now, thanks." Thinking for a moment that I might be forced to eat at knife-point, I hurriedly changed the subject. "One of the neighbours said you hadn't been too well recently. That's the main reason I came round."

Norman stopped eating. He wiped his mouth with his sleeve and shook his head violently.

30

"Not me, cock. Never been better. Don't want to take notice of these buggers round here. Don't know what time of day it is, some of 'em." His eyes narrowed. "Lot of bother round here. People interfering, and that. Got two court cases coming up soon. Blow the lid off this place, no mistake. Somebody's going to get the chop. Not just your councillors, local MP and the like. Right up to government in whatsisname, parliament."

I was just digesting this last morsel when he waved his arms in the air and shook his head from side to side.

"No, you've got it all wrong. Look – it's Eddie you want, not me. He's not been well at all. Somebody's given you the wrong message. I'm OK. It's Eddie. No really – " he said frowning and shaking his head, " – no really, my whatjermercallit, sister, came round this morning and said he wasn't well and that's a fact. I should get down there if I were you."

I could see that I was going to get nowhere. I took the address of Eddie's place and went to my car. Norman was not completely in touch with reality to be sure, but he didn't seem to be a danger to himself, or anyone else either. Eddie lived only a couple of streets away, so I decided to go there first and then maybe come back and have a chat with Norman or one of his neighbours, if I could find one. This sort of situation always filled me with foreboding: if the patient was frankly raving mad it was a straightforward case for admission under the Mental Health Act, but anything short of this was difficult to deal with since out-patient appointments were impossible to get within a reasonable space of time and, meanwhile, support from the social services and neighbours was almost non-existent. I was likely to be plagued by neighbours over the phone or in person about the patient who was "being a nuisance and lowering the tone of the street, and something will have to be done, doctor."

Eddie's house was a few streets away in a similar type of terrace but it was made to look even more dismal by the fact that the approach to it was an unmade road riddled with mud-filled pot-holes. When I approached the door I could hear the thunderous babble of a radio and TV playing simultaneously. When Eddie's sister opened the door I was nearly knocked backwards by a wall of sound. Nonchalantly she beckoned me in, screwing her eyes up against the smoke from a cigarette which hung limply from the centre of her mouth. Eddie was inside sitting in front of the TV and didn't look round when we entered the room.

"Do you mind if we have this lot off?" I bellowed at the top of my voice. Eddie didn't move his head, and his sister shrugged her shoulders and lit another cigarette. I stepped across the room and fiddled with the TV controls, wincing at the din. Eddie jumped up from his chair, kicking over a pile of newspapers which had been stacked untidily on the floor near his feet, pulled me away and turned the controls up even higher.

"As a matter of fact I do bloody mind, thank you very much!" Eddie yelled, his face contorted in anger.

"I've only come to help!" I bawled back. "Somebody called a doctor this morning and here I am!" I began to giggle. The whole thing was so ludicrous.

"You want to help?" shouted Eddie at the top of his voice. "Right – you can piss off for a start!" He began to stumble round the chair with a menacing look on his face, his false leg clanking and squeaking as he stepped over the old magazines and papers. I decided to concede defeat. I backed out into the street and in doing so, bumped into a middle-aged woman who was standing outside. She grabbed my sleeve and began jabbering in a loud, high-pitched voice about giving Eddie a shot of something. She was accompanied by another woman who joined in a moment later, but by this time I wasn't listening. I was just wishing I had specialised in skin diseases. I called some words of reassurance and turned towards my car. I could hear Eddie coming out of the house yelling his head off – then there was a scuffling sound which made me look back over my shoulder. Eddie had rolled up one trouser leg and was fiddling furiously with his false leg, cursing at the top of his voice. To my amazement he suddenly disarticulated it at the knee, scrambled up on his good leg and, brandishing the prosthetic like an axe, made great loping hops towards me. I turned and jumped into my car, looking in the rear-view mirror just in time to see him become a victim of his own forward momentum. On his single good leg he was unable to maintain equilibrium and he pitched forward behind the car, at the same time managing to deliver a sickening blow to the rear offside wing with his prosthetic. Afraid he might wreck the vehicle altogether, I took off as fast as I could, bouncing and dipping over the uneven surface of the street. My hands were so clammy I could hardly hold the steering wheel.

On the way back to the surgery I began to reflect on the unresolved shambles on my hands. I certainly couldn't leave things as they were: although the evidence was pretty thin, I was not impressed with the stability of either Norman or his brother Eddie. I didn't know Norman well enough to say whether this was his normal behaviour, odd though it was, but in the case of Eddie I knew that this violent outburst might herald a complete breakdown which could endanger himself or others. On balance I thought it best to get one of the local psychiatrists to visit Eddie and give his opinion.

I dropped Norman's notes off at the surgery and told Miss Cope that I was going up to Wishton General to speak to the psychiatrist in person rather than ring up. I wanted anyway to see what the surgeons thought about Thorley Meade, and the short drive up there would be pleasantly relaxing, with neither the threat of a patient tapping on the window wanting a prescription for elastic stockings, nor the phone ringing.

Wishton General Hospital, which stood not far from the foot of the Pennines, about fourteen miles south-east of Manchester, had originally consisted of an H-shaped brick building when erected in 1892 by Samuel Broadbottom, a local cotton baron. Broadbottom's vast cotton-spinning empire had made him a rich man but in the process had ruined the health of most of his mill-workers who clacked along dark cold streets in their clogs to start their shift at dawn and who returned exhausted in the damp foggy evenings. In his advancing years, as death made beckoning gestures, Broadbottom's passage through the eye of a needle had been assured by his final act of philanthropy. Thus Wishton General was built. As I passed through the main door from the car park, the bust of Samuel Broadbottom glared down from a mahogany pedestal in the main entrance hall onto the cracked wall tiles and the dangerously fragmenting marble floor. The expression on his face, with its slightly bulging eyes and down-turned mouth, seemed to indicate that he had not got good value for his money.

I crossed the corridor and left the building to walk up to the psychiatric block which was the oldest part of the hospital — in fact it had been a work house many years ago. This part was built of Derbyshire stone, now black with years of industrial grime. It overlooked the town of Wishton at the front and the Pennines at the back. It was quite separate from the red-brick main building, with its cluster of prefabricated annexes, the concrete and glass high-rise of the new maternity block, and the stock-brick huddle which housed the outpatient department, casualty and laboratories across the road. It was a chaotic hotch-potch of structures with no apparent cohesion of style or quality, and I couldn't help thinking that the hospital's physical appearance reflected faithfully the uneven quality of its administration and its medical care. Like all busy non-teaching hospitals where the main emphasis was on the constant turnover of work at breakneck speed in order to serve the needs of the huge local population, insight and self-criticism amongst the medical and administrative staff was a scarce commodity.

I wandered inside and had to go through a maze of fire-doors before I finally came into the main office. Standing in the middle of the large room was John Stopford, one of the consultant psychiatrists. He was surrounded by four girls who were filing case notes and typing with verve but without accuracy. They kept glancing nervously at Stopford as if they wished he would go away. He just stood, with a mug of coffee in his hands, staring morosely at the floor in front of him. He looked up for a moment when I came in, nodded and stared at the floor again. This deadpan greeting was entirely in keeping with his phlegmatic personality. After many years of waging war against bureaucracy in an attempt to get more money and better facilities for his department, he viewed his ever-increasing work load as if it was a tidal wave that must inevitably overwhelm him. When confronted with yet another psychiatric case he would take on a look of resignation and despair, muttering about assaults on his coronary arteries and acts of sabotage to his health in general. Yet he was a good psychiatrist and was liked by local GPs and their patients, which was to his credit. Under the same conditions, when the hospital administration displayed such insensitivity and poverty of vision, a lesser man would have folded up long ago.

I sketched out the events of earlier that morning with Norman and Eddie, knowing that Stopford knew them as well as David Neale, his colleague. The psychiatrist put his hand over his eyes and groaned.

"Oh God, don't tell me. Just don't tell me. I know the whole family. They've shortened the odds on me ever seeing sixty-five." He raked his hand over the parting in his thin hair, and the thought of what he was saying made him look older than his fifty-two years. "I don't know. I really don't. I mean... there's no answer. There aren't any empty beds anyway, even if we wanted him here. It's just getting worse, coming in from everywhere. What do you do with them? Get them a bit better, send them home, then they get back into their old ways and in no time they're back again. We're all going round in circles, that's all." He turned and looked out of the windows, took a deep breath and blew it slowly out of billowed cheeks. "Anyway, if you want a domiciliary visit you'll have to count me out. I've got a damn big clinic this afternoon. David is next door, though. He'll go, I'm sure."

"Oh that's fine," I said. "That'll be a big help if one of you takes a look at Eddie. I'd feel happier about it, anyway."

The phone rang, and one of the girls called across the room.

"It's sister in out-patients. She says there are quite a few patients waiting already and the hospital secretary is down there as well. He wants a word with you." She held out the phone towards him, and he looked at it with distaste.

35

"Tell her I'm on my way, and I'll speak to him down there. God knows what he wants," he sighed. He picked up a bundle of medical journals still in their wrappers and threw them in the waste-basket.

"Look at that lot," he said, pointing to the waste-basket. "Hundreds of hours spent by learned men compiling articles on how to improve our standards of care and here am I too bloody busy to read any of it. And I've no doubt that this administrator fellow wants to discuss where we can put the tea-dispensing machine, when I've not enough beds and the next admission will probably have to sleep in the toilet. I don't know what the answer is, I really don't." He opened the door and turned round. "I mean, what can you *do*?"

He left, still shaking his head slowly from side to side. One of the girls jumped up and showed me through to the other office. David Neale was sitting hunched over some case notes on his desk. His chin was on his chest and his whole body was convulsing with silent laughter.

It would be difficult to imagine two more contrasting personalities than John Stopford and David Neale. Short, broad, in his late thirties, David was a bubbling, enthusiastic man with a tremendous sense of humour. He seemed able to see the amusing side to practically everything. Difficult clinical problems usually sent him fizzing around restlessly, his eyes gleaming, exclaiming "fantastic" and "really amazing", and so on. I found him likeable mainly because he neither took himself too seriously nor did he take many of his consultant colleagues seriously. He waved me to sit down and began giggling.

"I've just seen this patient who was referred to me from the orthopaedic department. Fellow complaining of impotence. He's got a prolapsed disc, so they've got him in a bloody enormous plaster cast encasing him from his armpits to about half-way down his thighs. And then they wonder why he's complaining of impotence. Oh, Christ!" He collapsed into laughter which was partly muffled by the huge spotted handkerchief he had pulled out of his top pocket to wipe his streaming eyes.

I told him about Eddie and asked him if he would go and see him. He beamed with pleasure and anticipation.

"Great, sure. Sounds very promising. Of course I've dealt with the family before – to little avail I'm afraid – but anyway I'll whip round this afternoon and let you know. You might as' well sign your half of the section form now just in case I have to get him in. It will save you a job later."

I thanked him, signed the form and left. I wanted to see what the surgical registrar had found inside Thorley Meade, amongst other things, so I didn't want to hang around too long, even though David was always entertaining.

I was not able to speak to the registrar personally but got the impression from the houseman that, pending confirmation from tests, Mr. Meade had got a malignant growth obstructing his bowel. I went to the medical library and half-heartedly looked up a couple of things I wanted to know, then went to see a patient on the GP Maternity Unit. Before I knew it, it was time to get back for the evening surgery, so I went straight there without calling on Norman as I had intended. Miss Cope greeted me as I came through the door.

"Did Overton Police manage to contact you? I told them where you'd be," she said.

"No – they must have rung while I was on my way back. Why?"

"There was a disturbance at Eddie Young's house this afternoon." She closed her eyes and shook her head. She always did that when something "didn't bear thinking about".

"What happened?" I asked, feeling my tongue go suddenly dry.

She took a deep breath. "Not long after you left his house Eddie set fire to the living room, then took all his clothes off and was wandering about the street with just his false leg on. There were two fire engines there. Apparently not much damage was done, but the police were called and had a bad time collaring Eddie. They rang several times asking if you would attend."

My heart sank. Just what I didn't need when the surgery was filling up was to be called out to deal with a mess like that. I was just turning to leave when the phone rang. It was David Neale.

"Hullo, hullo! Just to let you know I've sorted Eddie out. A really super case! The whole street was milling about with police and firemen and screaming women. Eddie was really in orbit, an absolutely incredible sight! Anyway I got him in after a bit of an argument. Needless to say he wouldn't go in voluntarily."

"Thanks, David. I'm sorry you were landed with all that."

"Oh no, no, not at all. On the contrary – a great case. Really enjoyed it. Anyway I must dash – got to go and see someone who thinks he's Jesus Christ – just nailed himself to his kitchen door or something. Really amazing, isn't it? Right then – cheerio!"

He rang off. I felt enormous relief that the psychiatrist had been available to tie up the ragged ends of a messy afternoon. It was ironic to think that in the case of Eddie the problem had defined itself so dramatically and spontaneously and in doing so had in a way shaped its own solution.

Down the corridor I saw that the waiting room was nearly full, and I pressed the buzzer to summon the first patient.

# 5

Ian and I walked up the wide steps of Overton Town Hall and through the revolving doors into the entrance hall where corridors and offices turned off in all directions. At the far end was a stairway which curved out of sight to the next floor. The place smelled strongly of Mansion Polish.

The reception was upstairs and as we went up I could already hear murmuring voices and clinking glasses. The smell of cigar smoke drifted from above.

We entered the large reception room which was full of people. They were mostly grouped in bunches of four or five, clutching their sherry glasses against their chests and swapping harmless anecdotes with confident ease in the knowledge that, at a gathering like this, no one is expected to come out with an original idea or a remotely uncomfortable sentiment.

"Don't make a wave, eh?" said Ian gently as if he was reading my thoughts. "Come on, let's get a drink at least."

Friendly waitresses with frilly white aprons jostled through the crowd to serve us with sherry. One of the girls giggled shyly when she saw Ian.

"Good day to you, Mary," he said in his gravest Presbyterian voice.

"Oh hello, Dr. McDonald. My word, fancy seeing you here. It's only a couple of days since I was in the surgery with our Jack..."

"Quite so. Now then..." he reached forward and took two glasses from the tray which wobbled in front of him. "We really mustn't delay you on your errand of mercy, now must we?" He handed me a glass, laughing softly and nodding to his patient before edging away to a safe distance.

"Severe case of plethorarthria," he muttered as he sipped his sherry.

"Sorry?"

"Plethorarthria. Never stops talking. Now come along, Steven, this sherry is appalling. If we must poison ourselves, let's do it pleasantly." He put down his glass on one of the large tables and poured out a glass of white wine. I did the same and was surprised at the quality of it.

As Ian looked round the room I helped myself to some nuts and crisps and listened to a nearby gathering of women from the Rents and Rates Department, who were discussing the relative merits of the various tranquillizers they were taking. I couldn't help reflecting that between ourselves and the pharmaceutical industry we had transformed their department from an anxiety-ridden bedlam into a state of euphoric immobility: a year or two ago they had known that two and two made four but worried themselves to death about it – now they thought that two and two equalled five point six and didn't give a damn.

We drained our glasses and helped ourselves to some more. Ian began to say something, but just then a tall untidy man stumbled through the crowd, his wild lank hair falling down in front of his eyes. He held out an outstretched hand as he approached and his eyes blinked nervously as he flicked his hair off his forehead.

"Hello, Dr. McDonald. Didn't know you'd be . . ."

"Hello, Tom. Keeping the wheels in the town hall moving I hope?"

I took a large gulp of my wine and nearly choked on it. I had known this man on and off for years and he had been throwing sand in the face of enlightenment for as long as I could remember.

"Well, well, well, if it isn't young Doctor . . ."

"Ah yes – this is my new partner, Steven Rushton. This is Councillor Tom Brinkley – helps run the town."

Brinkley's handshake was warm and clammy. He stood back for a moment, fidgeting and sweating.

"Have you both got a drink?" he said, as we raised our half empty glasses. "Ah yes, of course you have, ha, hah!" He gurgled and sweated some more. I was sure that at any moment he would do a couple of cartwheels or handstands in the few silent seconds it took to empty our glasses. He rushed forward and poured the wine clumsily, managing to splash a glassful up my right sleeve. He spluttered an apology, turned round abruptly to get a napkin and in doing so, bumped violently into a solicitor whom I vaguely knew. The solicitor in turn spilled his drink down the neck of a buxom woman in horn-rimmed glasses. She was passing a bowl of nuts and the shock made her throw the nuts like rice at a wedding. The effect was like a chain reaction, Brinkley being the bombarding neutron hitting the critical mass. About a dozen or so people were eventually involved, each spending the next minute or two brushing nuts out of their hair and wiping sherry off their lapels.

It was probably the wine, but I was beginning to enjoy myself. Ian turned and began to chat to an old golf acquaintance who every so often took a couple of cigarettes from a box on the table and put them in his pocket whilst he was talking. I got pinned down by a smart, very gushing lady who introduced herself as Mrs. Doris Peel, a big wheel in the WVS. She started to talk about compassionate caring and I switched off pretty early on, smiling and nodding and listening to the conversation of the two Irish GPs behind me, whose voices I recognised. Mrs. Peel eventually terminated the conversation by asking a question which I hadn't heard. She smiled, showing teeth which were a credit to private dental care and I gathered from her expression that the answer to her question should be yes. I nodded and agreed, hoping to God it wasn't an invitation to open a bazaar.

"Oh good. I'm sure he'll be free in a minute and I know he'd love to speak to you." She nodded in the direction of the Mayor who stood, leaning backwards as Mayors tend to do, holding court in a loud, surprisingly coarse voice to his eager entourage. Mrs. Peel went over to the group looking back and smiling briefly as she did so. I gathered that she wanted me to have a word with Bevan. I got another drink and joined the two Irish GPs who were busy consulting their diaries, in the process of figuring out which drug firm booze-up or luncheon they could go to that week. In this, they had a highly organised strategy like a war-game: they had a chart on the wall of their shabby surgery round the corner on which were dotted drawing-pins at different points in various colours to indicate evening or lunch meetings, dates and whereabouts, generosity of different firms in giving samples, etc. Unlike the medicine they practised they had brought this particular speciality to a fine art. Patrick Dougan and Sean O'Malley were even more Irish than their names suggested, but despite their outrageous style of medicine with its mind-boggling limitations, they had a large and devoted list of patients. It wasn't hard to see why: the slightest hint of anything more complicated than a bad back or a runny nose and they sent the patient to casualty. ("He doesn't mess about – took one look at me and rushed me straight to hospital. I'd had this pain in my heel for weeks. D'you know what it were? Piece of leather broken in my shoe. My word, if it hadn't been for Dr. O'Malley rushing me to hospital I should have been suffering yet!") They were the casualty officer's nightmare and their letters of referral were a source of amusement and despair to the junior staff. ("Dear doctor, this patient has been poorly since a.m., please see and advise.") Ian, although he did not much admire their style, argued convincingly that their success lay in the fact that they did no actual harm, and indeed may have contributed more to the well-being of the local population than their over-zealous colleagues in the research units with their probes, scanners, radioactive isotopes and God knows what else, which they seemed intent on inserting into every bodily orifice.

Dougan was heavily built with a mass of dark bushy hair. He spoke quickly and impatiently, and beneath his vexed brow his restless eyes were unreceptive. O'Malley, on the other hand, was a pale, wan figure with thin fair hair, who looked like a chronic invalid. He spoke in a nearly inaudible voice with a very pronounced Southern Irish accent. He didn't smile much and when he found something amusing the nearest he got to expressing approval was to close his eyes and nod almost imperceptibly. It was at this point that he always looked as if he was going to keel over and faint.

"Hello there, Doctor ... Rushton, isn't it?" said Dougan.

"Hello. I think the last time I saw you was at..."

"Fareham's Pharmaceuticals. Lunch, Boar's Head, Hiley," snapped Dougan.

"In June, wasn't it?"

"June — that's right, that's right. Poor do, if I remember. Not enough to eat and only sherry before lunch. Plenty of samples, though. Always good wid the samples, Fareham's."

"Hmm. Can't remember what they were promoting, can you?" I said to O'Malley.

O'Malley shook his head and looked at his drink "No ... I don't tink I can. Den of course all dese drugs sound the same don't dey?"

Dougan poured himself another drink. He looked at me over his spectacles. "Will you be going to the evening meeting at the Belfry on Friday? Fingleheim are holding it. They're always very good. Free drinks during the whole evening. Take your wives. Tell me, doctor — you're up on all these modern diagnoses and things — I got this pain in my back now for a couple of weeks and it's worse when I cough — of all the things you ever heard — and what's more the pain shoots down my leg and I get pins and needles in my toes. What d'you make of that, doctor?"

I smiled politely and shrugged. "It, er, sounds like a P.I.D. to me."

"A what?"

"P.I.D. Prolapsed intervertebral disc."

"Is that a slipped disc?"

"The same thing"

"Well, well, well, now there's a thing. I was wondering about that. But what about the pain in my leg? What d'you think that is?"

I glanced at O'Malley to make sure Dougan wasn't joking. "That's when the sciatic nerve gets trapped in the back." I tried not to sound embarrassed.

"Well now, would you believe that? Fancy getting a nerve

trapped in your back and getting pain in the leg. Well, well, well, have you ever heard of that, Sean?"

"I ... seem to remember..." mumbled O'Malley faintly.

"A P.I.D. you say?" And what do you do about it, then?"

Thankfully I didn't have the chance to discuss it further, because Mrs. Peel came over and invited us all to meet the mayor. We went over, and Ian joined us.

Billy Bevan was a short, square looking man who had run a greengrocer's shop off the centre of Overton for years. It had a large notice on the window: "Billy Bevan buys direct from Heaven." He was pretty successful as greengrocers go, but had attained a certain notoriety for his drinking habits. He did most of his drinking in both the Conservative Club and the Labour Club, with occasional forays into the Liberal Club. He was chairman of the Overton Shop Keepers Association, a freemason, and was linked to various local charities, so that his circle of acquaintances was wide. During his spells at the Conservative and Labour clubs over the years he had collected a fund of ammunition for and against local politicians and it was inevitable that he would become mayor sooner or later in a town like Overton. What he didn't know about local dignatories and fellow councillors wasn't worth knowing and what he did know put the fear of God into most of them.

He stood fingering the tiny sherry glass in his large stubby red hands which were made for grasping pints of beer. Short, coarse black hair stood out on the backs of his hands and fingers, and although he was nearly bald, he grew hair in profusion nearly everywhere else. He had a very dark seven o'clock shadow on his plethoric face which looked like a bizarre tattoo, and out of his wide nostrils and large ears tufts of thick coarse hairs emerged looking like a swarm of crustaceans poking out their antennae to feel the air. Doris Peel introduced everybody to each other and we all immediately forgot who was whom or what function, if any, he or she had. The only thing I could remember was that Billy Bevan was Mrs. Peel's father, which surprised me because they were so physically dissimilar. I recognised one of the gathering as Stanley Bertenshaw, a gaunt-looking young man with an ill-fitting striped suit whose pockets bulged with pencils, erasers, sellotape and other mass communication hardware. I remembered Stanley at the Grammar School. His father owned a stationer's shop and Stanley was the envy of the school with his limitless arsenal of coloured ball-point pens and pencils. Stanley could never remember whether Greenland was above or below the equator but his maps were always a riot of living colour.

"Hello, Steven ... er ... doctor ... haven't seen you for a long while. Still jazzing on the old trombone?" he said across the circle of people. I smiled.

"Trumpet, Stanley."

"Oh, aye, that's right, trumpet. Still – you know – doing a bit, are you?" He gave what he imagined was an accurate mime of someone playing the trumpet but in actual fact it looked like someone doing a sword-swallowing act. For Stanley, though, it was close. I shook my head, ignoring the blank stares of the others in the gathering.

"No Stanley, I'm not doing too much at the moment. I've got other things on my mind just now. How about you – still going strong with the multi-coloured ball-points?"

Stanley grinned enthusiastically. "Oh no, it's fibre-tips now – they're far superior. You can get fluorescent ones which..." He looked round in embarrassment, and his voice trailed into silence as he realised that everyone was listening with polite incredulity at our banal exchange.

"Hm, I see you two know each other," said Bevan with some irritation. He turned to me. "And of course, I know you as well. Knew you when you were a lad. Tell me, what made you come to Overton to practise when the world is your oyster, so to speak?"

"Well I suppose I've always wanted to practise in an underdeveloped area, really," I replied, without thinking. There was a disapproving murmur and I saw Ian roll his eyes up and take another mouthful of wine. "What I mean is, I wouldn't have minded going to an underdeveloped country for a spell, but of course I changed my mind, family

45

considerations and so on." What terrible crap, I thought. It must have been the wine.

"Quite sensible, doctor. Family unity..." The speaker was an elderly vicar and I looked at him in amazement and gratitude for having saved me from further embarrassment.

"Plus the fact dey don't pay you anything, dese lads," barked Dougan, waving his glass around airily. "All you'll get out of that sort of missionary nonsense is a damn great overdraft and a big dose of..."

"Yes, yes, yes," broke in Mrs. Peel to the relief of the others, "But of course, Doctor Dougan, things are different now, you know." Dougan grunted and glared at his empty glass.

"Anyway, it's good to see some young blood in the medical field in Overton," said Bevan, eyeing Dougan coldly. "New ideas. Have you got any, Doctor Rushton? New ideas, I mean. Heard you were interested in one of these here health centre places. What's that – like a group practice, a mini-hospital or what?"

I began to outline the idea of the health centre – about better facilities and decent surroundings for the patient and the doctor, but the Mayor wasn't listening. He kept looking over the heads of the others and out of the window. Every now and again, as a substitute for intelligent response, he turned to Stanley Bertenshaw.

"Have you made a note of that, Stanley?"

"Well no ... did you want me to ..?"

"Make a note of that, Stanley."

Stanley rummaged in his pockets and pulled out a virgin note-pad and a finely sharpened pencil.

"No, you don't need to write it down," said Bevan irritably. "Just make a mental note for the next meeting."

The wine had given me a bit of momentum and I blathered on for a bit longer. I could see that Bevan didn't really understand what I was talking about.

"That's what we need," said Bevan, expansively. "A mini-hospital in Overton. We can have our own X-rays as well."

"They are expensive, you know, Billy," said one of the

46

gathering.

"I know that, but Wishton have got one. Why shouldn't we have one?" he said somewhat peevishly.

"What about the staff?" someone else asked.

"We can get them," said Bevan. "I know lots of girls willing to work those things."

I looked at him in amazement. "They do have to be trained, you know. Anyway a health centre isn't geared for that sort of thing. Not X-rays."

"We'll have one in Overton if I've got anything to do with it. You'll see," he replied.

"I'm afraid you're wrong, you know. That isn't the purpose..."

"No I'm not," scowled Bevan. "And another thing – make a note of this Stanley – we'll have the doctors man a twenty-four hour casualty station in the health centre, so the patients won't have to go to Wishton."

"You can't do that, either, you know," I said doggedly.

"Oh, and why not, may I ask?"

"For one thing you can't get the back-up staff and equipment..."

"And another thing," said Dougan vehemently. "Who's going to pay us for sitting there all night, have you thought of that now?"

"We'll see about that!" Bevan looked a bit flustered. He had got into difficult waters and the whole conversation was becoming irrelevant.

"Before my term of office ends, I will personally make sure that this project is at least on the drawing board, if not already built and ready to occupy. And we'll have X-rays and a casualty station. Make a note of that, Stanley."

"I think you're wrong about those last two things," I said wearily.

"So you keep saying, but I don't think I am."

"Sounds like manna from Bevan to me, that's all."

The group shuffled back a pace, staring at me in some distaste. Ian coughed. "Can we take it, er, that at your next council meeting, you will bring the matter up to give it urgent

47

consideration? The plans have been drawn up, and the money is available. We simply can't seem to get a site."

The Mayor looked uncomfortable. Committing anything to paper, however mundane, when it was a matter which might mushroom in scope in the future, was anathema to all local politicians and administrators.

"Well of course, a lot depends on the people at County Hall..."

"Can we have your backing in principle on a local level?" Ian persisted. Bevan grunted and looked quickly round the group.

"Yes. I think you can take that as read. I would like to be remembered as a forward-looking mayor who during his period of office played his part in the idea."

Ian caught my eye and winked. "There is a degree of urgency in this, you know. Quite a few of the older practitioners will be retiring in a few years and the younger incumbents will want to see something of this sort being built. I would like it to be ready before we have to vacate our present surgery. Our lease runs out in a couple of years."

"You won't have anything to fear about that."

"But you do understand, we don't want the prospect of spending two years practising from a pre-fabricated cabin waiting for the centre to be completed after we have vacated our present surgery. I want to be absolutely sure that the thing will be built, otherwise we might as well go ahead and build our own surgery, providing we can find the land..."

"Doctor McDonald, I give you my word, and let these gentlemen here be my witnesses, that as long as I've got anything to do with Overton Town Hall that will not happen. You shall have your health centre and long before your lease runs out." He sounded like a fairy godmother in some dreary northern pantomime, but his witnesses nodded approvingly and drained their glasses. Bevan looked at his watch.

"Well gentlemen, I must be off, I've got an important meeting to attend. Come, Stanley, and ask Tom Brinkley to follow us."

Stanley excused himself and disappeared to the other side

of the room. Ian nodded towards the door and we made our exit.

"Just one place I must go before we get back to the surgery," he said, and I followed him.

The men's toilet and cloakroom in Overton Town Hall was very large, and the urinals themselves were partitioned from the wash-basins by a high panel which did not reach the ceiling. As we were paying our respects to Sankey & Co Ltd the door opened and two men entered. They stood talking inside the door. Though I couldn't see them I knew by their voices that one of them was Bevan. They washed their hands noisily.

"I don't like being told I don't know what I'm talking about, don't care who he is."

"I don't think he meant that, exactly, Billy."

"Sounded like it to me. Anyway, you know what these doctors are like — blow hot and cold on everything. I don't think we need rock the boat at County Hall too much. These doctors will probably lose interest after a while, and God knows there's quite a few other things we need a site for in Overton."

"New swimming baths, for one," said the other voice.

"Aye, that's true. And then there's that business of the new supermarket that Matco want to build. That's got to be central. Anyway there's no harm in getting the idea off the ground. Get the press on it. Always good for the office, that, and then there's the elections next year. It might be useful, there, you know."

"Oh, I know what you mean, Billy. Still, don't want to get too concrete on a site, if you'll pardon the expression." They both laughed.

"No, I'm keen that our association gets first bite of the site for a new shopping precinct, and the supermarket, when they've decided on where the new road will be going. Put the health centre where they bloody like so long as the precinct's where we want it. Anyway, once we put the idea to County Hall they'll sit on it for years, and then again, re-organisation will be on us next year so it will go out of the window then, I should think."

"D'you think so, Billy?"

"Oh aye. Be bloody chaos for a decade. So as far as I'm concerned, once I've made sure of the shops this health centre can come when it likes. Health is all very well, but it's commerce as makes a town tick and puts money in people's pockets – and votes."

"Know what you mean, Billy. Very true."

"Aye, well think on. You lads can give it plenty of leather at this stage, it'll look very good for next year. But you're right about the site. Go easy, throw it back to County. It'll take time. By then I should think the doctors will have got sick and tired of the idea. They'll have to stand on their own bloody feet like the rest of us."

"Well, I must say, Billy, you were speaking fighting words for the idea in there, you know..."

"Aye well, them's only bloody words aren't they..." the door opened and then shut again. There was silence.

"What price a tape recorder?" I murmured. Ian grunted with disgust.

"Makes you want to throw up, doesn't it? However, it does give us unprecedented insight into the workings of the local administration. Now we know where we stand. We'll have to keep at it, at everyone, until we see results." He said it without conviction and I knew as well as he did that this could well take a lot more energy and persistence than we had time for.

# 6

It had been three or four weeks since I sent Thorley Meade into hospital. I had kept in touch throughout that time and was delighted to learn that the old man's malignancy had been confined to the bowel itself. The surgeons had not only managed to excise the tumour, which was not large, but had also been able to join the two ends of the bowel up again, thus avoiding the necessity of a colostomy. When I got the usual notification of his discharge from hospital I decided to leave the visit until the very end of the day, after I had finished evening surgery. I was looking forward to being able to tell Thorley all the facts of his case and at the same time reassure him of the really good prognosis. At his age he was likely not to have any further trouble with his cancer and would probably die of old age.

It was still a couple of weeks before Christmas, but as I walked up the garden steps in the dark of evening I could see that someone had placed an oil lamp decorated with holly in the porch. It gave a warm, reassuring light and made a visitor feel welcome. It was only a simple thing but it was like a beacon put there by the family who, though I knew they were not particularly religious, obviously felt they had to symbolise their joy and thanks that the old man they all loved had been delivered from the darkest of diseases.

They must have heard me coming, for as I went through the porch door, the inner door opened and Thorley's daughter stepped to one side, waving me in. I could see that she was beside herself with pleasure. Her eyes were moist with tears, but these were different tears from when I had last seen her at the house.

"Oh come in, doctor, come in. He'll be right pleased to see you. We thought perhaps you wouldn't come until tomorrow, with it being so late on, but anyway I'm glad you came tonight. We've got a few of the family to welcome him home, like."

I followed her down the hall into the lounge where Thorley was surrounded by his family, including three grandchildren who sat cross-legged on the floor listening with rapt attention as he talked to them. I stopped and savoured the sight and sound of this old man with his rich memory and his attentive family round him. After a moment Thorley saw me and waved me in.

"Well, well, come in, lad. Set yourself down on the settee. I'll just finish this and then I'll be right with you. Get the doctor a cup of tea, Margaret." He nodded to one of his daughters who jumped out of her chair and disappeared into the kitchen. Thorley was in charge again. He finished his tale, then turned and told me all about what had happened to him in Wishton General. It was very clear that he was pleased with himself.

"Can't say enough good about the staff in there. And Mr. Rowley – well, he's a real gentleman if ever there was one. He told me everything, and what a surgeon! Look at this." He parted his dressing-gown and showed me his neat, well-healed scar, much to the amusement of his family. When the tea arrived in the best cups and saucers I told him more or less what he already knew about his condition. He let me carry on because he knew that was what I had come for and it was what he wanted to hear, and he nodded his head slowly and thoughtfully, looking round at his admiring family one by one. Though he was tired, he was enjoying this declaration of a new lease of life.

We drank our tea together and talked some more. Then, for no apparent reason, he leaned forward and screwed his eyes up as he looked across at me.

"How long d'you reckon you'll be in that owd surgery of yours before your fancy new centre's built?"

I was surprised at his question, but knowing that he didn't miss much of what went on in Overton, I just sat back and shrugged. "That depends. Why?"

"Oh ... nowt much. Heard a rumour, that's all."

"What about?"

"Big supermarket chain. Matco. Got their eye on your property. Not surprising, when you think on. Prime position, next to all the bus routes. I heard they're trying to buy out Frank Lucas, knock the place down and build one of their bloody cut-price supermarkets. As if the place needs another." He spat out a tea-leaf from the tip of his tongue with contempt.

"We've still got a bit of the lease to run," I said.

"Aye, and it'll have to keep on running if they can't find a site for your new centre. You'll be in a bonny mess if they knock your surgery down before that's ready."

"Oh, I don't think the local authority would allow that to happen," I said vaguely.

"Don't be so bloody sure, lad. Where there's brass talking, owt can happen. I've seen it all before."

"You sound as if you know something that we don't."

"Oh well, when you've lived in this town as long as I have, you hear things." He got up slowly and smiled. He wasn't going to enlarge on it. "Anyway, think on. Don't trust any bugger. Well – it was nice of you to call in. I didn't thank you much for sending me in there but I thank you now for what you did." The other members of the family nodded their agreement, and I left.

Thorley Meade's words were still in my head as I drove home through the back of the town into Hiley, then up to Joel Cross which lay at the foot of the hills known as Loweth Heights. Joel Cross was the old part of Hiley, away from its bustling brightly lit centre, and consisted of a narrow main street lined on either side with rows of small stone cottages. At the far end of Joel Cross, Loweth Lane rose like an escarpment straight to the top of the Heights where it turned sharply right onto the gently undulating summit with its occasional huddle of farm buildings. As I crossed the top I looked over the low thorn hedge to the right and I could see clearly down and across the whole of Greater Manchester. As far as the eye could see were the street lights which made a breathtaking pattern against a sky black as shellac. I never failed to feel elated by the drive up here. The speed at which the warm, narrow nestling streets of Joel Cross were left behind for the peace and freedom of Loweth Heights with its windy deserted grass slopes was, I guessed, as exhilarating as an ascent in a hot-air balloon. But now, I had forgotten Thorley Meade's word of warning.

I stopped the car by the side of the road, switched off the engine and gazed down at the hypnotic sight below. I could only hear three sounds, each of which seemed paradoxically to magnify the silence around me: the tiny metallic ticking which the car engine made as it cooled; the distant bark of a farm dog; and the feathery sound of the wind as it buffeted against the windscreen. I gazed for some time until I began to shiver as the temperature inside the car dropped below a comfortable level. I started the engine and pointed the car down the hill on the other side of Loweth Heights, down the steep twisting road which eventually led to Comshaw, only a mile or two from home. The road was lined on either side with steep grassy banks interspersed with craggy lengths of stone wall, and the bright halogen beams threw them into fierce relief as I swung round each bend. The road was dry and there was no frost yet. I drove through the narrow main street of Comshaw, into Lower Malper, swung right up the steep hill into Malper, across the narrow canal bridge – then home.

We bought the house we now lived in only a short time after I joined Ian in the practice, and although it broke the bank we loved it so much we were prepared to do without practically everything else in order to have it, for it was a fine early Victorian stone house built with all the skill, strength and confidence of those days. Its massive walls seemed to insulate its spacious warmth and friendliness as a family house.

When I went inside our two sons, Carl aged four, and Stacey, aged two, were crawling on all fours in the hallway trying to catch the cat. Tanya was putting out the evening meal and yelling for everyone to come and sit down. I collected the children, opened a bottle of wine for no particular reason, and we sat and ate.

"Our younger son has excelled himself once again," said Tanya. She had a habit of twitching up the outer half of her wide generous eyebrows when she was about to tell me something important or unpleasant. "A patient rang up about half an hour ago and while I was talking to her Stacey took a pair of scissors and cut the tassels off the three-piece suite."

"Oh, great. Did you really?" I turned to the lad who opened his dark brown eyes wide, nodding enthusiastically. There was no point in making a major issue out of it now. I knew that he had already been corrected, for there was a dry tearstain on his cheek.

'It was Mrs. Sutcliffe," said Tanya, smiling. "Her husband is the Reverend Sutcliffe."

"Oh yes, I know them. What was the trouble?"

"Apparently he has just sold his car ... and before the buyer collects tomorrow he thought he would siphon the petrol out of the tank. He swallowed a mouthful in the process, of course."

I burst out laughing, nearly choking on a piece of pork chop.

"I know what you're thinking," she said. "What a pretty ungenerous gesture for a man of the cloth. Practical, though. Anyway I told his wife not to make him sick, to give him milk to drink and tell him not to light a cigarette."

"My God, your life in their hands," I said, and we both laughed, even though it was perfectly sound advice. Although Tanya had had no formal medical training, she had picked up enough from what I had mentioned in conversation and this, combined with her rare common sense and ability to distinguish quickly between the important and the unimportant, meant that she could handle these calls as well as any GP.

After we had eaten I rang Mr. Sutcliffe and established that he had in actual fact only managed to get a very small taste of the petrol. I pulled his leg a fair bit which was taken in good part.

We settled the children into their beds then sat talking across the table drinking our wine. I started to tell Tanya about Thorley Meade and what he had said about the supermarket people looking over the surgery property with a view to buying it up, but I could tell she wasn't listening. As she put the wine glass to her lips her eyes smiled across at me over the rim of the glass.

"What...?" I asked.

She put down her wine, licked her index finger and gently stroked the rim of the glass. "I was going to ask you to take a specimen for a pregnosticon, but I don't think you need bother."

"Are you sure?"

"Oh yes. I'm sure. Number three is well and truly on the way.

I looked at her and knew that she was right. We hugged each other and I was so happy I forgot about the surgery, Matco, and everything else as we twirled round the kitchen, slightly drunk, Tanya laughing softly in my left ear. We went to bed and coiled round each other, each enjoying the warmth and contact of the other like pups in a litter. Then, later, we lay concave and still as spoons and I prayed there would be no more calls that night.

# 7

The next morning I woke to the phone ringing in my left ear and I looked at my watch. Six thirty-five. Bloody hell.

"Hullo, Doc. Hiley Police Station here. We haven't woken you up, have we?"

I grunted. "No. I always lie awake at six-thirty in the morning awaiting your call."

"Oh good. That's all right then," the voice chuckled. "The lads will be relieved to hear that. Anyway, Doc, we've got a dead body for you to see in Hiley. Someone hanged himself, it seems. CID are at the house and asked if you would attend. Number twenty-eight, Shepherd Street.

"Twenty-eight, Shepherd Street."

"Correct, Doc. Cheerio."

"Cheerio." I put the receiver down and lay back, staring at the ceiling. I felt Tanya stir next to me but she did not waken. I reached across and ran my hand over her left iliac crest, then across her firm flat stomach which rose and fell gently with her breathing. This was a hell of a time to get out of bed to answer a police call, and the inevitability of it seemed to double the gravitational force of my body. What a mug's game this was. I had been the police surgeon for this area for the past year or two, ever since old Doctor Grundy had died. Of course, it helped to pay the bills, but most of the work was at night or in the small hours. It was all right for Grundy – he had a small practice and was semi-retired so it didn't affect him too much. He was one of those rare physicians whose bizarre work-pattern, although entirely worked out to suit himself, earned him the respect and admiration of most of his patients. After a game of golf or a visit to the cinema he would sometimes do a house call on a patient so late at night that he had to knock on the windows to get the whole family out of bed. His theory was that, during the day, never to be available led to him being appreciated better. His patients used to say in awe: "By God, there's a real doctor for you. Works all the hours God sends!"

All the same, I enjoyed the job in spite of the odd hours and the fact that most of the work was mundane, like taking blood samples from drunken drivers. Occasionally there was an assault case, a rape, or a dead body, when extreme care in the examination and reporting was necessary. But what made it most tolerable was my contact with the police, whose members ranged from the highly intelligent to the frankly dim, and from the morose to the comical. No different, in fact, from doctors or solicitors or any other professional group for that matter, except perhaps that their sense of humour in grisly circumstances was highly developed. Which helped, sometimes.

I got up, dressed, and drove away from the house without waking Tanya or the two boys. Fortunately I knew where Shepherd Street was and with a bit of luck I could get there, do what was necessary and still get to my surgery on time.

When I turned into the street I could see which house it was because a panda-car was parked outside and a constable stood in the small front garden with his radio squawking and crackling away. A CID man whom I did not recognise stood in the doorway. It was grey, misty, and very cold with a fine drizzle, and as I went straight in and down the dark hall out of the wet, I was surprised to find that somehow the house seemed even colder and damper than it was outside. At the end of the hall I was met by Inspector Jim Hardcastle – a large, plethoric, uniformed man of great experience who had a healthy disrespect for experts.

"Hullo, doctor. Not the best way to start your day, is it?" he said.

"Not really," I mumbled, shivering and yawning with the cold.

"Apparently this chap lived alone, a bit of a recluse. Hadn't been seen for days. Neighbour gave the alarm today. He's in here."

We went through into the kitchen. The body lay face upwards in the middle of the floor and the suffused face with its bulging eyes and swollen protruding tongue was an unpleasant sight. The rope was buried deep into the skin round the neck until it was almost out of sight, but a short length was visible trailing out onto the floor where it had been cut, by one of the officers, from the clothes rack which hung from pulleys on the ceiling. A chair stood to one side and it was easy to see the grim simplicity with which this man had committed suicide. From the post-mortem colour changes in the skin I guessed he had been dead for a day or so. He was a big man and I didn't roll him over to inspect him further. The body had already been photographed and I hadn't the stomach at that time in the morning to do anything more. I stood up and looked round. The kitchen was virtually bare. The cupboards contained a few biscuits, some tea and sugar but little else. The whole place was dirty and utterly desolate. On either side of the corpse had gathered four officers: Hardcastle and a constable on one side, and on the other, two CID men one of whom was Detective Inspector Early. Early was tall and slim with thinning hair and a small moustache. Even in these dismal surroundings I could see an impish twinkle in his eye as he sucked on his ever present pipe.

"Morning, doctor. Not a very nice day for it," he said taking his pipe out of his mouth and stuffing his finger into the bowl. I pulled a face and said nothing. The five of us stood there gently stamping our feet now and again against the cold. There was silence for a few seconds.

"What's your diagnosis, doctor?"

"Well, he's certainly dead all right," I said.

"Ah. That's a relief." Early turned down the corners of his mouth, closed one eye and nodded slowly. "Isn't it, Jim? A relief to know that." He looked at Hardcastle, who nodded and looked back at him, poker faced.

"Oh aye. Mind you, we had our suspicions about that, didn't we, Colin? We came in here earlier on this morning and thought – ayup! This man looks dead. It's just a feeling we got, wasn't it, Colin?"

59

"That's a fact, Jim, you're right there. Thirty years in the force and you learn to sense these things. Still, it's a relief to have our suspicions confirmed by the expert, isn't it, Jim?' He looked back at Hardcastle and they both nodded solemnly.

The young constable looked uneasily from one to the other then cleared his throat.

"I – I wonder what drives a man to do a thing like this?" he asked nobody in particular. Hardcastle glanced sideways at him, then slowly pulled out a huge bag of boiled sweets and handed them round.

"Glad you asked that, son. Difficult to answer." He slowly unwrapped a sweet and put it in his mouth.

"What do you think, Les?" He stared at the other CID man, crushing the bag back in his pocket.

"Economic situation, shouldn't wonder," replied the CID man, "the price of beef..."

"The falling pound," said Early. His voice was nearly unintelligible for he had jammed the boiled sweet to the back of his mouth with the stem of his pipe. He held both hands behind his back, gently tapping the back of one hand into the palm of the other, and kept raising himself up and down on the balls of his feet, all the time looking up at the ceiling. "On the other hand it could be the Anglo-Soviet Trade agreement..."

"Increasing pollution in the Baltic," said Hardcastle with a grave finality.

"Increasing pollution in the Baltic?" Early gagged on his pipe and boiled sweet, snatching his pipe out with one hand before he choked. "Bloody hell, Jim, that's a bit far-fetched. Pollution in the Baltic!" He turned to the young constable. "Ignore that last remark, son, your senior officer is being facetious. Beyond the bounds of credibility, you might say." He turned to me, grinning broadly. "Well, doctor, thanks very much. You've done your bit – you must be wanting to get away now, eh? You're quite happy about there being no *prima facie* evidence of foul play in this case?"

"Oh, yes. That's pretty clear." I replied. I'd had enough of this and I moved out of the kitchen into the hall. Early called

60

from the kitchen.

"You're absolutely and completely happy about it, then?"

"Yes. Completely".

"Well, that's all right, just so long as you're happy, doctor. We were all wondering about the knife sticking in his back, that's all."

I froze on the front door-step. My God, I hadn't turned him over!

"The what?" I gasped. My response was greeted by a chorus of guffaws and I blushed with anger.

"You're an insensitive bunch of bastards!" I growled and stormed out to my car. Before I could start the engine there was a tap on the window and I turned to see Early stooped down with his face close to the glass. I wound the window down and smelled his ash-tray breath.

"Hang on, Doc. Haven't taken umbridge, I hope. Not by what you heard in there."

"I just . . . I suppose I'm not as hard-nosed as you people."

"Listen, Doc. I've seen more bloody stiffs than you've had hot dinners, but it still knocks me a bit sick. I've pushed a few full plates into the middle of the table in my time after a nasty shift, believe you me."

"I can imagine."

"No you can't. When you get home tonight that lovely wife of yours'll take the edge off your bad day with a plate full of meat and two veg and Christ knows what else, whereas it'll be a Chinese carry-out in front of the TV for me. My wife left me years ago because she couldn't put up with all this shit." He glanced back at the house, then turned and winked. "We all have our ways of softening the blow, eh? Cheerio, Doc."

I drove thoughtfully to the surgery, feeling chastened and depressed.

I was late and the waiting-room was full. I cleared my mind as best as I could and summoned the first patient.

Through the door waddled May Wrigley, beaming broadly and panting loudly as a result of rheumatic heart disease, high blood pressure and gross obesity, the last problem being the

61

result of a lifetime spent eating away the profits of the family business. She and her husband ran a fish and chip shop. She was sixty-two and in spite of her increasing breathlessness she had no intention of stopping work. That day she wore a thick overcoat which made her appear almost spherical. Whatever her faults she was always in good humour and never complained about anything.

"Hallo, doctor – had a nice lie-in this morning, did we?" she said breathlessly, hoisting herself into the small chair by the desk. Her eyebrows jiggled up and down and she grinned, putting her hand on her heaving chest.

"Here's the sample you asked for, doctor," she said. She reached into her large handbag and brought out a small slim glass bottle with a plastic clip-top. I remembered that she had come the other day complaining of one of her many episodes of cystitis. I had given her a sterile container which I was going to take to Wishton General Hospital laboratory to be cultured for bacteria, and I had spent some time explaining to her the procedure – about taking care not to touch or contaminate the bottle or the contents in any way. As she passed the bottle over I detected a strong smell of Dettol. She saw my puzzled expression.

"Oh, I put plenty in," she said, looking pleased with herself. I opened the top and realised immediately that the bottle contained more Dettol than urine, which meant of course that the sample would be impossible to test and was therefore useless. I groaned and threw it in the waste-bin.

"I can't test that, Mrs. Wrigley. What did you put all that Dettol in it for?"

"Well you see, I remember you saying that my water had a germ in it, and, well, I didn't want anybody at the hospital catching it, so I put plenty of disinfectant in. Have I buggered it all up?"

I began to laugh, and so did she. It was quite funny in a way. With the best of intentions May had managed to dismantle all my efforts at scientific diagnosis in one single act. I wrote out a prescription for a course of tablets and she looked at the prescription, still laughing.

"You have to laugh at these things, though, don't you?" she said, standing up and gasping again. "Oh, are these the pills you gave me before?"

"Yes. The same."

"Well, they worked all right last time. Anyway, doctor, that laugh has done me more good than knowing about all them germs in my water, I can tell you. You must get some queer folk in here. Ta-ta, doctor." She lurched out, still cackling and gasping.

I felt quite a bit better after that, and ploughed my way through a very routine session. At about eleven-fifteen I looked at the last card on my desk. Glenys Booth.

Glenys was a tall, gangling eighteen year-old with untidy flaming red hair and severe acne. She stooped in a round shouldered way and invariably looked unhappy, which was hardly surprising when you saw her mother. Mrs. Booth was a large aggressive woman who always accompanied Glenys to the surgery and rarely, if ever, let her get a word in edgeways. She never hid her disdain at my efforts to treat the family and for that reason it puzzled me at first why they always came to me rather than Ian, until I came to realise that I probably gave her more reason to complain, and as she had a great need to complain she therefore preferred to see me. She didn't present me with symptoms or problems, only a series of challenges. Every move on my part was matched with a counter move until we reached stale-mate. I could see, from her grim smile as she leaned back in her chair and filled her ample lungs by a slow, noisy intake of breath through her flaring nostrils, that her opinion of me as an incompetent fool had been confirmed. Consultations with her always followed the same sort of pattern, like well rehearsed sword play:

"Isn't there anything you can do for my back?"

"Well, it would help if you went on a diet and reduced weight."

"Don't eat anything as it is."

"Well I could give you some tablets . . ."

"Those pink ones you gave me last time?"

"Yes."

63

"They were no use at all."

"Mm. Well, in that case we'll try these."

"I'm allergic to those."

"Oh. All right, I'll give you some medicine."

"Can't take medicine. Makes me heave."

"Have you thought of acupuncture?"

"Can't abide needles."

And so on, each step a parrying challenge to my efforts at effecting a solution against apparently insurmountable obstacles. She was aware that she was difficult to get on with but genuinely believed that these intractable problems of hers, while they were beyond the help of medical science, were themselves the cause of her aggressive personality. When I once asked her whether she had considered the possibility that it was the other way round, she gave me a look of such outrage that since then I had rarely dared to draw her fire. Instead, I had taken the step of retreating behind a succession of useless placebos at each consultation which, although I knew it was not very good medical practice, had prevented me from being physically assaulted and had kept her relatively happy.

They came into the consulting-room together. Mrs. Booth sat down, signalling Glenys to stand by her side. Glenys stood biting her bottom lip and staring gloomily over my head. Mrs. Booth sat clutching her handbag on her lap, bolt upright, knees together, jaw sticking out, glaring at me. She produced a bottle of pills and slapped them hard on the desk. I recognised them as a simple vitamin compound.

"Those haven't done Glenys an ounce of good," she said, widening her eyes slightly and tipping her head back a fraction of an inch. "She's no different than when she came a month ago." My move. A powerful feeling of *déjà-vu* enveloped me. I remembered that Glenys had come in at that time feeling run down and irritable. That is, according to Mrs. Booth. Glenys herself had been unable to get a word in as usual and in the end I insisted on Mrs. Booth leaving the room which she had refused to do. Glenys didn't wish to be examined and the whole thing had been a time-consuming charade.

"Still feeling run down, Glenys?" I asked.

"I'm not so bad," replied Glenys, shuffling her feet awkwardly.

"Oh yes you are," interrupted Mrs. Booth. You're shocking – tell him." She turned to me. "She's shocking."

"In what way, exactly?" I asked, feeling my brain glazing over. It was going to be a repeat performance. Mrs. Booth turned to Glenys again.

"Go on – tell him."

"Well, it's..." Glenys mumbled.

"You're bad tempered, tired all the time and what about your leg?" Mrs. Booth turned to me again. "One leg's bigger than the other, she won't tell you that. It's swollen if you ask me. She wants a damn good check up, that's what she wants. Show him your leg, Glenys."

Glenys blushed and her acne became irridescent. She was miserable and embarrassed as hell. She lifted up her ankle-length coat and I leaned forward in my chair and reached out to inspect her legs, suddenly feeling a paralysing yawn enveloping me. I stifled it with tremendous effort, screwing up my eyes and feeling my jaw go into a quivering painful spasm as I struggled to keep my mouth from gaping open. It was then that I touched a thick, heavily stockinged leg which recoiled at once. As I opened my eyes and looked through the blur of yawn-induced tears, I realised that I had grabbed Mrs. Booth's leg in error. It was an easy mistake to make since mother and daughter were so close together. Her look of shocked disbelief cleared my brain immediately and I turned my attention quickly to Glenys's legs. To my astonishment the left leg *did* look thicker than the right leg, and when I told her to pull her dress right up to her bottom I found that the leg was quite swollen right up to the thigh. The diagnostic possibilities set my brain racing and I asked Glenys to lie flat on the couch so that I could have a proper look. She was beside herself with embarrassment which seemed to be out of all proportion to the situation, even taking into account the menacing presence of her mother. By the time she had clambered slowly and sulkily onto the couch I had already decided what would be the most likely possibility and dreaded the next few minutes. When she pulled up her dress I saw a gently bulging abdomen. I placed the flat of my hand on the swelling and felt the unmistakable flickering movements of a six month-old foetus. I glanced quickly at Glenys who looked up at the ceiling. I stood with my hand on her abdomen for quite some time, totally absorbed in thinking how the hell I was going to break the news. Mrs. Booth interrupted my thoughts.

"It's her leg — not her stomach, you know," she said impatiently.

"Yes ... yes, I know. It's important for me to examine the abdomen, though, because there's something here which may be connected with the swelling of the leg," I murmured. I turned to Glenys. "Have you any idea what this swelling is?"

She nodded her head vacantly from side to side.

"Any guesses?"

She looked up at the ceiling again. Oh God, I thought. Here it comes.

"Well, Mrs. Booth. Glenys is about six months pregnant ..."

"Rubbish! How could she be? I would have been the first to know!" she said indignantly. I had no reason to doubt that last statement at all, knowing Mrs Booth.

"And anyway, why is that leg swollen?" she said, her voice rising in pitch and volume.

"Well, I'm sure the baby has been pressing on a vein in the pelvis and it has blocked the drainage of fluid from the leg," I replied. Mrs. Booth's eyes bulged and she began to twitch in the chair. Glenys remained impassive on the couch. I signalled for her to get up.

"She'll have to go into hospital today, I'm afraid, to see about this blocked vein." I sat down and looked at them both. Glenys suddenly became tearful, and the truth was dawning on her mother.

"D'you mean to tell me that our Glenys is going to have a *baby*?" she cried incredulously.

"Yes. In about three months' time." I gritted my teeth. Did I actually have to put lantern slides up to get it through this woman's head?

"Well! That's a disgrace! I hold you personally responsible for it coming to this!" she yelled, standing up. I nearly fell off my chair in amazement, and Glenys burst into noisy sobs.

"I beg your pardon?" I said slowly.

"Well she must have been in this state when we came last month and you did nothing about it, did you?"

"Mrs. Booth — if you had allowed your daughter to speak for herself and if she had allowed me to examine her then, I would have reached a diagnosis, but it would not have altered the picture, would it? Your daughter is pregnant now, has been so for six months and if nothing untoward happens, will continue to be pregnant for the next three months as well."

In the few seconds of silence which followed I became aware of poor Glenys's sobbing obligato and I felt suddenly sorry for her, for she was being totally ignored by myself and her dreadful mother. I asked the girl to sit down and explained to her what I intended to do. Any threatened interruption by her mother I quickly squashed by throwing my hand in the air like a policeman on point duty. Mrs. Booth simmered and quivered menacingly but I ignored her until I had finished.

After some time Glenys recovered and looked balefully once or twice at her mother. As I rang Wishton to get her admitted I heard Mrs. Booth mutter several times: "Just wait until your father finds out. *Just wait.*" Mrs. Booth was about as comforting as a basking shark.

As they both left the surgery Glenys smiled weakly, while Mrs. Booth's breath hissed in and out of her flaring nostrils. She had the look of a stallion which had just backed into a barbed-wire fence. Her departing glare convinced me that this was not going to be the end of the story by any means, but I was equally sure that it would be some time before the concluding chapter was reached.

Ian came in shortly afterwards and I brought up the Matco rumour. He seemed unconcerned.

"No danger of anything like that. I heard the same story recently. I've checked with Frank Lucas and they've no plans to sell up. We're safe here until the health centre's ready. Anyway, the council and health authority wouldn't allow it in the face of public opinion. Don't worry."

"In spite of what we heard in the gents at the Town Hall?"

"In spite of that. These fellows blow a lot of hot air but they're sensitive to public opinion. We'll be OK, you'll see. Let's just concentrate on looking after the patients – the rest will take care of itself."

I said nothing, for I did not share his optimism. I had an enormous regard for Ian's integrity and clinical judgement. He had been a general practitioner in Overton over thirty years, but if he had one fault it was that he fully expected his kindness and conscientiousness towards the welfare of others to be reciprocated. While this was true of his patients, I was not convinced that it was going to be true of the newer breed of administrators and local politicians who were waiting on the side-lines to step into the arena of local government re-organisation when it came next year.

# 8

The Weaver's Arms was on the road home, so when I got a request to visit the landlord's wife I arranged my visits that morning in such a way that it would be the last call before lunch. It was early January and the bright, hard morning sun had not thawed the frost which had formed overnight, even though it was now past mid-day. An icy wind had kept the temperature around zero and had also kept the patients away from the surgery. As a result, there were many more home visits that particular day and it was clear that the brief euphoria of Christmas had been replaced by the harsh realities of winter ailments. People were keeling over left, right and centre with sore throats, bronchitis and influenza.

The Weaver's was an attractive stone-built pub separated from the road by a very narrow flagged pavement which at lunch time was invariably lined with customers' cars. That day was no exception and I had to park at a distance and walk back to the entrance. As I approached, someone stepped out and through the open door came the magical bubble of warm air carrying the smell of draught beer and home made soup, like a package from heaven.

Beryl Sefton, the landlord's wife, was a quiet, efficient woman in her late forties, whose basically attractive features were somewhat spoiled by her perpetually unhappy expression. Her husband, Gerald, treated her at times like a dog, which more or less explained her long face. He had very little in the way of a sense of humour and his idea of fun was to make spiteful, humourless jokes or comments at her expense. His attempts to draw the attention of the customers to his cretinous jokes usually made them cast their eyes down into their beer with embarrassment. This never bothered Gerald Sefton much, simply because he was supremely insensitive.

I went inside. Round the polished oak bar stood a dozen or so men in sober suits clutching gin and tonics, whilst round the fire at the other side of the bar sat a huddle of older retired locals in heavy overcoats and scarves talking quietly and drinking beer. The group at the bar wore no overcoats, for they had jumped into the pub directly from their warm BMWs and XJ6s. They were local business men, estate agents, solicitors and so on, who were grabbing a snack and a drink during their lunch hour. There was much back-arching laughter amongst them as Gerald – who was on his own behind the bar apart from a young girl helper – vented his feelings about the lads from the local technical college who played darts all through the lunch hour and only bought half a pint of mild.

"Doesn't cover the cost of the light over the board," he grunted. "They could all do with a wash and a hair-cut, the whole lot of them. A day's work wouldn't do them any harm." There was an approving chorus of "Quite right, squire!" and a rumble from one or two members of the group about bringing back National Service and flogging.

As I approached the bar one of them turned round and nodded in my direction. It was Dick Wainwright, a retired local business man whom I had known since I was a child. I didn't like him then and liked him even less now. He had been on every committee and organisation you could think of and had spent most of his life holding forth on matters he knew little about. Long before his retirement he had become a Conservative councillor and had devoted himself entirely to self promotion, getting his photograph in the local paper on every conceivable occasion, whether it was presenting a cheque to one of his worn-out ex-employees or congratulating an old lady on getting an inside toilet put in her house after she had waited twenty years.

"That's right, isn't it, doctor?" he said, waving his glass around airily. "About these lay-abouts, I mean. Scrub 'em down with carbolic and send 'em on forced labour. When I was in the forces we used to throw 'em in jankers for going

70

round looking like that. Should be bloody flogged, that's what I say."

It was difficult to smile at someone like this, but I managed it anyway. I wanted to get him to talk about the surgery problems.

"We still seem to be in limbo with the health centre plans – I don't suppose you've heard any encouraging news?"

He cleared his throat and leaned back, put his free hand in his pocket and jangled a handful of loose change. "No, I'm afraid not, doctor. There's a problem about finding a suitable site, you know, I'm sure you realise..."

"I notice you found sites quick enough for the new swimming baths and that new shopping precinct next to the market place at the end of last year. They would have been ideal for the centre," I said coldly.

He stared at the ceiling and frowned. "Yes, but there were certain technical difficulties about priorities and such-like ... and of course County Hall have been dragging their feet on your centre."

"What about the possibility of our present surgery being knocked down to make way for a supermarket? That's going to leave us up the pole if you haven't even found a site for the new centre."

Wainwright looked a trifle uncomfortable and took another drink. "No chance, doctor. A thing like that just couldn't happen. Too much at stake. I'm sure I don't know where you got that idea from. I've heard nothing." He looked at his watch and put his drink on the bar. "Well, I really must get away – now stop worrying about the health centre. There'll be a site found soon enough and no one at the Town Hall's going to pass any planning permission to demolish your surgery, leaving you nowhere to look after the patients. The idea's ridiculous. Quite ridiculous." He turned and waved and I stared at him as he disappeared through the door, still thinking about what Thorley Meade had said about trusting no one. Or maybe I was just getting paranoid.

I made my way to the other end of the bar nearer the fire and asked Gerald Sefton where the patient was. I was puzzled

71

when he started to behave in a very odd and secretive manner, first pointing his finger in the air then putting his hands together as if in prayer, muttering "Ah, yes, mm, right." He buttoned up his blazer which had a large RAF squadron crest on the breast pocket. He was very fond of wearing it: presumably it gave him an air of authority when advising a dose of National Service to long haired youths. He strutted very close up to me at the other side of the bar and nodded his head to indicate that we should both move even closer to the far end, where he poured out a large whisky and put it on the bar top. When he saw my questioning look he shook his head.

"On the house. I want you to pop up and take a look at Beryl. It's her bronchitis."

I took a couple of sips of the scotch, saying nothing, and to my surprise he poured another large one into the same glass.

"Have another," he said in a low voice. He was speaking out of the side of his mouth and as I listened I noticed for the first time that his handle-bar moustache hid a mean, paper-thin upper lip. "Now, she's not well and I would like her to go to her mother's for a few days and I want you..." He leaned closer and dropped his voice even lower "... I want you to see to it that she *goes*. I'm sure you'll think it's best. She'll get a rest and it will give her a chance to build herself up again."

I stared in amazement at Gerald's novel concern for his wife, and wondered what the hell was going on. I noticed the bar had gone rather quiet and I glanced round at the group at the other end. They were visibly leaning in my direction, straining to hear but at the same time looking at their drinks.

"Another one, doc?" Gerald asked, grabbing my glass.

"Hell no, I'd better see your wife."

I turned and went round the back, climbing up the narrow winding staircase to a large landing on the first floor. I was still wondering about Gerald's weird behaviour.

Beryl Sefton was sitting up in bed sipping a hot lemon drink and sifting listlessly through a pile of newspapers and magazines which littered the bed. Her hair was uncombed, and she had no make-up on her face. She looked up when I came into the room and smiled thinly.

72

"Did Gerald send for you?" she said suspiciously.

"He did. Why, don't you think you need a doctor?"

"That depends, doesn't it?"

"Depends on what?"

"Depends on what sort of remedy you had in mind." She blew her nose on a tissue and eyed me coldly.

"Well let's see what we're dealing with first," I muttered, ignoring her look. I took a brief history and listened to her chest. She had got bronchitis and I wrote out a prescription for the relevant treatment, sitting on the edge of the bed as I did so.

"Will you get enough rest here, d'you think?" I asked, putting the prescription on the bedside table.

"What do you mean?" she said sharply. I was surprised by the hard edge in her voice.

"Well, I believe your mother is willing to have you stay with her for a few days. You know – so that you don't get dragged into helping in the bar before you've had chance to pick up properly."

"Did Gerald tell you to suggest that?" she said, her lower lip quivering.

"Well he did mention..."

"Ha!" Her harsh exclamation made me jump. She looked angry and tears came into her eyes. "Yes. He bloody well would suggest that, wouldn't he?"

"I don't..."

"Oh, give over! You're all the same, you men. Swines. Well, you can put that prescription away and go downstairs and tell Gerald I'm not going to my mother's, no matter who suggested the idea." She turned her back and closed her eyes. That seemed to be that. I was flabbergasted by all this because Beryl Sefton had always been quite pleasant on previous occasions. I got up slowly and went downstairs. When I entered the bar again Gerald bounced over quickly from the other side of the room.

"Well? What did she say?" he said brightly. I reached out for my whisky on the bar top.

"She's got bronchitis. She'll..."

"Yes, yes, yes, I know all that," he interrupted impatiently, "but what about her going away for a few days?"

"She won't go on any account," I said flatly. I was just closing my hand on the whisky glass when he swept his hand across the bar top and snatched it up like lightning, putting it on the till behind him.

"She *what*?" he hissed, looking furious.

"She doesn't want to go, and that seems to be that."

"Well dammit — I thought you might have been able to persuade her," he said through his teeth.

"What's all the fuss about? She doesn't want to go ..."

"Never mind. Forget it. Sod it." He flapped his hand in front of his face as if he was brushing away a fly and I could see that the man was beside himself with fury for some reason. There was obviously more to this than met the eye, but neither of us were in the right frame of mind to go into it further. I turned to go. By this time the whisky was giving me indigestion which it always did when I took it on an empty stomach, and I was looking forward to getting home for lunch. The Seftons would have to sort out their own problems.

On my way out of the door I noticed that one or two of the group at the bar were chuckling while the rest of them were winking and nudging each other, but by now I didn't really care what the hell was going on. I stepped outside, and the icy wind made me gasp. As I was getting into my car Ian drew up and leaned out of his car window to ask if all was well. I walked over and told him about what had just happened. He roared with laughter.

"You didn't know, then?" he said.

"Know what?" I asked irritably. I was getting cold.

"Why Gerald Sefton wants his wife away? Hell, he's always paying for her to take little trips and holidays, so he can go and see his fancy piece in Gloston. No wonder he wanted you to advise her to go to her mother's to recuperate! Beryl Sefton hasn't been away for a couple of months so I suppose Gerald must be desperate. God, I thought you knew!" He laughed again and waved, then drove off.

I stood for a moment feeling angry and foolish. Not angry with Sefton in particular but more angry with myself for being so slow-witted not to have spotted the manoeuvring a mile off. As I drove home I couldn't help feeling that, although I had learned a lot since I first went into general practice, I had – in this instance at least – underestimated the hidden complexities in the apparently simple equation of diagnosis and treatment. I still had a lot to learn about the infinitely variable element in the equation: the human factor. I remembered reading somewhere that it is as important for the doctor to know what sort of person has the disease as to know what sort of disease the person has. Without a knowledge of both, the consultation can have unexpected results for both patient and doctor alike. If I mastered this, then diagnosis and treatment would take care of itself and I might conceivably become reasonably good at my job. I absent-mindedly changed down going up a steep rise and crashed the gears. I cursed. One thing at a time, one thing at a time.

# 9

It was February. The low stone wall of the churchyard afforded no protection against an icy wind which ripped across the gravestones as they stood black and irregular like bad teeth. Between the graves and the stone-flagged paths, tufts of coarse grass bent and hissed in the wind, and silent groups of people, hunched against the cold, shuffled desolately into an already packed church, some of the men with tears in their eyes which were not entirely due to the biting wind. The sunlight, slanting low through restless willow trees, was the colour of fresh-cut sodium and threw long thin writhing shadows across the churchyard and against the huddle of mourners as they filed slowly through the church door.

Stan Hamer had promised his funeral would be a "big do" and he was quite right about that. Inside the cold church I noticed that the vast congregation contained familiar faces; many were patients and some I noticed were people with whom I had been at school. Others I had not seen since I had last been in the church over twenty-five years ago.

Before the service began, the subdued whispering of the congregation and the rustling of their clothes as they arranged themselves in the packed pews created sybillant echoes against the high oak-beamed ceiling. I thought about the many people I had known who had accepted, with varying degrees of equanimity and bravery, the diagnosis of their untreatable cancer – and its implied death-sentence – but I could not recall anyone quite like Stan Hamer in this respect, especially since the disease had killed him at the age of thirty-seven.

I had known Stan for as long as I could remember. In fact we had grown up together, disrupting the same Sunday School as boys, wriggling impatiently in stifling, glass-partitioned rooms with dusty teak floors, longing to be out in the sun of those endless summers catching fish, climbing trees and playing cricket. I remembered those games of cricket best of all, played sometimes in bumpy meadows where the long grass whipped our shins and cuckoo spit smeared our knees as we ran. Other times we played with wickets chalked on walls and made new rules every day: you're out if you're caught one-handed off a wall, last to bowl gets first bat, six and out if you thump one into Johnson's yard. Later, in our early and late adolescence, when the jars of Brylcreem and Valderma became more important than the cricket bats autographed by Cyril Washbrook, we attended the local dances and youth clubs to eye up the local talent, and breezed into the local pubs to get sick on Craven 'A' and Chester's bitter.

I lost track of him for a time as we went our separate ways, but on coming back to Overton I was pleased to discover that he and his family were on our list of patients – although I seldom saw him in that capacity. The rare consultations that took place usually consisted of a few laughs and jokes and humorous references to earlier days, for Stan Hamer hardly ever had a significant illness. The last time he had been at all unwell had been twenty-five years ago, when he lay on the couch in the front room of his parents' two-up and two-down, smiling wanly after swallowing some small change on the way back from the chip-shop. Stan always seemed to be swallowing things like that, in those days. It was a standing joke that each trip to the toilet was, for him, a voyage to discover a treasure-trove of previously swallowed objects.

As I sat waiting for the service to begin, I thought back over the last year. I had been called to the house the previous spring. That was how it began. Doreen Hamer greeted me at the door with a cheerful smile. As we exchanged a few words in the hallway I noticed more lines in her pleasant, round face than when I had last seen her. I went upstairs and, after a bit of light-hearted banter, gave Stan a cursory examination and confirmed that he had influenza or something very like it.

While I was telling him that he would have to stay in bed for a few days, young Colin Hamer walked in. He was twelve and remarkably like his dad, with a ruddy complexion and fair hair, stocky and confident.

"Does that mean my dad can't take me to the cricket this week-end?" he said in a voice which indicated that he knew the answer. I nodded and the boy pulled a face and walked away. When I turned back again it only struck me then how pale Stan was. I turned down one of his lower eyelids and looked at the conjunctival sac. He was quite anaemic. I told him to come down to the surgery in a few days for a blood test and left it at that.

A few days later he came in and in the cold light of the surgery I was shocked to see how awful he looked. I measured the haemaglobin, finding it to be about one third of the normal level, and a few questions revealed that he had been getting very tired recently – with that level of anaemia it was amazing that he could walk about at all. His history of dyspepsia, especially after beer, suggested a duodenal ulcer, and when I made a rectal examination there was evidence of a large and very recent haemorrhage, presumably from the stomach. I silently thanked my good fortune in spotting this, for a sudden further haemorrhage could have been disastrous. Stan looked at me in amazement when I told him that he must go into hospital immediately. His main concern was that a lot of work had piled up that needed his attention – couldn't it wait for a few days? I shook my head. No.

I was pleased to see him a couple of weeks later looking much better after receiving several pints of blood in hospital. A barium meal had shown a questionable tiny duodenal ulcer which was doubtlessly the cause of the problem. He was going to be summoned for review in three months' time. I made some reassuring noises and as he got up to go he smiled.

"They're pretty good down there at the Royal. Looked after me very well. The only thing is – why have I still got this dull ache in my belly?" He pointed to the lower right quadrant of his abdomen.

"Is that where you were getting your indigestion before?" I

78

asked.

"Yes. It's always down there."

"OK — let's have a quick look." I waved him onto the examination couch. It was probably nothing, but still...

As soon as I placed my hand on the abdomen I realised that there was something seriously wrong. Low down on the right, underneath my hand, I could feel a hard mass as big as an orange. I had no doubt at all that it was malignant, and it fitted perfectly with the symptoms and the bleeding: carcinoma of the caecum. Under my breath I cursed with anger and disbelief that it had not been felt before, either by myself or while he was in the Royal. Stan looked up and caught the expression on my face.

"Go on. Don't say you've found something else."

"I'm afraid so," I said as casually as I could.

"Oh great. D'you reckon it's cancer?" His directness, even for him, I found unnerving. It demanded a similar response, but I softened my reply by being evasive.

"Can't rule that out, Stan. Whatever it is, it's serious and needs sorting out quickly."

He jumped off the couch, got dressed and then began to chuckle.

"What the hell's so funny?" I asked.

"You."

"What's that supposed to mean?"

"Well I've only been here twice in the last five years and both bloody times you've sent me into hospital. I'll have to take my illnesses somewhere else — it's causing havoc at the firm, you know." He was smiling ruefully and I found myself smiling as well. "Anyway, I can't go today, I've got too much to do, but I'll go tomorrow," he said.

The next day he went back into the Royal and I called in at the house to have a word with Doreen Hamer. I told her what I thought but she expressed little surprise.

"I thought it might be something like this, Steve," she said in a resigned voice. "He's been ill for a few months, you know. He could hardly get up the stairs without losing his breath, just recently. But he wouldn't admit to anything like that, as you know." Her face suddenly looked tired and drawn and I knew that the next few weeks or months were going to be an enormous test of strength for her.

I was in touch with the Royal a few days later. The diagnosis had been provisionally confirmed and a laparotomy was performed later that week. At operation, they found a large malignant tumour, but it had been possible to remove the whole thing and there was no evidence that it had spread to the lymph glands or anywhere outside the bowel. The right half of the colon had been removed and an end to end anastomosis was made. On that basis they could be guardedly optimistic about the prognosis and this information I relayed to Stan's wife. She was thankful and relieved.

I called to see Stan when he came home from the hospital and found him to be in really good spirits. We openly discussed all aspects of his illness and he was left in no doubt that although his cancer had been removed, the next few months would reveal whether the removal was a complete success or not, since if it did recur it would probably do so within the first year.

He came to the surgery for a routine check after a few weeks and I examined his abdomen. The scar had healed perfectly and he was putting on weight. I felt over the operation site. Was there a hint of a lump there? Or was it scar tissue? I couldn't be sure, and I was relieved to hear that he was due back at the Royal in a few days for the routine follow-up. At least that meant that someone else would be looking at his abdomen as well, which would clarify the nagging doubt in my mind.

I didn't see him for about eight weeks, but knew from Doreen that he had been working the whole time. When he did come in I detected a subtle but distinct change: he was his usual, cheerful cocky self, but there was an unhealthy, sallow appearance to his skin and his face was thinner. He complained that he felt sick, couldn't eat, and that beer tasted like metal in his mouth. He climbed onto the examination couch and pulled up his shirt, looking at me steadily and with

80

no sign of fear in his eyes, only sadness and disappointment.

"Can you see what I can see?" he said quietly.

I nodded. There was a visible mass in the abdomen larger than a grapefruit and its significance was clear. Not only had the malignancy recurred, but its rate of growth displayed an almost obscene, rampant vigour. I realised that whatever was done now, the outlook was hopeless and he would be dead within a few weeks.

"Doesn't look too good, does it?" he said.

"No. It doesn't look good. It doesn't look good at all," I replied flatly. I avoided his eyes, fiddling with a pen on my desk. I began to compose another letter to the Royal, not wanting to talk about it very much, although I knew I must.

"Does this mean another operation?" he asked, sitting down by the desk. I put down the pen and looked up.

"I don't think so. The growth has recurred..."

"Oh bloody hell," he said. There was no anger, fear or bitterness in his voice. He said it as if he had just spilled egg on his tie.

"I don't think this can be treated by surgery ... not on its own, anyway," I said.

"That means I've had it?"

"There are quite a few anti-cancer treatments now. They are being improved all the time," I replied, avoiding his question. "I should think you'll have to receive drugs and maybe some radiotherapy..."

"And what are the chances?"

"It may be possible to slow down the rate of growth of this tumour – or even stop it. I don't know. I really don't."

"You don't reckon much, do you?"

"No, I can't say I do. But a lot depends on how you respond to the treatment."

There was silence for a few seconds. I bit the end of my ball-point pen and it broke off.

"Anyway I'll give you the letter, ring the Royal up in the morning and get you in to start things off." I wrote the letter quickly and handed it to him in a sealed envelope.

"Aye, O.K." said Stan thoughtfully. "Hope I won't be in

too long. Got some big jobs coming up that I want to get done."

"Sure. Well, I can't tell you how long, but after they start things off, maybe you will have the treatment done as an out-patient."

He nodded and shrugged but said nothing. He got up slowly and pushed the chair back.

"I'll not let a thing like this beat me. Not bloody likely," he said, staring at the manilla envelope and pressing with his finger and thumb round the edges absentmindedly. "The only thing is ... the youngster. Our Colin. That's who I feel bad for, it'll be hard going for him..."

"I know," I said. "But I'll keep in touch..."

"I know you will, and I'm grateful for that. It'll help." He smiled and we shook hands before he went out.

The next few days were not easy because Doreen Hamer came in nearly every day to give me a report on Stan's progress and the stress was showing on her face. After the initial euphoria following the operation, she now felt a profound sense of disappointment, of having been let down in some way — as if Stan's quick recovery had been part of a conspiracy which now made the truth seem even more cruel. If she was bitter and resentful about this, she did not show it. She adopted an attitude of quiet resignation to what now seemed to be an inexorable decline in Stan's condition, for over the next few weeks the response to treatment was frankly negligible.

About six weeks after he began receiving the fearful cocktail of anti-cancer therapy, he came into the surgery looking quite pleased with himself. He showed me his abdomen and it seemed that the tumour had diminished in size very slightly.

"If it carries on like this I'll have beaten it," he said, chuckling, "I told you I would."

I could not share his optimism and said nothing beyond making a few encouraging noises. I couldn't take my eyes off the change in his face, which had become grey and hollow-eyed, a mask which mocked his strength of will.

"Oh I know what you're looking at," he said, drawing his hand across the sunken cheeks. "I see this every morning in the mirror when I shave. It's those bloody drugs – they knock me about something shocking. Thank Christ they haven't made my hair fall out yet." He laughed. "That's about the only thing they haven't done to me. Anyway I can put up with it if I know they're working."

A few weeks later he came in again. He was getting very severe pain in his right leg and hip and the leg muscles had shrunk to half their normal size. It was obvious that the growth had spread to involve the pelvis, the spinal nerves, or both. By this time he was also getting side-effects from the treatment, but he made light of it and was content to take as many pain-killing drugs as were necessary. To my amazement I learned that he had been working the whole time, driving back and forth from Birmingham where the firm had a big contract. He drove the whole way there and back sitting on a bed-pan because of the agonising, uncontrollable diarrhoea. It seemed incredible that in spite of the terrible effects of the disease and its treatment he was able to function so well, for under similar circumstances most individuals without the same drive and determination to survive would have been bed-ridden, if not dead, by now.

Then one day, about two months after his treatment had started, Doreen came in, sat down and lit a cigarette.

"Stan's gone," she said.

I must have looked nonplussed, for she smiled and shook her head.

"No, I don't mean that. I mean he's left home."

"Left home? I don't follow..."

"Well, you wouldn't know. He's gone to live with a girl in Mottley. A receptionist at his place. Oh, I've known about this girl for a long time but this is the first time it's come into the open. I don't think any the less of him for it, though, don't think that. He's been a marvellous husband and father over the years. I just think it's like a sort of..."

"Last fling?"

"Yes... I suppose that's it, really. He really doesn't know

83

what he wants. And some of the time he has so much pain and he's taking so many tablets he doesn't know what he's doing. It's young Colin I feel sorry for. The poor lad is so confused – he can't understand it at all." She smiled briefly but her eyes were moist.

"Has Colin said much?"

"Not really. We've talked about it and I've tried to explain how Stan is feeling at the moment but it's very difficult. He can hardly cope with the fact of Pauline – that's the girl's name – as well as his dad being so ill. The thing that really worries me – Pauline doesn't have any idea how seriously ill Stan is."

"Oh come now – it must be obvious when she looks at him, surely," I said.

"Well, she visited him when he was in overnight at the the hospital last week and brought a load of holiday brochures to plan a winter holiday."

"That doesn't mean very much, I think. It may be simply to give him encouragement."

"I don't think so. I've talked to her. The thing is," she bit her bottom lip and stubbed her cigarette out slowly, "What will happen when he ... well, you know ... towards the end. I mean, he'll have to have someone to look after him, won't he? What will he do? And how will he know when he can't carry on?"

"He'll know. He'll become very tired and will want to sleep a lot."

"Then it's started already. He came to see Colin and me for the day on Saturday and he could hardly walk. God knows how he drove all the way back to Mottley. I'd just like to be sure that when it comes to, you know, the end, that he'll ... come home. That's all." She wanted to cry and I wished that she would, since it would have been less distressing to watch her cry than to sit by helplessly and watch the emotionally exhausting efforts she made at fighting back the despair that welled up inside her. I felt very sorry that the whole thing was taking this turn, more so because of the boy. Young Colin worshipped his dad and if, after all this time, the last few difficult weeks turned the lad against Stan, and created bitterness instead of love and understanding, it would be a pity. I tried as best as I could to reassure Doreen that when the chips were down Stan would finally come home.

He came in to see me a few weeks later. He had been in and out of the Royal for treatment and the reports from the hospital had been more gloomy each time, until the last letter indicated that only one further treatment was being attempted. No effort was made to hide the fact that this was a last desperate shot and that further therapy was not contemplated because of his worsening condition. We sat and talked for a few minutes, then he got up to go. He looked exhausted and his face was drawn and lined with pain. He was due to go into the Royal overnight for the final large dose of therapy, which he knew would leave him feeling wrecked for the next few days.

"There's one thing about it – we'll soon know whether this treatment has worked," he said. "One more dose of the stuff and here's hoping. Otherwise, there'll be a lot there." I knew that he was referring to his funeral and said nothing. "Aye, it'll be a big do, all right," he added. He laughed quietly, waved and walked out.

A few days later he rang from Mottley, but his voice had lost its usual cockiness. He sounded afraid and slightly incoherent. I guessed it may have been the drugs, but it was also something else. He was due to go into the Royal for treatment later that day, but during the night had had severe rigors and sweating. He couldn't control the cold and shivering: it was the final onslaught of the disease on his shattered defences. I told him to go without delay to the Royal as soon as I had ordered the ambulance. He hesitated.

"No. I'll go home first. Collect a few things. That's the best thing. Go home first. Thanks." That was the last time I spoke to him. He went into hospital and for a time his condition miraculously improved. He surrounded himself with paperwork connected with his business and worked furiously, sorting out all his affairs, bank accounts, insurance policies and so on. He even worked out the precise arrangements for his funeral down to the last detail, making a list and checking by telephone the availability of the pall-bearers. He did all this in between bouts of drugged stupor, not out of morbid obsession with his own demise, but simply to make things easier and smoother for Doreen and the family. After a couple of weeks, however, I rang the hospital and found that he had deteriorated badly. The following day I went down to see him, for I knew that he could not last many more days.

As I approached the ward I met the house surgeon – a pale, untidy, very bright-looking man with a bunch of ball-point pens in his top pocket.

"How's Stan?" I asked.

"Comatose, I'm afraid. You his GP?"

"Yes."

"Mm, well he'll maybe last today, not more. Tell me, what sort of character is he?"

"Why?"

"Three days ago I went to see him and he asked me if he was going to die, and if so, when did I expect it?"

"Yes, that sounds like Stan all right. What did you tell him?"

"Well I've never been asked like that before. It – it was a bit nerve-racking, I can tell you."

I smiled grimly, knowing how he felt.

"Then, when I told him, he looked at me and said: 'By the look on your face I feel more bloody sorry for you than I do for myself.'" The house surgeon shook his head as he walked away.

I went into the side-ward. Stan lay covered with a single cotton sheet, sleeping restlessly. His weight loss had made him virtually unrecognisable and I was shocked to see the profound change which had taken place. I looked round to see the whole family there in the room: On one side of the bed sat Doreen, and next to her, Stan's parents, Bessie and Jim Hamer. They got up as soon as I came in and started fussing around. Bessie handed me a cup of tea off a tray and Jim offered to get me a sandwich in case I hadn't had lunch. They had all been there more or less night and day for the past week and it was typical of them that they gave no thought to their own discomfort and impending loss.

At the end of the bed sat Colin Hamer, his head cupped in his hands, looking rather lost as if he did not belong to this gathering. On the other side of the bed was a dark-haired young woman carefully re-arranging the bed-sheet. Doreen introduced her as Pauline and I presumed this to be the girl from Mottley. There was no embarrassment or awkwardness in this introduction. She smiled, and carried on with what she was doing.

We spent some time talking about old times, but it became a little heavy-going after a while. Jim Hamer could scarcely control his quavering voice and his face showed his distress. I felt at that time very close to them. Although I had known them a long time I was moved by their warmth and enormous dignity, as well as by their total lack of bitterness. I made a move to leave for I had a few other calls to make. Jim Hamer shook my hand and looked at me with tear-filled eyes.

"Thanks Steven. We've known one another for a long time and I'm glad it were you looking after Stan. Thanks for all you've done..." He took a great sobbing breath and turned away to look out of the window by the bed. I looked round at the rest of the family and excused myself. Doreen Hamer phoned the next day to say that Stan had died. It was all over.

After the funeral service I left the church and walked through small groups of people talking quietly to each other. Leaning into the icy wind, I walked across the churchyard to my car which was parked nearby. I was not looking forward to finishing off the morning surgery which I had left an hour before.

As I was getting into my car an old man, whom I vaguely knew, walked slowly past and nodded towards the church.

"Sad day for some," he said, pulling down the corners of his creased mouth. I nodded, and the old man walked on.

# 10

The passage of the next few weeks saw the winter warm into a bright dry spring which in turn blossomed into an early summer of hot days and warm sunny evenings. The unusually good weather did not ease the work-load in the practice one bit, and both Ian and I continued to see full surgeries each day. The welter of upper respiratory infections was replaced by hay fever as the commonest reason for consultation and in spite of giving courses of de-sensitising vaccine to many dozens of patients, there were more cases each year whose complaints ranged from a few sneezes to the whole range of symptoms attributable to pollen sensitivity. The pollen count was particularly high that year. Many patients had such acute disturbance as to become temporarily incapacitated: their eyes swelled and streamed incessantly and they wheezed for days on end. Adults had their work routine and their social life brought completely to a standstill and many children had to be kept indoors – a restriction which in their case added unhappiness and frustration to an already miserable affliction.

The long, warm evenings had another effect which was obvious when driving home after surgery: crowds of men in their shirt-sleeves quenching their thirst at the end of a long hot day, amongst the white painted wooden or iron tables and Martini parasols which always appeared, as if by magic, all over the back gardens and adjacent pavements of nearly every pub during a spell of good weather. Some of the men were still in their working clothes, straight from a late shift, sinking pints of mixed, whilst freshly washed young men drank draught lager which made them belch languidly as they nodded and smiled at their girlfriends' animated conversation. Young children dashed in and out of the car parks and amongst the tables and chairs, spilling their crisps and lemonade and squealing with laughter, their parents enjoying an hour of relaxation before putting them to bed. Even the odd admonishing wave of the finger from dad at the noisy excesses from some of their offspring, together with the occasional snarl of, "If you don't behave yourself, Darren, I'll leather your backside!", did not seem to carry much conviction on evenings like these. The snag was that at closing time quite a few of these characters would climb into their cars with a blood alcohol level which would not be consistent with remaining conscious — let alone driving a car. As a result one or two of them would be stopped by the police and I would end up being called out at around midnight or so to take a blood sample at Hiley or Stallbrook Police Stations.

It was one such evening in early June. The children were in their beds, but they sat up wide awake for a long time before lying down restlessly, as the light came through the bedroom windows from the sun which hung like an orange, low in the sky. Tanya and I sat on the lawn for a while, talking and drinking beer before the lengthening shadows of the house cooled and darkened the garden. A light breeze began to blow gently rustling the leaves of the beech and ash trees which surrounded the rear of the house, but it was still quite warm. Tanya's pregnancy was advancing nicely and the bulge of her abdomen was sufficiently large by now to make her change her position frequently as we sat and talked. Life seemed pleasant and uncomplicated and for the last couple of months I had not even given any thought to the health centre, let alone discuss it. We idly reflected on my chances of being called out that night. I knew Tanya was hoping that I would stop doing the police surgeon job, especially now our third child was on its way. I had given it some thought on several occasions, but when the cheques arrived in the post I put it off each time. Even as we talked about it the phone began to ring and I immediately jumped up, spilling my drink, and ran in to answer it. As I ran into the hall, wiping beer off my shirt, I wondered how many years would pass before the sound of the telephone ceased to make me jump like that. I cursed my

89

own response as much as the fact of the phone ringing.

It was the police station at Stallbrook. There was a case of rape and I was requested to examine the victim. I took a shower to waken myself up, told Tanya not to wait up, knowing that this sort of case could take a couple of hours to sort out, then got into my car and drove off. The roads were surprisingly clear so I put my foot down and was there in about ten minutes.

Stallbrook nestled amongst a series of hills. Newer development, built long after the decline of the cotton industry, had spread like fingers up the sides of the surrounding slopes from the densely packed centre of the little town. The big new police station was right in the middle, but so close were the adjacent buildings that only from its small asphalt car park could it be seen from a distance of more than twenty yards. It was flanked on the other three sides by warehouses, the market hall, and the ponderous black lintels and Doric columns of the public swimming baths.

I walked up the steps to the glass doors, in front of which stood Jim Hardcastle. He nodded.

"Evening, doctor. It's about time you got an altimeter fitted to that bloody vehicle of yours. You passed one of my lads on Dootson Road and he thought it was a low-flying aircraft. Just radio'd in now to let us know. I appreciate your enthusiasm at these cases of ours, but we're not thinking of putting landing lights in the car park, you know."

"Yes, I'm sorry about that. I was gathering a fair bit of momentum down that stretch," I replied guiltily.

He smiled. "I should bloody say so. Exceeding the speed limit by a factor of three, according to my lads."

"I must have had my mind on something else," I said. He laughed, and the deep throaty sound echoed round the car park.

"Oh Christ – driving without due care and attention as well, eh? Best not say anything else, doctor." He half turned and gazed over the tops of the nearby buildings and over the town. "Just stand here a minute, doctor, and look around you. D'you know," he said, with mock wonder in his voice, "it's difficult to imagine, I mean to say you'd never *think*, looking at the town *now*, that a hundred years ago..." he waved his arm slowly from one side of the horizon to the other, '.... a hundred years ago it looked ... exactly the bloody same." He shook his head sadly, and we both went inside.

Dusk was gathering and the bright neon lighting of the interior made my eyes ache as I stood in the central office. At one side of the large desk which occupied nearly half the floor space, a young constable gloomily typed out a report. His right index finger hovered over the typewriter, occasionally plunging down the keys like a hen picking out corn amongst its own droppings. He silently mouthed the sound of the words, syllable by syllable.

It was warm and airless in the place in spite of the open windows, and the station sergeant fanned his face with sheets of foolscap as he leaned over the humming banks of the radio equipment in the radio room. The adjoining glass door was fully open and I could hear the dead-pan conversation.

"Ah – Panda, ah – Three, are you ah – receiving me? Over."

Squawk, crackle, click.

"Panda Three receiving, over."

"Ah – Panda Three, ah – proceed immediately to Lin Chow's on ah – Market – ah – Street, understood ah – Panda Three? Over."

Blip, scratch, scratch, blip.

"Understood, Stallbrook. Have we got trouble there again? Over."

"Ah – negative, Panda Three. Collect and pay for, – ah repeat ah – pay for, two ah – chicken curries and ah – three bottles of ah – Tizer..."

I cleared one corner of the desk of plastic cups, ash-trays, carbon papers and disposable ball-point pens and took a couple of things from my bag which I would need for the examination. I filled out a few forensic labels to save time while I waited for CID to come downstairs with the victim's statement and to fill in on a few details. After a few minutes Detective Inspector Early came down in shirt-sleeves, sucking his pipe as usual. He sat down in a chair by the desk, shook his head slowly and rolled his eyes up to the ceiling.

"You've got a right one here, doctor. I mean, this good lady tells a tale that has that indefinable, ludicrous quality known to you people as fantasy. In short, you might say, she has told us a lot of cock."

He tapped his pipe and puffed it thoughtfully, first glancing at me and then gazing out of the window into the darkening shadows of the town outside. I grunted and rummaged in my bag for my torch, which to my annoyance was not there.

"Just to put you in the picture, doctor. You can read that in a minute." He handed me the hand-written statement which covered two or three sides of foolscap. "The lady's name is Brenda, Mrs. Brenda Wagstaff. Mother of five children. Husband is away a lot, a long-distance lorry driver. Well, she went to a dance last night with a man friend who on the way home allegedly raped her in the *front seat* of a mini, now there's a thought."

"Last night?"

"Correct, doctor," he replied, pursing his lips and nodding. "Only, tonight, her husband got back unexpectedly and the boyfriend at the dance turns up as well to take her out again. Brenda gets the wind up and screams rape the night before. Husband thumps them both, drags Brenda round here and here we are. Before you ask, we've interviewed the boyfriend and he says it all happened with full consent in a field at the back of the dance-hall. And I think you may notice – correct me if I'm wrong, doctor – bits of grass still in her hair. Anyway, I'll leave you to decide the medical evidence."

"Fair enough," I said, getting to my feet. "Have you got a torch by any chance? I've left mine somewhere."

Early opened a drawer in the desk and searched around, finally pulling out a huge black waterproof torch which looked as if it was used by deep sea divers to examine oil-rigs for signs of metal fatigue.

"There you go, doctor. Just the job, that. Hey up, what's this..." He pulled from the drawer about ten feet of stout mountaineering rope and threw it across the desk. "Now *that* might come in handy. I should tie one end to your feet and the other end to the radiator just in case you fall in while you're taking samples."

I smiled at Early's coarseness, for I knew the man had a reason for being like this: when investigating serious crime he was correct and meticulous, sometimes ruthless with his subordinates, yet on the other hand he could be charming and extremely kind to old ladies who had lost their pet cats or canaries. But when he felt his leg was being pulled and his time wasted he usually responded in this way.

"Are you trying to tell me something?" I said as I walked to the office door. Early smiled and put his pipe in his pocket.

"In a way, doctor, in a way. Here we are, both of us busy men — you wanting to get back to your bed and me wanting to get to grips with all the problems of keeping law and order in this teeming metropolis — and here we are, pricking about with a silly nonsense like this. It's a waste of valuable professional time and public money."

"Sure. Still, it's got to be done..."

"Oh, absolutely, doctor," said Early, nodding his head vigorously. "You're right there, no question. Justice must be seen to be done and so forth. Oh yes, far be it from me to say ... anyway, do your worst, doctor. I'll come back here and get one of the lads to brew up once I've introduced you to the distressed victim." He led the way to the examination room.

Brenda Wagstaff sat in the examination room talking quietly with the policewoman in attendance. The WPC was being sympathetic and kind and stood back politely when we went in. Brenda was short and rather plump, with heavy mascara which had run with tears earlier in the evening. The mascara was smeared round her forehead and cheeks where she had repeatedly wiped it with her hands, and she had a bruise on the right side of the lower jaw and a puffy eye where presumably her husband had taken a swing at her. She was a sorry sight and it seemed that she did not have a great deal to look forward to, whichever way things turned out. Inspector Early introduced me and when he had gone she slowly began to take her things off for my examination. The WPC did what she could to make her feel less apprehensive, but Brenda naturally felt both resentful and miserable about the whole thing.

The actual examination was really a dead loss, but I did all I could and took all the necessary specimens, the only positive findings being the presence of a few grass fragments in her hair and in her tights. I collected the specimens together with all the relevant labels and went through into the main office. Early looked up from his pipe and raised his eyebrows with a silent question.

"Not easy to say anything definite, really," I said. "No sign of violence, all her clothing intact – they are the same clothes she wore last night apparently."

"Yes, we'll have to send them off to forensic when she goes home and changes," Early said in a weary voice.

"And then of course, she has had five children, which made things even more difficult..." I continued.

Early leaned forward and put his elbows on the desk. "Are there any signs of intercourse against the will of this lady, with signs of violence, a struggle or whatever?" he asked.

"Intercourse, probably, but violence or signs of a struggle ... no, not at all. The facial bruising was caused by the husband, tonight."

"Right, doctor. I think we have gone far enough with this one. It's getting late, I'm getting hungry and there's a tidal wave of crime sweeping across the town while I'm tied up with this stuff." He smiled and winked mischievously, then got up and beckoned me to follow him to the examination room. In the corridor he stared down thoughtfully at the floor as he walked. Outside the closed door of the examination room he turned slowly on his heel and jabbed the stem of his pipe at my tie. He spoke softly and very gravely.

"Now then, doctor. I want you to observe most carefully in the following few minutes, for what you will see and hear can only be truly appreciated by a keen and probing mind. I shall now demonstrate some of the subtle nuances of police interrogation." He turned again and we went into the examination room. Brenda and the policewoman were talking about the price of vegetables as we entered. Early took a small upright chair, turned it round so that it was facing him, then sat astride it and leaned forward so that his forearms rested on the back of the chair. He sucked at his pipe quietly for a few seconds, screwing his eyes up against the haze of blue smoke which drifted slowly to the ceiling. Then, still with his pipe in his mouth, he cleared his throat and looked at Brenda with a quizzical expression on his face. His voice was bright and cheerful, very conversational.

"Well now, Brenda love, what's all this bloody shit about you being poked in the front of a mini?"

Poor Brenda was a bit shaken by this, but she soon recovered.

"What's that supposed to mean?" she retorted, stubbing out her cigarette furiously in an ash tray on the desk. "I told that other detective how it happened so don't come that. You're all the rotten same, you lot!"

Early riffled through her statement which he was holding. "It says here," he said with a very, very small hint of incredulity, "it says here, according to what you told my detective constable, that the man, one Henry Hinchcliffe, pulled down your tights while you were sitting in the passenger seat, and while he was in the driver's seat, and he then raped you."

"That's right, he did!" cried Brenda indignantly. "Well," she added less forcefully, "he didn't pull my tights *right* down. About six inches or so, that's all."

Early dropped the statement papers in front of him in the chair and took the pipe out of his mouth.

"Now let's get this right, Brenda. You say he pulled your tights down six inches, and raped you while he was in the driver's seat and you were in the passenger seat?"

"Well ..." Brenda looked somewhat rumpled and dejected. Her shoulders slumped. Early stood up and looked at the ceiling with half closed eyes.

"Then I put it to you, Brenda," he said in heavy measured tones, "I put it to you, that in order to do *that*, Henry Hinchcliffe would have to be an acrobatic dwarf with a prick two feet long and shaped like a boomerang." His head jerked down and he looked straight at Brenda with his eyes wide and his eyebrows raised as high as they would go. Brenda's mouth suddenly curled down and she burst into noisy tears.

"Ooooh, I'm sorry," she sobbed, "I only said it because I knew if my husband found out he'd beat the living daylights out of me. When he finds out what happened he'll kill me..." The words dissolved into great convulsive sobs and she stuffed a very small patterned handkerchief against her nose and mouth with such force that I thought that she was going to end it all there and then by suffocating herself. Early turned to the policewoman and smiled benignly.

"Make Brenda a cup of tea, love, and then we'll see about this statement of hers." He gathered up the foolscap sheets and led the way out of the room, this time striding quickly back to the central office. We sat down by the big rectangular table and Early filled his pipe again.

"Well, doctor, I hope you took careful note of my cunningly devious approach."

"Oh yes," I replied, "Very Machiavellian."

Early closed his eyes and sucked his unlit pipe.

"Mmm, very Machiavellian. Very *Machiavellian* ... that's very good, doctor, very apt. I like that. Mind you," he opened his eyes again and began searching for matches in his bulging trouser pockets. "That's where I missed out, you see. Lack of classical education. You lads are lucky, university education and so forth. Opens up the mind, that does. Although to be quite honest with you, doctor, when you come right down to it, all these degrees and diplomas are not worth much if we can't communicate with one another. I'll give you an example." He found his matches and took a long time to get the fresh tobacco lit. He was nearly lost in a billowing cloud of smoke before he continued.

"Some of us here, for our sins, get sent on refresher courses now and again, designed to broaden our outlook, so to speak. We were at one in Lancaster last year. Had a lecture on 'The Value of Communication in Present Day Society', I think it was. There we were, sitting in this hushed lecture hall, forty burly coppers looking down on a young lecturer with very thick spectacles – a real egg-head, looked as if he had come from another planet. In a very twee voice this lecturer bloke just says, 'Gentlemen, we live in a confusing world, do we not? Good. Now, I would like one of you to define the word confusion. Define ... the ... word ... confusion.' He looks round to see a sea of stony unflinching faces in front of him. 'One of you. Define. The. Word. Confusion,' he says again, very clipped, very precise. Nothing. By this time he starts to get a little impatient and struts up and own and we're all looking at him as if he's growing another leg. Then he points at one of us in desperation and asks him to have a go. Well, this big lad stands up, a very big lad he was, from Birmingham, I think. Anyway, without batting an eyelid..." Early burst into laughter and in doing so blew ash from the bowl of his pipe all over his shirt and the table in front of him, "... he says: 'Confusion, sir, is when an Irish cat has a crap, then scratches a hole in the ground and buries *itself!*' Now that, doctor, warmed my heart to hear that man, and whilst it was perhaps none too elegant, it was very pithy. Very pithy indeed, I thought." He laughed to himself and brushed ash off his shirt. "Buggered if I can remember the point I was trying to make," he added. We both laughed and helped ourselves to cups of tea which stood on the desk in a shallow tray advertising Swales Oat-Meal Stout. Early always had a fund of anecdotes which he loved to relate and I knew that if I didn't rouse myself out of the chair I would be stuck for the next couple of hours, which had happened many times in the past. I packed up my bags, deciding not to write my report there and then as I usually did: I would do it in the morning. As I was filling out the claim for my fee a detective constable came in and spoke to Early.

"You'll have to have a word with Brenda's husband, sir, won't you? Now you've heard what she had to say. He's in the front office." The DC was perspiring freely and to my amazement was wearing a heavy tweed sports jacket in spite of the warm night. He must have been very uncomfortable since the temperature hardly seemed to have fallen since early evening. He saw me looking at him and could tell what I was thinking.

"Have to wear this tonight, doctor," he said cheerfully. He

turned round and lifted up the back of his jacket. Most of the back of the shirt was missing from just below the shoulders. "Had a bit of a misunderstanding with one of the dogs earlier on. Sorting out a disturbance at the front of the station, we were."

Early grunted. "From what I heard, you looked highly bloody comical, son," he said. "Dog-handler grappling with two layabouts, you on your hands and knees in the road with that big alsation on your back. It's a wonder nobody threw a bucket of water over the lot of you." He shook his head and groaned, then slowly got out of his chair, brushing more ash off his trousers. "Well, come on, let's have a word with Brenda's husband and try to keep some semblance of order and dignity about the place."

I went down the corridor to the main door and as I left I heard Early open the door of the front office where Brenda's husband was sitting.

"Well, now, Mr. Wagstaff," he said in a cheerful voice as he went in, "We've just had a word with your good lady wife..." The rest of his sentence was obliterated as he closed the door.

I walked out of the front door of the station, down the steps and into the street. A light, cool breeze gusted gently down from the direction of the market square and as it funnelled into the narrow street between the police station and the market hall it disturbed a small collection of debris: empty potato crisp packets, newspapers and tissue-paper – the sort used for wrapping oranges and grapefruit. They tumbled and scraped their way along the kerb and into the gutter as if pulled by invisible wires. As I crossed the street to the car park on the other side I caught the smell of uncollected garbage from the market stalls, and the warm waft from an oriental restaurant up the street welded the various smells into an unpleasant amalgam; it had a foetid quality and I imagined it to be like the stinking breath of a bilious prehistoric reptile. It was almost as if the town, after languishing in the sun all day and pouring vast quantities of beer and food into itself, had belched with satisfaction before settling down for the night.

# 11

The month of June that year sprawled out lazily into a series of shimmering hot days, each fulfilling the breathless promise of its still, misty dawn. By the time August had arrived I had seen the dawn quite a few times whilst driving home from a confinement or from a visit to Hiley or Stallbrook Police Stations. Although usually dead beat, my face feeling like a greasy mask through lack of sleep, it was still good to be up early on days like these to smell the damp earth and see the dew like glass beads on the grass — the precipitation of the breath of night. Even senses dulled by fatigue became aware of the beauty of such mornings. Sometimes, though, I parked the car in the drive at the back of the house and fell asleep in the driving seat, waking up to other sounds which were a sort of morning overture of civilised man: the flushing of a toilet; the clank of a dustbin lid; the snatch and whine of a battery-operated milk-float; clinking bottles; footsteps, whistling, coughing, slamming doors, starter-motors, car engines, moving traffic — building up gradually in intensity like a colossal orchestra warming up its instruments before the sounds imperceptibly merged into the more distant diapason, a sound so low in frequency that it could be felt rather than heard.

One of these mornings that August I arrived back at about 6.30 am after attending a home confinement. It had been a simple, straightforward affair which only needed my attendance to put a couple of stitches into the perineal tear — but there had been a lot of talking and tea-drinking and so it had taken longer than usual. By the time I got home it was too late to go to bed, so I made some toast and sat in the garden drinking tea. After a short time the two boys joined me and we rescued wasps from the marmalade for some time before

Tanya came down. She was by now about two weeks overdue with her pregnancy. She carried a cup of tea and the morning mail, consisting mainly of advertising literature from the drug companies, which I gave to the boys to scribble on. They ran inside for coloured pencils.

"Aren't you tired?" asked Tanya, smiling across at me as she sat down carefully on a garden chair.

"Not really. I'll probably deteriorate after lunch-time though," I replied. "How about you?"

"I'm not really looking forward to going in tomorrow for induction with this dispute," she said.

I'd forgotten about that. The ancillary staff were on strike and there was no food or laundry for the patients. Eating sandwiches and lying on paper sheets was not an appealing prospect for someone in labour.

"I think I'll take a large dose of castor oil and then mow the lawn this afternoon," she said thoughtfully. "That should do the trick. Then have the baby at home."

I smiled at her philosophical, practical approach "OK. We've got the local midwife's number. Just wait until I finish evening surgery." I looked at my watch. It was time to go. "Sure you'll be OK?"

She laughed and shook her head, which made her long auburn hair fall forward, framing her face and making her look incredibly attractive.

"Wait until you've finished surgery? Yes of course, I'll try not to go into labour during surgery hours. God knows, we mustn't inconvenience the patients."

"I didn't mean..."

"I know. But it would be nice if you were around this time. You always seem to be on duty when I go into labour."

"Don't remind me. The last two times were a bit of a shambles," I said ruefully. I thought back to the time in Edinburgh; an ice-cold top flat, fleeting visits to the Simpson Maternity Unit and not being there when it mattered, running back to pick up the fraying pieces of a disintegrating career in surgery. The second time was no better. I had not been in the practice very long and I was simply trying to do too many

100

things in too short a time, the net result being that I did nothing properly.

"I'll be home early, whatever happens," I said. "If you do start, just ring me and I'll drop everything. I promise."

"I will. You'd better get going now." She smiled and lifted her face as I leaned down and kissed her.

I drove to the surgery by way of Breadburn. It was an aptly named place, being dominated by Bailey's Giant Family Bakery. I marvelled that such a delicious smell could emanate from a place which baked such bowel-paralysing bread.

Early mornings in August were characterised by small groups of elderly people with suitcases standing at street corners or outside newsagents' shops, waiting to be picked up by coaches to take them to Blackpool, Skegness or Torquay. For this was the holiday month and many of the shops and businesses closed down for two weeks. Younger families left the town by means of their family saloons, sagging with roof racks piled with badly-stacked suitcases, infants' trolleys and the odd plastic potty – the latter representing the emancipation of the infant bladder: in the family saloon you could stop where you pleased. Gone, for these parents, were the days when they passed pub after pub with "No Coaches Allowed" signs outside, while their children whimpered and wriggled, red-faced and sweaty, as their tiny bladders filled beyond endurance.

I pulled up at the traffic lights where there was a sizeable collection of holidaymakers talking animatedly. They were all well beyond middle-age, the men wearing new sports jackets and flannels and each carrying a transparent plastic raincoat tucked in a small bundle underneath his arm. Some of the women checked the contents of their handbags for the third or fourth time, others their magazines and knitting which they carried in string bags. Their conversation floated across as they shuffled about, occasionally peering up the road and glancing at their watches to see if the coach was coming on time.

"We've been going to Alice Clegg's Guest House every year since dad died..."

"Like home from home, like."

"Got a big colour telly."

"Just the thing when it's wet."

"The food's lovely..."

"That counts for a lot."

"Cups of tea whenever you want..."

"Makes all the difference..."

"And as much bread and butter as you can eat..."

"Well, I mean, what more can you ask for?"

The lights changed and I drew away from the little gathering, catching a brief glimpse in the driving mirror of their hesitant jostling as I swung round the corner at the traffic lights. I drove past the empty, brightly-lit supermarket on the right and then turned down the narrow drive into the dilapidated open garage of the surgery. Ian had already arrived and Miss Cope was talking to a patient on the telephone, so I went through to my consulting room.

A few minutes later Ian stuck his head round the door.

"Ah. It's yourself. A quick word – you had better come into my room."

My heart sank. A quick word usually meant a half-hour discussion. Still, Ian looked pretty solemn so it must be important. A glance at the record cards on the desk showed that there were already quite a few patients waiting. I got up and went into the other consulting room to find him pacing up and down, staring at the floor as if he were trying to establish the exact dimensions of the room.

"Bad news," he said gravely, handing me an official-looking envelope. "First of all, Miss Cope has announced her intention of retiring in the new year." He looked aghast, as if, hearing it spoken aloud in his own voice, he had registered the fact for the first time. He shook his head slowly. "That's a terrible blow. I don't know how we'll replace her."

I agreed. The fact was we couldn't replace her, not at the pittance we paid her. Sixteen years she had been in this practice and she knew the patients inside out, knew who was on the phone and who had a neighbour or relative with a car to bring patients to the surgery to save us visiting. She made and checked Ian's appointments, arranged his visits, sharpened his pencils, and did a thousand other things to make the surgery tick over. Since my own methods of working were haphazard and ill formed as yet, I probably did not appreciate Miss Cope's qualities as much as Ian, whose methods over the years had been honed and polished into a careful, regular routine. Miss Cope blended beautifully with this routine and could therefore anticipate his every move, more or less, which to Ian was the epitome of a good working relationship. The problem, as I saw it then, was that Ian's experience and careful methodology might not compensate for his corresponding decline in ability to adapt and improvise in entirely different conditions. Once we had got through the business of finding a replacement for Miss Cope, the next year or so would be an uneasy transition through unchartered waters.

"Well, it's a little time off before it happens," he said. "We need to think about what we're going to do."

"Well the first thing is . . ."

"We'll have to think about it for a bit," Ian repeated firmly. I took this to mean that he didn't want to discuss it or even think about it for as long as possible. Anything that might upset the status quo made him agitated. I nodded in agreement and opened the letter he had given me.

"Oh yes," he said gloomily, "that's the other matter."

I looked at the letter. It was from Parfitt, Johnson and Snead, local solicitors on behalf of the owners of the building, part of which we occupied. It was brief. It simply stated that the lease on the surgery expired in twelve months' time and that we would be required to vacate the premises to make way for development.

"This can't be right, surely?" I said in amazement. Ian sat down and stared blankly out of the window.

"It is, I'm afraid. I've checked."

"But the last time you spoke to Frank Lucas he said there was no danger – "

"I know what he *said*. But apparently they've been offered a big fat price for the whole premises and land from some big supermarket chain. The rumours were correct, and they want us out."

"Christ – another supermarket! The place needs that as much as ..." I trailed off as I thought about all those official reassurances.

"Oh yes, I'm well aware of all that. My God, I've worked my backside off in this town for over thirty years and to think it should come to this. Getting thrown out of my own surgery!"

"But that's the problem really, isn't it? I mean – we don't own it, only rent it," I said.

"Same damn thing." Ian was angry and bitter. "We pay the rent. What a bloody thing! It's indecent. Anyway, maybe the new health centre will be ready by then and ...'

"Oh come off it Ian! They haven't even found a site for it yet, let alone started to build it."

"Hm. That's true." Ian swivelled round in his chair and stared at his hands on the desk. "What's amazing is that it's actually seven years ago since I first got the ball rolling for the health centre. Hell – we've had meetings with the architect and all those bloody administrators, and after all this time, what is there to show for it? Nothing. Not a brick laid, not even a site found. If I responded to patients' illnesses in the same dilatory way I'd have been crucified by the GMC before now."

"The fact is we are going to be turfed out with no suitable premises to go to, unless of course we contemplate going into a temporary building while the health centre is being completed." As I said this I realised that the logistics of moving all the surgery equipment, phones and records twice within the space of a year, would be horrific – quite apart from the expense, which would of course come out of our own pockets.

"No, I'm not having that," said Ian. "We'll stall. Put it in legal hands, that sort of thing. Get the public behind us. They *can't* throw us out. We'll stall until the health centre has been completed and then we can move in."

I smiled. "I wish I could share your optimism. You

remember I wrote to the Area Health Authority a year or two ago warning them of the urgency?"

"I do. And they wouldn't commit themselves to a damn thing. Yes, I remember. Typical. And what about the local council? What a shower they turned out to be. Bloody terrible. All wind and water and no use at all. Can you remember all that claptrap at the Town Hall? And all those official denials about development? I mean, without a decent building who is going to come to Overton to replace the likes of me when I retire? There's a couple of GPs in the same boat. Bond – he's sixty-odd, should retire soon. And there's McClean – he's nearly sixty. Who's going to replace them when they retire?" He leaned back in his chair, his voice becoming calmer, more reflective. "Reorganisation of the National Health Service. My God, what a charade. I wonder what we've let ourselves in for."

I wondered, too. Since reorganisation early that year a giant spanner seemed to have been thrown into the entire business of decision-making, and we had groaned from one meeting to another without any discernible progress being made. It had been intensely frustrating; the old welfare clinic was due to be demolished very soon to make way for the by-pass and yet there was still no sign of the health centre even being started. It was difficult to believe that the town and its people would be deprived in such a way but this had suddenly become a real possibility. I could only curse the new structure of the NHS with its mind-rotting pyramid of committees whose inner chambers echoed all the way to the hallowed temple at the Elephant and Castle; those committees which were like intellectual mortuaries where original or dissenting ideas were laid to rest pending further examination. The only certainty was that if things did plod on in this way then the people who stood to suffer most were the patients. But then, that would be nothing new.

We agreed to discuss things further when we had more time and I returned to my consulting room to start the morning surgery. I went through the whole surgery mechanically, thinking about the problems we had just discussed, and at the

105

same time wondering how Tanya was getting on.

When I had seen my last patient Miss Cope came in and told me there was someone waiting to see me. I grunted unenthusiastically. She brought in a young couple with a baby whom at first I did not recognise. Then I realised the girl was Glenys Booth. I was amazed, because she looked attractive with a modern hair-style and her acne had pretty well disappeared. She introduced me to her new husband who was a motor-mechanic in Chester. Apparently she had been kept in hospital the whole time until the baby had been delivered, and had then gone straight to Chester to live with her new in-laws, which is why I had lost track of her. I expressed my surprise.

"Didn't my mum tell you, then?" said Glenys.

"No, she didn't, as a matter of fact. She was in here a few weeks ago . . ." I blushed at the memory of it. No wonder she didn't tell me. I remembered that I had been up all night the night before and Mrs Booth had started to tell me a long dreary story about her aching legs. Her voice had had the effect of an overdose of curare and sodium pentothal and I had fallen deeply asleep while she talked.

"Oh well," said Glenys brightly. "Just to say thanks for what you did, doctor, and that we're very happy, especially that we don't see much of my mum. I feel sorry for you, doctor, in a way, having to look after her. She told me to tell you that she'll be coming in to see you again next week."

They said goodbye and I sat back, wondering what God-awful miasma of pathology her mother would present me with now, especially since her only daughter had left and obviously did not need her any more.

When I got home that evening I found that Tanya had mowed the quarter-acre lawn and was having regular uterine contractions. Though she was physically restless and uncomfortable she was mentally very calm and did not want any medication. I put the children to bed and wandered about checking and re-checking my obstetric bag and making coffee. It never occurred to either of us to ask for assistance in what we anticipated would be a perfectly normal labour.

About eight-fifteen the membranes ruptured and I rang for the local midwife who arrived within ten minutes. She was a cheerful middle-aged woman with a scrubbed shiny face who took charge right away. Fifteen minutes later our third child was born – a boy, nine pounds. My own professional contribution was thankfully confined to making tea and keeping a supply of hot water at hand.

When the midwife left I crept into the bedroom where Tanya lay with her eyes closed, the only sound coming from the cot where the baby quietly whimpered and sucked his fingers. With growing elation I examined him in detail, noting with wonder and amazement his perfect form. Tanya opened her eyes.

"Another boy," she murmured. "Everything all right?"

"Fine. No problems. How do you feel?"

"Exhausted. Come and sit here."

I sat on the edge of the bed and we gazed at each other, saying nothing. Then we threw our arms around one another and Tanya burst into sobs of joy. An overwhelming emotional response surged through me and my hands shook uncontrollably as I stroked her hair. She pulled away, laughing through her tears.

"Come on, let's drink to the best delivery of all three of them."

I went down to the cellar and opened a bottle of champgne from a case which I had bought for the obstetrician who had looked after Tanya during the ante-natal period. After tonight, we felt entitled to drink some of it ourselves. We drank a couple of glasses and Tanya sat back on the piled up pillows.

"We did quite well, didn't we?" she said.

"You did. I didn't do anything, really."

"You didn't have to. I felt relaxed, fully in control. It's different in your own home. And you were here, which is what mattered. That's all that's ever mattered."

I took a large gulp of champagne and the fizz brought tears to my eyes. At least I think it was the fizz.

# 12

I took the next few days off to help out with things at home, then Tanya's mother came and took over, leaving me redundant. I didn't want to use up all my holidays, hoping that we could get away later next month, so I went back to the surgery which fortunately was fairly quiet for the next week or so. We avoided discussion of our lease, and Miss Cope did not mention her retirement next year. We carried on as if nothing was going to change.

By Wednesday the following week I was beginning to feel restless. Not only had we kept all these problems to ourselves but in the last few days I had seen an endless string of trivia in the surgery which a boy scout could have handled. There was an overwhelming number of gnat-bites, sunburn and nettle rash cases which had affected young children on holiday from school, whose mothers had not the slightest idea of treatment. It seemed incredible. Their indignation and astonishment, when I indicated that these problems could be dealt with by common sense and simple household remedies, radiated from their faces as if I were expounding on quantum mechanics. The mention of Calamine lotion brought looks of mute disbelief as though I had mentioned medieval sorcery, and likewise my dogged explanations of simple everyday bodily functions seemed to some of the young parents as incomprehensible as $E = MC^2$. Where are the grannies of yesteryear, I thought, to lay a foundation of common sense onto these vacant lots? Probably re-housed from their former dwellings, sitting in centrally heated maisonettes in some distant, clean, windy estate dreaming of the donkey-stoned steps and flagged backyard where they used to live before they had to move for re-development: it weren't much to look at but we had good neighbours across t'yard, and there were

108

always family popping in, you know, like, being as they only lived across t'street. Hello, gran, hello our Colin, hello our Pam, hello gran, love, brought you a jug of stout from the off-licence, ooh yer 'avin' tripe and elder by 'eck that's a bit of all right I say that'll put hairs on yer chest, club man's just this minute gone, thanks I will have a cup of tea, come across tomorrow we're only having spam but there'll be plenty of Turog and butter, our Brian'll come round tonight, I'll have to go now, tar-ra gran, tar-ra Pam love, tar-ra Colin, tar-ra Gran, tar-ra, see yer.

Now in silence, she waits in vain for a knock on the door. Perhaps the welfare will call, better than no one at all...

I definitely needed a holiday away from all this. My enthusiasm was dwindling and I was having difficulty concentrating.

Then, quite suddenly, I was jolted awake by Emily Parker, whom I very rarely saw. She was a fairly large seventy year-old who lived with her bronchitic husband, and since she had retired she had been active in all sorts of cancer-relief campaigns. She was quiet but very firm and only very reluctantly would she allow herself to be examined. A deliberate undoing of the very top button of the blouse, for example, accompanied by a rather prim expression, indicated that the physiological wonders of her cardio-pulmonary system would have to be assessed by a swift examination of the two square inches or so of bared skin she revealed just above the sternal notch. She once turned down my offer of a rectal examination for her piles, presenting me instead with a few square inches of blood-stained toilet paper. This was evidence enough for Mrs. Parker, for she had no wish for an unnecessary and improper examination. Still, she was kind and generous to others when they were ill and within her self-imposed limitations I found her quite likeable.

Today, however, she complained that her stomach was swelling and that she could now no longer wear her corsets. All other enquiries I made were negative: she had no other symptoms. Only after a lengthy argument could I get her to agree to an internal examination, which was just as well

109

because I soon found the cause of her trouble. She had a very large ovarian tumour which felt malignant and which was about the size of a twenty-eight week pregnancy. I explained this to her and recommended that she see a gynaecologist with a view to possible surgery.

"Is this completely necessary?" she asked warily.

"Yes, of course it is, Mrs Parker," I replied, "otherwise I wouldn't have suggested it in the first place."

"Hm, I see. More examinations, more humiliations – that's what it means."

"What it means," I said as patiently as I could, "is that if we do something positive *now* it could save you a lot of unnecessary trouble later on. Surely all this work you do with cancer relief must have shown you that?"

"Aye, well, it's not the same thing when it's yourself," she sniffed. "Well anyway, I'll let you know presently."

I had already started to fill in a referal form. "What's that supposed to mean, Mrs Parker? I'm just about to write off to the hospital now."

She shook her head. "Well you can put your pen down. I'll let you know what I've decided when I'm good and ready."

"But how long…"

"When I'm good and ready," she said with heavy emphasis. "When I've had a good think on it."

"Well, it's up to you…"

"You're right there, lad. It *is* up to me. I thank you for your trouble, but I must think about it. You do see how it is, don't you?" She smiled, and I did see how it was. She had always been used to making up her own mind about everything and did not like being swept along passively by something she did not understand. I knew that I would have to wait for her to make up her mind on whether we took this any further, and that was that. She thanked me again and left.

I collected the visits and did them as swiftly as I could. There was nothing in them which required a great deal of time – two cases of chicken pox, a case of mumps and a post-natal visit. I got through them quickly and decided to call at Smallwood House which was more or less on the way home.

110

Smallwood was a local authority old people's home built on the edge of the new council estate between Overton and Overdale. I remembered that they had asked me to call some time that week but there was no urgency, "only when it is convenient, doctor". The staff of Smallwood were friendly and very competent and we got on well. I had acquired quite a few of the old folk in the home, some of whom were my own patients who could no longer cope in their own homes, but quite a few were patients who had moved from other areas too far for their own GP to visit. I liked old people and enjoyed my visits there because the problems were relatively simple, medically. This was partly because they were well looked after by the staff and on the whole didn't get depressed or lonely. It was therefore unnecessary to give them a mountain of multicoloured tablets to keep them happy, since they adjusted themselves to their various physical limitations fairly quickly.

I drove through the estate and remembered it as I had known it thirty years ago when it had been rolling fields and copses. It had been prize conker country. Over on the other side of the estate was an old sealed off ventilation shaft of a coal mine, a reminder that, underneath the endless fields I had known as a schoolboy, lay a rich coal seam a century ago. This area had been called Collier's Meadow. It was curious how place-names in the north, even outside the towns, still echoed their gritty past. Just as older women wistfully remembered their first lover, so northern towns reflected the infatuation with earlier times when they had had their thighs spread apart by the industrial revolution, the greatest rapist of all time. No genteel southern-place-names here: Pit Street, Foundry Lane, Iron Street, Mill Lane, were all within a mile from where I now parked my car outside Smallwood.

I walked across the neat lawns and through the double glass doors which led into the main corridor of the single storey home which housed about fifty elderly people. Some of the residents were making their way slowly to the dining room where lunch was being served: a shuffling, trembling exodus of bent, arthritic frames supported by walking-sticks and

Zimmer aids. By the time the last, least able individuals reached the small tables in the dining room, the more robust residents would have slurped their way through the soup and be already half way through the main course.

Mrs. Garner, the Warden, showed me to the single room where the patient was. Ellen Bean had caused me some anxiety a couple of weeks ago when she had suffered a brisk rectal haemorrhage, the cause of which was not clear and which showed no signs of stopping. In spite of her age (she was ninety-five) I had had no option but to send her in to the Royal. Fortunately, without any interference or investigation, the bleeding stopped spontaneously and she was discharged back to the care of Smallwood. The chances were that the bleeding was due to either carcinoma of the large bowel or diverticulitis, but because she was not physically fit for any sort of abdominal surgery, the diagnosis – and therefore the investigation – was largely of academic interest. I was quite surprised when Mrs. Garner showed me a letter which had arrived from the Royal the day before, indicating that they wanted to admit Ellen for a few days to perform, amongst other things, a sigmoidoscopy and a contrast barium enema – two investigations which on their own would have been hair-raising, even for a young fit and healthy individual, let alone a frail old woman of ninety-five. It seemed an instance of the system being more important than the patient.

We went into Ellen's single room which was small, light and airy. There was, in common with all the rooms in Smallwood, a wash-basin in one corner with clean towels draped over the rails under the sink. In the immaculately kept bed under the open window in the corner, Ellen Bean sat against a pile of pillows. With her eyes screwed up tight she lifted a spoonful of soup in a wavering, uncertain arc from the soup-bowl on her bed-tray, to her mouth. Mrs. Garner went over to her and announced loudly in her right ear that the doctor had come to see her. Ellen jumped and spilled tomato soup all over the yellow counterpane. She became agitated and began to wipe the soup off with jerky little movements of her knobbly hands while Mrs. Garner moved away the soup and bed-tray.

"Mrs Bean, I just called in to see how you were," I said in a loud clear voice. She stopped wiping up the soup and screwed up her eyes as she looked at me, her wrinkled mouth working away silently. She put her hand behind her ear and turned to Mrs. Garner.

"Who is it? What's he say?" she piped.

"It's the doctor," said Mrs. Garner, enunciating the words with the usual triad of movements which people make when speaking to the very deaf: the exaggerated mouth movements, the widely open eyes and raised eyebrows, and the rhythmic up and down nodding of the head.

"How are you today?" I yelled.

"Oh, not too bad," she replied. Mrs. Garner shook her head.

"Actually, doctor, she's had tummy-ache this last day or two, that's why I asked you to call."

"Any more bleeding from the rectum?"

"No, none at all. Bowels completely normal."

"All right. Let's have a look at your tummy, Mrs. Bean."

She nodded and smiled and slid down the bed to be examined. In spite of being ninety-five and fairly deaf, she was not mentally slow and it would have been easy to fall into the trap of treating such a patient as if she were a seven-year-old child. With a reasonably active brain she could observe and experience the inexorable decline of the rest of her body with its increasing dependence on others. I could not think of a worse humiliation than being spoken to in the kind of patronising banter which doctors and nurses, in particular, were in the habit of using, when talking to their elderly patients, under the misguided impression that they were treating them like members of the human race: it was the last twist of the knife.

With some difficulty and the help of Mrs. Garner, I managed to lift Ellen's nightie, which seemed about twenty-seven feet long, from under her bottom so that the abdomen was finally revealed. I placed my right hand flat on the dry wrinkled skin and Ellen gave out a cackle of laughter, a

113

surprisingly loud, harsh sound to come from so slight a frame. She lifted her head off the pillow and looked at me with her faded blue eyes.

"It's a long time sin' I had that happen – I say it must be fifty years sin' I had a feller's hand on me belly!" She laughed again and shook all over. The examination became a bit of an irrelevance since all three of us were laughing so much and I couldn't find anything unusual anyway. When she had tucked her nightdress down the bed again I sat down and explained to her about the test which they wanted to perform at the Royal. Her face quickly changed and she looked apprehensively at Mrs. Garner. She took a deep breath, and when she spoke she sounded almost apologetic.

"See here, young man – I know you doctors are all trying your best, but when you get to my age you don't want to be mucked about so much, you know. Any road, I'm feeling all right now, so I don't want to go down there and have them poking about with their instruments and taking X-rays or whatever. It'll all cost a lot of money and I'll be using a bed that's best used for someone a bit younger than me. I don't think I could face going down again – I mean, they were very kind and all that, but I don't want to leave Mrs. Garner here." Her eyes started to fill with tears and her voice took on a softer, more pleading quality. "Don't send me down there again, doctor. If me time's come I'd sooner see it out here. You won't send me, will you?"

I shook my head. There wasn't a single argument against what she had just said and I reassured her as best I could. She looked relieved and thanked us both profusely before we left her room. I went back to Mrs. Garner's office and we sat and discussed the old lady for a while. We had the telephone number of her niece, the closest relative, and I decided to ring her up to let know what was going on. Fortunately she was at home and I told her about the letter from the Royal and her aunt's feelings. She seemed to grasp the situation instantly and to my great relief agreed with her aunt's sentiments about choosing to die with dignity rather than be subjected to futile and unpleasant investigations. I immediately rang the

114

secretary in the surgical office at the Royal and told her that Ellen was declining their invitation. She sounded annoyed.

"Hm, well, we'll have to rearrange things now, you know. How is it she's not coming? Has she died, or something?"

"No, she hasn't died. She hasn't somethinged either. She just doesn't want to come in. I have spoken to both her and her closest relative and I agree with her decision."

"I see. Well that is most unusual..."

"Not really. Anyway, just cancel the arrangements. She won't be coming."

"I don't think the Professor will like this, you know."

"Well he's not the patient, is he?"

"That's not the point. The Programmed Investigation Unit can't just grind to a halt, you know. I'll need this in writing about the patient changing her mind." I could visualise her tonsils wobbling with authority.

"Are you serious?" I said. "Has she signed some form of legally binding contract to have a sigmoidoscope shoved twenty centimetres into her ninety-five year-old rectum?"

"No, but..."

"Then do me a favour. Have a word with your boss. I'm sure he'll understand. Cheerio!" My God, Ellen Bean had thrown the department into turmoil. She had held up a wizened, ancient hand in the path of the steam-roller of technological medicine. She had said no. I had no idea why but her response gave me a feeling of intense satisfaction.

I looked at the clock above the desk where Mrs. Garner was sitting writing in a patient's folder. It was nearly one o'clock and time to go home. I leaned back in the chair by the phone and looked out onto the lawn and rose bushes outside.

"You're very quiet, doctor. What did the secretary say at the hospital?" Mrs. Garner asked.

"Oh, nothing much. Wanted me to put it in writing. About Mrs. Bean not wanting to go in."

"Really? Whatever will they think of next, I wonder."

"I wonder sometimes, too. Anyway it's all taken care of so don't worry about it. If there is any change in her condition let me know, otherwise leave well alone."

"Right you are, doctor, we'll see to it."

"Right. Cheerio, Mrs. Garner. Probably see you next week."

"Yes, OK. Cheerio, doctor."

I went out into the sweltering sunlight and got into my car which was as hot as an oven and stank of plastic and leather. I drove into Overdale Road then turned left before I reached Overdale itself, descending the steep slope of Mill Lane into Hiley. As I coasted down the hill I glanced over the roofs of the council estate on my right and saw the patchwork hills of Loweth Heights. Gathering on the sky-line were banks of slate-blue cumulo-nimbus, a threatening fortress of storm clouds on the horizon.

# 13

The next day was my half day and I spent most of it asleep in the garden. I awoke feeling guilty: for the first time in several days I had had the opportunity of playing with the children or at least behaving as if I were part of the family, but that afternoon I had neither the energy nor the inclination to do either. I made a mental note to get my haemoglobin checked.

It was not necessary to look at my watch to appreciate that the afternoon had sneaked into evening while I was dozing, because the whoops and yells of the boys, as they played with endless energy and invention, had deteriorated into long silences punctuated by increasingly ill-tempered exchanges and pointless arguments. An oppressive blanket of hazy cloud blotted out the sun, giving the light a steely, almost theatrical quality. It had become unpleasantly airless and humid.

I had arranged to do an all-night session in Wishton Casualty that night because they were short of casualty officers. I ate my tea silently, regretting having agreed to help out. Afterwards, while Tanya bathed the baby, I read the two older boys an abridged version of the shortest short story I could find, and when I had finished it was time to go. As I rummaged unenthusiastically for my car keys the phone rang. It was Emily Parker.

"Doctor Russell, can you come round?"

"Has something happened?"

"No, not like that. I'd like you to come round, tonight. It's very important, doctor."

I groaned inaudibly because it didn't sound too urgent and it was going to make me late for casualty. I could tell she wouldn't be put off so I didn't bother to argue over details.

I went upstairs to let Tanya know that I was leaving and

stood at the bedroom door watching her as she carefully dressed the baby. She looked up and smiled briefly.

"What's the matter? Do I look like hell?"

"No. Just tired, that's all"

"That means I look like hell."

I stepped across and held her close, absorbing the warm fragrance of her body which was even more erotic through her thin summer dress. I felt guilty because I was taking, and giving nothing back in return.

"That's the last time I agree to do one of these sessions," I murmured in her ear. She turned away.

"Yes. Until the next time they ask. Now go on – you'll be late if you've got a call to do on the way." She smiled briefly with moist eyes.

When I got to the house, Mrs. Parker opened the door as I walked up the crumbling asphalt path. Behind her, a younger man and woman shuffled about uncertainly in the narrow hall. Mrs. Parker, on the other hand, looked quietly self-assured, ushering us all into the front living room, where Mr. Parker sat in one of two small upright chairs which were placed next to each other in the middle of the room. Next to Mr. Parker, who sat staring at the floor with his emphysematous chest heaving visibly under his open-necked flannel shirt, stood a small boy vacantly picking his nose. Behind them was a woman in her early thirties. She slapped the boy's wrist lightly and he jumped with surprise, then blushed with embarrassment. Mrs. Parker sat down on the empty chair next to her husband and the other two people came into the room, arranging themselves like one of those faded sepia family poses from the turn of the century. Mrs. Parker cleared her throat.

"I'm sorry to have dragged you out, doctor. I know you must have plenty of others to see to, but I've brought the family round as you can see, to talk over what we discussed in the surgery this morning." She looked round at the gathering and the rest of the family nodded gravely. The young boy looked restless.

"Gran, can I have an apple?"

118

"Wait, Kevin..."

"But you said I could have one before we went back home."

"All right, run and get one. There's a bag on the shelf in the pantry, that's where they are. Sit and eat it in the kitchen, Kevin love, there's a good boy, while us grown-ups talk to the doctor." He nodded and ran out of the room.

"You won't know my family, they live in Breadburn. Kevin's dad — that's my son-in-law — couldn't come on account of he's working tonight, but everyone else is here." She smiled a proud and contented smile which seemed to soften her normally quite stern features. "We're a close family, you see, doctor. We always talk these sort of things over together before deciding what to do. You do understand, don't you?"

I nodded and sat down. At this point it would have been easy to start looking at my watch and, anticipating what they were going to say, wind up the whole procedure and leave as quickly as possible, mumbling about a prior engagement. But this would have been a mistake, for this rather formal ritual was of tremendous importance to Mrs. Parker, and even though I knew more or less what she was going to do and say (which would in itself be an anti-climax) it was essential to listen, to let the ritual play itself out, and in listening, to be part of the ritual. It was a familiar scene which I had witnessed many times in the past, and its links were with the traditions and beliefs going way back in the history of working class families in this part of the country. When it came to marriage, birth, and death the mother came into her own as the head of the family, and it followed that when matters of health or welfare of any member of the family cropped up, the mother's judgement carried the most weight. Mrs. Parker was now faced with a major crisis in her own health, and although she was afraid of its implications, had drawn comfort and strength from those same traditions of behaviour in her own family background going back for generations — traditions which she probably could not put easily into words even if she were consciously aware of them.

119

She was, in a way, not only telling me about her immediate decision regarding her ovarian tumour, but also showing me what sort of people she and her family were. It was a demonstration of strength and solidarity in the face of ominous uncertainty, and it reminded me of Stan Hamer and his family as they faced their own crisis. As I sat down Mrs. Parker looked momentarily embarrassed.

"Oh I *am* sorry, doctor. I should have asked you to sit down before. You must think we're very rude."

"No, not at all. Now, tell me what you have decided, that's what you wanted to do, wasn't it?"

"Well, yes. Now, I know I could have come up to the surgery to tell you the same thing, so I hope you won't think I've wasted your time but ... well it seemed proper, somehow, to tell you here in my own house – on familiar ground, so to speak. What I've decided is this. I will go and see a specialist like you suggested this morning at the surgery, only I'll go private if it's all right with you, doctor."

"If that's what you want to do. But there's no need to spend..."

"Listen, doctor, it *is* what I want. I don't want umpteen doctors and students looking all over me, so I got the address of a specialist from a friend..." She fished a crumpled manilla envelope from her apron pocket and handed it to me. On it was written the name and consulting room address of a well-known gynaecologist in Manchester.

"Do you know him?" she asked anxiously.

"Oh yes. He's very good. One of the best in the area, so they say."

"Well, that'll do me. Now I know full well I could go on the National Health – and God knows me and Dad here have paid our fair share of stamps and that – but we've put a bit on one side and this seems as good a way as any of using it."

Mr. Parker coughed his gurgling, bubbling cough that seemed to shake the roots of his bronchial tree. "Aye, Mother's right enough, there," he rasped. "And as you know, doctor, I've had my fair share of treatment on t'National Health. And any road, what is this here cyst Mother's got?

120

Can you tell us?"

I explained what I thought it might be as best as I could. The younger relatives asked one or two thoughtful questions, then, on seeing the clock on the fireplace was showing ten minutes to nine, I stood up.

"What happens now?" asked Mrs. Parker. "Do I just go down and see the specialist, or will I need a letter from you, or what?"

"Yes, I'll sort the letter out, if one of you could pick it up tomorrow from the surgery. Now don't worry any more about it. You're going to a very good man, you know."

We all shook hands and I made my way outside. Mr. Parker and his wife came to the door.

"Thanks for coming, doctor. Mother were a bit bothered really, although I know she hides it," Mr. Parker said. He waved and went indoors, but Mrs. Parker followed me to the gate. As I opened it she grabbed my arm lightly and I was surprised to see that her eyes were moist and she was trembling.

"I'm very grateful to you for coming, doctor. With the family being here as well. I've seen a fair bit of sickness in my time but when it's yourself, well, it's not easy and I must say I'm a bit nervous about these things. Well I mean, you're bound to be, aren't you?"

"Yes, I suppose that's..."

"And just another thing, doctor. Don't think I'm niggling, but I was taken aback this morning when you started scribbling that letter out for the hospital. I mean, you hardly gave me a chance to get dressed, you know."

"Yes I suppose I was a bit swift. I'm sorry if..."

"Oh don't worry, lad. You were pulled out of the place yesterday morning from what I saw. No, but just bear in mind these things take time to sink in, you know. Anyway, thanks a lot for coming. I feel much happier now – it meant such a lot you coming when I had the family round me." She smiled and waved, then disappeared into the house.

I was twenty minutes late arriving at Wishton General. I glanced through the open door of the waiting room on my way in and saw a couple of bandaged hands, a restless child in the arms of an anxious looking mother and a couple of bored looking youths writing graffiti on the walls with a felt-tip. I walked into the small inner office and my face fell as I saw the bulky figure of Sister Eileen Brock sitting at the desk, peering into the mirror of her compact case and plucking her eyebrows with a small pair of tweezers.

"Mr. Nuthurst not on tonight?" I asked. The obvious disappointment in my voice annoyed her intensely as I had intended that it should and she stood up, snapped shut her compact case and made a big issue out of shuffling a bunch of case-cards around the cluttered desk.

"No doctor, he is not. Mr. Nuthurst is on his nights off, so you'll have to put up with me for tonight, won't you now?" She compressed her lips into a thin line and her head wobbled in the way it usually did when she was annoyed. She looked at her watch. "Anyway, doctor, you don't have long to do tonight. It's half past nine already."

"My, my, we are in dazzling form tonight," I murmured. "I am overwhelmed by your welcome." Actually, Eileen Brock was about as dazzling as a hippo in the mid-day sun. She was, to be fair, floundering on the dry beach of her menopause, dumped there a year or two before by the high tide of her reproductive life – but quite apart from that, she was painfully aware of her own physical unattractiveness and as a result she radiated a sort of bleak anti-charisma. It would have helped if she was good at her job, but after twenty years of nursing she seemed to have gained one years's experience twenty times. She was dim, insensitive and inflexible – qualities which were unfortunately shared by quite a few of her contemporaries. She handed me half a dozen case-cards and pushed back the chair from her desk.

"There's a few to be going on with. Your first patient is in the first cubicle. Youth with a foreign body in his eye."

"Oh yes, I saw his two pals scrawling obscenities on the waiting room wall as I came in," I said, laughing quietly. Her nostrils flared and her eyes widened like a stag at the sound of gunfire.

122

"Oh they were, were they! We'll see about that..." She bustled out of the office and down the corridor, her large body and ill-fitting uniform making a noise like a heavy load of washing going round a tumble-dryer, while the coarse nylon tights round her huge upper thighs scraped together with each step, creating enough static to light up a small town.

I went through to the treatment area and dealt with the assortment of cases which presented, working methodically and mechanically, without enthusiasm. I was praying that after midnight I might get an undisturbed night's sleep which I felt I needed badly, hoping at the same time that Brock and I would see as little as possible of each other. I could probably last out until then without overlooking something important or making some stupid error through fatigue.

After I had cleared the place of problems I went back to the office and was pleased to hear that Sister Brock had gone to one of the orthopaedic wards to see a friend who had fallen off a stationary bus and sustained a very nasty fracture of the neck of her femur. I couldn't help thinking that the sight of Brock at the bedside would be enough to cause those little osteoblasts, which were busily mending the fracture-site, to beat a hasty retreat, thus putting the healing process back at least a fortnight.

As I finished my third cup of coffee there was the sound of an ambulance and another vehicle tearing to a standstill in the yard outside, the light of the blue flasher streaking intermittently through the windows of the department. The auxiliary went to see what was going on and two part-timers, who had been doing the dressings and cleaning up the treatment room, rushed past the office to the admission area outside. A minute later the auxiliary returned, picked up the phone, and rang the female orthopaedic ward.

"Staff nurse? Can you please tell Sister Brock to come to casualty? She's there, I believe, seeing a friend... Yes, that's right... We've a serious head-injury just come in... Thanks." She put the phone down. "Ten year-old boy, fallen out of a tree earlier this evening. The ambulance men have put him in cubicle two. D'you want X-ray, doctor?"

"No, let me see him first. Has anybody come with him?"

"Yes. The mother and father are with him. They seem very nice people, but the little boy is breathing very oddly."

We went through to the treatment area where the ambulance men were folding up their blankets and wheeling the stretcher out. The parents of the boy stood by the examination couch. The mother, who was a smartly-dressed woman about forty-five years of age, stroked the boy's hair and spoke softly to him while the father stood with his hands thrust deeply into his pockets, staring blankly at the back of his wife's head in a totally distracted manner. He seemed so terrified and bewildered that he had switched off completely. When I appeared the boy's mother looked up only briefly but the father jumped with relief and grabbed my arm.

"Oh doctor, thank goodness. I'm glad there was someone available right away." He had a well-spoken voice, hoarse with anxiety. "Simon was playing with friends earlier on this evening. Apparently he was climbing a tree and fell down. By the time his friends found help he had been lying there for an hour."

"He appears to have some kind of concussion ... he will be all right, won't he?" said the boy's mother, looking round. Her face was very calm.

"Well ... let's see. If you just wait in the waiting room while I have a look at him ..."

They left the cubicle, glancing back at the boy as they went out. For the first time I had a clear view of the patient and it was evident at once that something catastrophic had happened to his central nervous system. His mouth was open and he took short, shallow, gasping breaths with what seemed to be abnormally long intervals in between. Apart from the spasmodic contractions of his neck muscles which occurred with each intake of breath, he did not move at all. He fixed his wide, terrified eyes on me and followed every movement I made. He was a healthy, good-looking lad with clear, tanned skin and a strong build. He was conscious, and even tried to answer my questions in a sort of gasping whisper. At first I couldn't make it out: the amount of brain damage seemed hardly consistent with being conscious, and the pupils were normal as well. That was odd. I lifted up the boy's hands and when I let go they dropped like wood back onto the couch. Then it dawned on me. I ran my fingers over the skull but felt no sign of external damage. Below the nape of the neck I gingerly felt the line of the cervical vertebrae, and there it was – a gap in the posterior spines which could be felt through the soft skin and muscle. I felt sick as the thought of the classical text-book description came to mind, for this boy was a quadriplegic – paralysed from the neck down by a high transection of his spinal cord by either a fracture or a dislocation of one of his cervical vertebrae. Most of his respiratory muscles were paralysed and he was only breathing with his diaphragm and a few of his neck muscles. He needed urgent help with his respiration if he was going to survive. I sent the auxiliary to get the radiographer who was up on one of the wards doing a mobile X-ray, then asked one of the part-timers to stay with the boy and the other one to make some tea. Cups of tea were the inevitable accompaniment to bad news in this department, and the parents of this lad were going to have more than their fair share this evening. I went quickly through to the office to ring the orthopaedic registrar. As I crossed the corridor I saw in the corner of my eye the parents standing at the entrance to the waiting room. I didn't look towards them but went straight to the phone, and as I waited for the switchboard to answer I heard Brock's voice at the end of the corridor.

"I'm afraid we can't have you waiting in this corridor, you know."

"We're the parents of the boy who's just been ..."

"Yes, well, relatives can't be cluttering up the corridor. This is where the stretchers come through. Can you go through to the waiting room until the doctor has finished?"

"But he's just come in with a very bad head injury ..."

"Oh but my dear, we have head injuries coming in here all the time. It's nothing unusual for us, you know – nothing out of the ordinary at all."

"If you'll pardon me for saying so, sister, it's far from usual with us."

"That's as may be, but the corridors in the department cannot be obstructed by relatives. We simply cannot run an accident department..." Her voice was cut off by a door closing down the corridor. She must have herded them into the waiting room. Jesus Christ, what a woman, I thought. My anger was subdued somewhat by the appearance of a pert little radiographer with short blonde-hair. She shoved an X-ray form in front of me and I filled it in.

"Cervical vertebra, AP and lateral. Tell the nurse to put sand-bags round the head, and X-ray him on the trolley, will you? Don't let those porters move him off there. And don't be long – he's pretty sick."

She smiled and shoved the form into her pocket. "Quick as a flash. We can wheel him down as he is. Won't need to move him, don't worry. Films won't be up to my usual standard though, on that trolley. I'll bring the films up as soon as they're ready. Don't you want the skull as well...?"

"Yes, sure," I said. She whisked away to get some porters. It was fortunate that this girl was on tonight because she was both fast and good.

"Dr. Rashid here."

I had almost forgotten that I was still holding the phone. Thank God it was Rashid. At least he was competent and made sense.

"Rashid, there's a sick child here. Looks like a high cervical transection, he's only got his phrenic nerve working his respiration. I'm getting him X-rayed now. Will you come and take a look or should I get him to the ward? He's going to need special care."

"I'll come and see. Then he will have to go to our Intensive Care Unit. I'll come now."

I put the phone down and smiled grimly. The Intensive Care Unit was something of a euphemism. In actual fact it was a small side room off the male orthopaedic ward. In it was a bed surrounded by a labyrinth of wires and leads to and from an oscilloscope and a small respirator. When there were

126

a couple of nurses in there "specialing" a patient, it was hazardous to even set foot in the room, let alone try to get to the patient. It was rather like holding an all-in wrestling match in a telephone booth.

Rashid came down and made a swift, silent examination of the boy who had come back from X-ray. His films followed soon after. They showed a fracture dislocation at the third cervical vertebra with severe displacement. Rashid pulled a face and shook his head.

"We don't have the facilities here to treat such a case. I will contact my consultant to see what he thinks. Don't worry, I will take over now. There is nothing you can do here, really. I'll get him in the ward meanwhile."

"While you're doing that, should I have a word with the parents or would you prefer...?"

"No, no, please, that will be quite all right. Have a word with them while I sort things out. I think he should go to a spinal unit."

I went down the corridor and into the waiting-room, taking a deep breath before I opened the door. The boy's parents stood up and the mother straightened the creases in her coat.

"How bad is he, doctor? Is it a head injury?" asked the father.

"No, there's no sign of head injury..." I said slowly.

"Thank goodness for that! I could bear the thought of him having any brain damage or anything like that."

"There is something – " I began, but the father's face had relaxed and he took out a cigarette, his hands jerking with tremulous movement. He wasn't listening. He carried on almost as if he wanted to block out any other possibility.

"He's our only child, you see – late arrival – and of course you know how boys are always climbing trees, and..."

"I think you ought to know..."

"Of course, we don't keep him wrapped in cotton wool – I mean, you can't watch them every single moment..." He talked very fast, taking no notice of anything. His reaction at the first scrap of information I had given him had triggered off a stream of relieved, almost hysterical chatter and he

127

perspired freely as he spoke. His wife stared at him apprehensively.

"Of course you expect these sort of bumps and knocks with kids at this age but he's tough enough to bounce..."

"Your son is – "

"He'll hate being laid up for even a short time, I know that – "

"Your son is totally paralysed," I said, clearly and slowly. I hadn't planned on telling them like this, and I felt sick as I realised that it was like letting go with both barrels at a bird in full flight. The boy's father immediately became silent. His face caved in and he sat down heavily with his mouth half-open. His wife remained calm, her voice very quiet.

"What has gone wrong? Why do you say he is paralysed?"

"It's the spinal cord, I'm afraid. The fall has damaged it at the neck."

"That's the nerve, isn't it, from the brain?"

"That's right. It's been very seriously damaged."

"But how long will it take to heal up?"

"We don't know the total extent of the damage yet, but I should tell you that the spinal cord has no regenerative powers at all. What I mean is, it ... it doesn't heal once it has been severed."

"But ... the paralysis ...?"

"The paralysis will remain permanent if the cord is severed. But we don't know that yet ..."

"Can't it be joined or something?"

"No. But we don't know for certain whether ..."

"My God. Oh my God," she whispered as it finally sank in. She sat down slowly next to her husband and said nothing else. He stared at the door, looking suddenly ten years older. His face was ashen. The door opened and one of the part-timers came in carrying two cups of tea.

"Here's some tea," she said in a bright voice. "I hope you like it strong, it does more good when it's strong, I always think, don't you? And I've put sugar in both. You do take sugar, don't you?" They took the tea, nodded stiffly and began to drank it. The nurse went quietly out when she saw the expression on my face. I started to move towards the door.

"I'm sorry . . ." The words came out in a mumble of fatigue and sympathy.

The father looked up.

"Yes, doctor. Can we see him?"

"In a moment. I think he'll be going to the ward now. The other doctor is arranging it. He'll be taking over now."

"Thanks, doctor."

"What . . .? Oh yes. Sister will let you know when it's OK for you to go through."

I went out of the waiting-room and walked right outside into the fresh air of the ambulance bay. I could hear steam hissing from a vent somewhere, and the occasional clatter of a stainless steel tray or bedpan echoed across the yard from the wards. I had only been standing for a minute or so when another ambulance screeched in with its blue light flashing round the yard. I turned and went inside to the office which was empty. The auxiliary had made more coffee and I drank another cup. It had gone cold. I sat back and closed my eyes. The lids felt as if they had got sand plastered on the inside. I heard the usual clatter and bang of a stretcher being brought in, but in spite of the noise I could feel myself falling asleep. Maybe they would turn round and go away, eventually.

After a few minutes Eileen Brock appeared at the door, looking a trifle breathless.

"I've just got back from taking that child to the ward. Did I hear something arrive just now?"

"Yes. I think you did, sister" I murmured, half asleep. I didn't move and she went off down the corridor to where all the noise was coming from. She returned a moment later holding a case-card.

"One of your own patients. Pregnant. Severe abdominal pain. Just had a fight with her husband."

I looked at the name on the card: Mrs. Ludnika Wilcinská. She was expecting twins and was about thirty-four weeks.

"I wonder how she arrived here instead of . . ."

"Apparently," Brock said, "the neighbours heard a big row and screams. Phoned 999. She's not too good, doctor. Blood pressure ninety over sixty. She's behaving very hysterically, though. Not helping herself at all, if you ask me."

I didn't say anything but went straight to the patient who was sobbing noisily on the trolley. The auxiliary was doing her best to settle her down while the two ambulance men stood nearby talking about their holidays. Mrs. Wilcinska didn't seem surprised to see me and gave a fairly good history once she had calmed down. It appeared that she had found out that her husband was seeing another woman and they had had a terrific row. He had knocked her downstairs and walked out. Shortly afterwards she had started with lower abdominal pain and someone had sent for the ambulance. That was more or less it.

She remained silent as I examined her, and every so often a tear squeezed out of the corner of her closed eyelids. She was in a fairly shocked condition. Her blood-pressure was low, the uterus was hard and tender and I guessed that she had probably had some form of intra-uterine haemorrhage. I took some blood off for cross-matching and set up a saline drip to run fast. When this was going satisfactorily I asked Brock to check the blood pressure again while I rang and arranged her transfer to the labour ward. When I got back the blood pressure had improved but she was now complaining of lower abdominal pain again which probably heralded the onset of premature labour. I gave her a large dose of pethidine, praying that doing this would confuse the diagnosis by removing the symptoms when she got to the labour ward. She began to sob again.

"It don't look too good, eh, dogtor?"

"You'll be OK, don't worry," I replied, trying to smile reassuringly.

"What about my babies – dey OK too?"

"Too early to tell. Try to rest. They're taking you up now."

"OK. If you see that swine my husband you tell him what happened, be sure now."

"Yes. Has no one come with you?"

"No. I got no one now. A neighbour, she look after the kids. I don't know what I do now..." She broke down completely and even Brock tried to reassure her before the ambulance men finally took her up to the labour ward. I went to the duty room, lay on the bed fully clothed and fell into a deep sleep.

I had left a message for the auxiliary to ring me at seven thirty a.m. and when the phone rang I woke up instantly, feeling clammy and dreadful. After a shower and two cups of coffee which made me feel no better, I went across to the labour ward to see Mrs. Wilcinska. During the night she had had twins, a girl and a boy, but only the girl had survived and was in the prem unit. They had to do a hysterectomy to stop the bleeding, and Mrs. Wilcinska was still flat out following her surgery. Sitting outside the ward was her husband who looked beside himself with remorse. When he saw me coming he got up out of the chair and stared at me balefully. His mouth opened to speak but no sound emerged. I shook my head.

"Look – what you do in your private life is no concern of mine, neither is your domestic life. Save your energies for seeing to your wife. She's going to need you, she's got nobody else. So don't screw it up." Mr. Wilcinska nodded slowly and sat down. I turned and went down to casualty again to collect my night bag. When I arrived the office was full of people. A couple of day-staff had arrived and were in the throes of arranging their hair and straightening their uniforms. Hovering outside, clutching a bunch of raffle tickets close to his mouth with both hands, his elbows tucked into his side like a praying mantis, was Lennie Higgs, ward orderly from male orthopaedic. His dyed blonde hair bobbed up and down on his collar as he tried to catch the eye of Brock who was buttoning up her coat to go off duty.

"Hello, Eileen, petal. D'you want to buy a raffle ticket for the Autumn Fair?" Brock scowled and shook her head.

"Oh come on, flower, there's lots of gorgeous prizes..." He glanced round as I reached in to get my bag off the desk. "Oh, Doctor Rushton. Just the person I'm looking for!"

There was a chorus of "oohs" from inside the office and even Brock managed to smile, but I was in no mood for pantomime that morning.

"What about the little boy – Simon something – we sent him to you last night?" I asked, feeling that the brisk clamour in the office now seemed almost indecent.

"Yes, that's what I was just going to say," chirped Higgs. "Rashid got Mr. Murray in, then he in turn got Mr. O'Hare in, the neurosurgeon from South Manchester. You couldn't *move* in the ICU. Then one of the plugs wouldn't fit on the videoscope and we were running about all over the place, well you never *saw* such a commotion in all your..."

"The little boy. What about the little boy?"

"Oh well ... died at twenty-eight minutes past four. Respiratory failure. Shame. D'you want to buy a raffle ticket for the..."

"Stuff your raffle tickets unless the first prize is a brand new intensive care unit," I snarled. I walked out of the department, got into my car and drove away from the hospital which was already humming with activity. What a bloody night, and what a start to the next day! But what about Mr. and Mrs. Wilcinska and the parents of that child who died after falling out of a tree? I wondered how *they* all felt that morning, how long it would be before they ceased to dread each haunting dawn.

# 14

When I had finished the morning surgery, which mercifully was light and composed of easily identifiable problems which could be quickly resolved, Ian brought his coffee into my consulting room and sat down.

"When are you having a holiday?" he asked.

"Week after next. I've marked it on the wall-calender in the office."

"Yes of course. Going anywhere special?"

"Not really. We're going to see a few friends in London, maybe tour round, depending on the weather."

"Hmm. Well, relax and enjoy yourselves. Forget about all this." He waved his half-empty cup around and spilled coffee on his lap. "Damn! Anyway, have a good time. You look as if you need the rest. Did they hit you hard last night?"

I told him what had happened and he pulled a long face.

"Pretty dismal, eh? Doesn't exactly set you up for a full surgery the following day. I think you ought to give it up at the hospital, along with all this police work. Mind you, when I was your age I used to do a fair bit of running round, too. Come to think of it, if I hadn't I wouldn't have been able to afford half the things I've got now. Then again, I suppose the hospital work keeps you in touch with all the latest developments."

I couldn't help smiling when Ian said this. I was thinking of the out of date apparatus, the incompatible plugs on the resuscitation equipment, equipment which lay around unused, still in its polystyrene packaging because the instructions had gone missing and no one was sure how to use it. I also thought about the deterioration in morale in the hospital: the ancillary staff seemed to have become more peevish and concerned more with their own status and what they were not supposed to do, rather than with ways in which they could be of help in the care of patients. Nearly all the good, experienced nursing staff had disappeared from the wards and were embroiled in a tangle of administrative clap-trap about procedures and management, while the resident medical staff seemed to spend most of their spare time discussing overtime payments. Meanwhile the patients shuffled around in their slippers and dressing-gowns like refugees in a transit-camp, bewildered and uneasy in the certain knowledge that if they all disappeared overnight their absence would not be noticed for weeks, such was the bureaucratic momentum of the institution. Yet in spite of this, an amazing amount of good work was done and many people actually benefited from hospitalisation.

Ian put his cup on the desk and stood up. He began to pace up and down. An earth-shattering decision was imminent.

"We really should have a get-together soon to discuss the problem of the surgery premises, amongst other things. I should have liked to talk about it tonight but something has cropped up. The fact is, I've been asked to take part in a four-ball this afternoon and you know how these matches can drag on into early evening..."

"That's OK by me," I said, feeling relieved. I was not in the right frame of mind to go through an evening discussing that sort of problem, and anyway I had received an invitation that morning to some drug-promotion meeting which was to be held in the evening. I rummaged amongst the mail and dug out a neatly printed card.

"Shard Pharmaceuticals are at the North Towers tonight. Buffet, film, wives invited. I think that's where I'll be. D'you want me to tell them you'll be along later? With a bit of luck you'll miss the film but be in time for the food and drinks."

"The main business of the evening? No, I don't think so ... Shard, you said? Shard, Shard ... aren't they the firm who make those pessaries for vaginitis and those little pink tablets – Eleval or something – for depression? Or is it the other way round? Might as well be, for all they're worth." Ian laughed quietly to himself.

134

"Do I detect an air of cynicism?" I asked.

"Oh no, not really. Still, when you've been treating patients as long as I have ... which brings me to the other thing I was going to mention." He turned and looked out of the grimy window, his voice becoming more reflective. "I had a patient in the other day who asked me if I thought she was on the change. I remember the day I delivered that girl into the world ... Wakefield was at one end of the bed dropping ether onto a mask on the mother's face and I was at the other, pulling this wee bairn out. She was really tiny but you'd never think so to look at her now. And she asked me if she was on the change! My God, have I really been around that long?" He turned round and smiled, then stared at his hands on the desk blotter. "So I've been thinking. It's time I cut down my commitment a bit. I'd like to do a lot less here, and that means looking for another partner. It means more work for you, but also a bigger share when you most need it."

I was taken aback. "This seems like a hell of a time to start looking for a new partner, what with Miss Cope leaving and all the surgery — "

"Oh I know all that but I don't agree. I'll have more time to sort out the surgery problem and it'll give you free reign to organise the work the way you think best. That way I can bow out gracefully over the next few years and live long enough to enjoy my retirement. I've no intention of working like a cart-horse and then dropping dead on the golf-course the day after I retire. I've seen that happen too often before."

He went on to outline his plans and it was typical of him that he intended to be scrupulously fair in the arrangement. He had obviously given it a great deal of thought over the last few weeks and he presented his argument in a clear-cut fashion that was difficult to fault. We agreed to leave things until after my holiday before getting down to the business of looking for a suitable partner. This last job I knew was going to be tedious and time-consuming, but the thought of more flexibility with the work and holidays, together with a greater share of the practice profits, more than compensated for that.

Ian stood up and pulled a scrap of paper from his pocket,

glancing at the names he had written on it. It was his visit list. He knew the patients so well that he rarely needed to put an address alongside. Sometimes he wrote down the number of the house but hardly ever the name of the street.

"We'll talk again soon about all this. Time's pressing on now. Have a good time tonight."

After Ian had gone I wrote the letter I had promised for Mrs. Parker and gave it to Miss Cope for one of the family to collect. She hovered around her desk as if she was waiting for me to say something.

"Did the doctor tell you that I would be finishing here later this year?"

"Ah, yes ... yes, he did. I have been meaning to mention it. I'm sorry to hear it, naturally. What's made you decide to retire?"

She smiled her enigmatic smile, turned away and sorted through a pile of prescriptions – more for something to do with her hands than from necessity.

"Well doctor, I have managed to save something during the years I have been here, although it hasn't been easy. I have been given a good offer for my house and I have always wanted to retire to the Fylde coast, you know, and now the opportunity has arisen for me to do so. Anyway, doctor, when you get your new health centre all your methods will be different. I don't think I'll fit in with that kind of set-up. You need someone a bit ... well ... with a more up to date approach."

"I don't think you're doing yourself justice," I said with surprise. "What makes you think you wouldn't fit in? Our methods in the health centre are not going to be that different, you know. All we are doing is using part of a larger building which will also house the district nurses, health visitors and so on. We'll be seeing patients in exactly the same way as we do now.'

She slowly shook her head. "There's a big difference, if you don't mind me saying so, doctor, between seeing your patients in your own surgery and seeing them in a health centre which will be bustling with all sorts of people from the local authority, interfering and looking over your shoulder. You won't have the same control over the running of the practice and I have the feeling, talking to the patients here, that a lot won't like it."

"How d'you make that out, Miss Cope?"

"A big impersonal place like that makes people apprehensive. With all those local authority folk around you may find they fear a loss of ... well, the personal touch, if you like."

"Oh, I doubt – "

"And there is another thing, doctor. Have you ever thought that there might be a change in attitude of the patients towards the doctors?"

"In what way?"

"I know Overton people. When they see that fancy building which will be open all day long, I think you'll find they may become more demanding, more difficult to please."

"That sounds depressing. Why do you think that should be? I hadn't thought about that particular problem, I must say."

"Stands to reason – in the minds of the patients, that is. They see a nice big expensive local authority-owned building and, by association, look on you as an employee of the local authority. They'll start demanding things as of right and behaving as though they're in the rates department at the Town Hall, or the social security offices. It won't be like a doctor's surgery any longer, and what's more, some of the patients won't look on you as their own doctor any more. You'll be just like another government employee to them."

"I'm afraid a few think like that already," I said, and smiled grimly. Her statement made me feel a little uneasy. This was the first time she had voiced her opinion on the health centre at such length. She was quite reserved and rarely expressed opinions unless she was sure they were based on sound knowledge or experience. And she wasn't daft. She had lived there all her life amongst the patients and she really knew how the local people ticked. Although these problems seemed secondary in view of the fact that we looked like being forced to find another surgery before the health centre was ready, I couldn't help thinking for the rest of the day about what she had said and wondering whether our decision to move into a health centre was the right one.

That evening when I got home Tanya and I talked for a while about Ian's plans for semi-retirement and for taking on another partner. She was pleased at the idea if it only meant that I could afford to give up the police work, so that we could have a few more undisturbed nights. I had put the doubts about the health centre out of my mind by then and didn't even mention it.

We waved to the babysitter and set off down Comshaw Road. I felt in good humour: it was our first night out together for a long time and it was to be at the expense of one of the country's largest pharmaceutical companies. It was a beautiful evening and the warm yellow light of the low sun shone through the screen, making Tanya's skin appear a delicious colour.

North Towers was in Bogsworth, on the Gloston Road. The three-mile drive was on a narrow snaking road through brightly-lit hills and into twisting gulleys made suddenly dark and cool by overhanging trees. When we arrived the car park was already fairly full and one or two people were standing in the open doorway drinking beer. Inside there was the usual large noisy collection of GPs. Their movement and conversation edged the locals into the far corner of the bar where they stared resentfully over their beer glasses at this unwelcome take-over. A densely-bunched, perspiring scrummage of earnest drinkers pressed forward towards the bar, laughing and talking loudly to each other whilst dipping their leading shoulder to get closer in and catch the barman's eye.

"So she's sitting there, pregnant as anything, and the boyfriend – two gin and tonics, when you're ready – and the boyfriend says: 'She hasn't seen her monthly for a bit, d'you think summat's up?' And I looked at him and said – I couldn't help it – 'Well, something *has* been up, lad,' and he just – "

"Brandy and – "

"He just – "

"Dumbfounded was he? Brandy and – "

"Just looked blank. It's a wonder he ever managed it in the first place. Gin and tonic, when you're ready!"

"I had one the other day . . . this is my drink isn't it? Right. No, hang on, *that* one's mine – that's yours, there. I had one the other day, examining this fellow's foot, came with his wife – "

"When you're ready, barman! Brandy and . . . oh hell, you could die with thirst in this place. Sorry, go on."

"So I took his other shoe and sock off to compare the other foot –"

"Don't tell me – it was bloody filthy. Another lager, please!"

"Right. Black as the hobs of hell. And his wife – and this bloody tickled me – his wife, she looked all disgusted – "

"Hold on. Grab that glass, it's yours. Or was it me that ordered the gin and tonic? Oh sod it, drink up anyway. Go on, his wife looked disgusted – "

"So his wife looks disgusted and turns to me and says, 'I can't abide that sort of thing – I make sure I have a bath once a fortnight, whether I need one or not!' I thought she was pulling my leg."

"Two down here just fainted with dehydration, barman, when you're ready! Once a fortnight, that's very good . . ."

Vic Unsworth, one of the Shard reps, stood with his back to the bar and towered above everyone, cheerfully passing glasses backwards and forwards over the heads of those in front of him. I remembered him at the grammar school which we both attended. Vic was a front-row forward, the largest in the history of the school, and he passed the glasses over now as if he were facing a ruck from the opposition. It was good to see his grammar school education being put to such good use. I mouthed an order for drinks for Tanya and myself and within a minute they miraculously appeared, vaulting over from the bar in Vic's hands which looked like large mechanical grabs at the end of his long arms.

We jostled around for a while, holding fractured

139

conversations with various people we knew. Normal conversation was out of the question, mainly because of the overall noise and the continuous movement of the closely packed crowd. Now and again the random jostling was disturbed by a shock wave from another part of the room, where the epicentre would be a spilled drink or someone falling over a chair. Within a few minutes I found myself at one side of the room face to face with a garrulous Scottish GP whose name I couldn't remember. The last time we met had been many months ago at Hiley police station when he had tried in vain to persuade me not to take a blood sample from one of the Scotsman's drunken patients, on the grounds that the patient had a bad leg, or something ludicrous like that. He waved his short arms around, causing onlookers nearby to draw away and clutch their drinks tighter. At the risk of being accidently knocked over by his flailing arms as he argued some point or other, I moved into the small space the man had created around himself. As a result the Scot directed his sweating, eye-popping tirade directly at me. I had no idea what he was talking about – not that it mattered much, since it was impossible to get a word in edgeways with this fellow when he was like this. Which was nearly all the time.

"Hey, you're moving into a health centre sometime, aren't you?" he said, poking me in the ribs with a stubby index finger.

"Sometime. Don't know when. Why?"

"Oh man, ye don't know what ye've let yerself in for. I tell ye, we moved in last year and it's been murder ever since. One big argument over running costs since the day we moved in and ye cannae get the receptionists to do a blind thing without them consulting their bloody contracts because they're all in this union. Noopy or Droopy or something."

"Don't you employ the receptionists directly yourselves?"

"Naw. Slipped up, didn't we just? We were told it would be simpler this way, but it's terrible. And administrators snooping round making sure you're not seeing too many private patients! Did I tell you the health centre administrator who's in charge – does bugger-all except wander round with a clip-board and pencil for about ten grand a year – she's got this anti-smoking campaign going and, Christ, I practically had tae go to the toilet before I could light a fag! Can you imagine that! Just like being back at school. Anyway, we sorted that little problem out in a civilised manner – I told her she'd get her arse kicked if she mentioned no smoking in my presence again. Have ye got your own place just now?"

"Yes, but not for long."

"Take a tip from me, son – stay where you are. Don't go in. Have they built it yet? Well – pull out. Dinnae get involved." He turned round and made for the bar for another drink. I looked past him and saw Tanya talking to a group of GPs wives over on the other side of the room. She looked across and cocked her eyebrow, pointing to her empty glass. I edged across and found her in conversation with Marjorie Snowden, a GP in Stallbrook who was in partnership with her husband. Bill and Marjorie Snowden, rarely, if ever, attended untidy thrashes like this: Masonic Ladies' evenings seemed more their style. They were always immaculately dressed and rarely put a foot wrong, and their urbane manner seemed out of place among the rest of the rabble. Marjorie was telling Tanya about the miracles that private education had done for their two teenage boys, and I wondered how they afforded private education for their children at all. Bill appeared with two sherries for himself and Marjorie and as he nodded his greeting I suddenly remembered that he was on all sorts of medical committees locally, having a penchant for medical politics. It might prove useful to get his advice on how to avoid getting kicked out of our surgery.

"Hello, Steven. Have they started your health centre yet?"

"Funny you should ask that. We've got a problem, you know. They haven't started it and what's more, it looks like we may be up the pole shortly with our present surgery."

"Oh really? In what way, precisely?"

"We've had notice to quit. Which means we may have to move out before the centre is finished. We were given the word that this would never happen."

"In writing?"

"Well, no..."

"Ah, then you are in trouble, whichever way you look at it."

"How d'you make that out?"

Bill Snowden smiled his committee smile which meant that he was party to information no one else had. "Unless you can use delaying tactics and stay where you are until the new centre's built, then you're going to be in a mess. And I doubt whether you could delay being thrown out of your present surgery if there's enough vested interest in knocking it down, because you won't get much local support."

I took a drink and my mind flashed back to the conversation Ian and I had overheard in the gents' toilets at Overton Town Hall. "What if we decided to sod the health centre and buy a place of our own instead?" I asked.

Bill laughed grimly. "Not a cat in hell's chance. Can you imagine the Town Hall giving you planning permission for a place of your own which would leave them with an empty health centre on their hands?"

"I don't see how they could stop us."

"They can, believe me. It's been done before. No local authority likes egg on its face. Expediency is the name of the game."

I was still trying to fathom out this last statement, at the same time reeling at the implications of what Bill was saying, when a loud barking laugh interrupted my thoughts. Bill winced and nearly dropped his drink. I turned round and saw Patrick Dougan and Sean O'Malley convulsing themselves over some private joke. O'Malley had his eyes closed and swayed backwards and forwards like a straw in the wind, while Dougan, with his brows still stern and knotted into broad lines across his forehead, laughed harshly into his glass of whisky.

"Ah, hello there, doctor, and how are you? Been busy in the practice have you?" he asked, swallowing the rest of his drink quickly. "Well now, this is a good firm, is it not? Very hospitable are these people, yes. Sean and me have seen this fillum they're showing tonight. We saw it three times last week, what do you think of that?"

"Really? How did you manage that?"

"Because they sent us a card along with a choice of four venues, all on different dates. Sean and myself just ticked all four, that's how we managed it." He laughed again, and I couldn't help thinking that if freeloaders were oranges these two would be Jaffas.

"And the film? What's it about?"

"Oh God, now don't ask me that. I don't ... Sean, d'you remember what was the fillum about ... ?"

O'Malley shook his head slowly. "Was it not about the arthritis ... ? Or perhaps it was not ... No, I can't think what it was, at all."

"Well, that's not the main thing is it, doctor?" said Dougan winking through his thick spectacles. "There's always lots of samples with this firm. And do you know that they're giving away these little bars of soap, just the job they are. We've really got enough now to last for ..."

Bill Snowden cleared his throat and started to move away. "Right, then, Steven. We'll ... see you again, no doubt. Good luck with the surgery thing." He glanced at Dougan and O'Malley with some distaste before he disappeared into the crowd.

Vic Unsworth ushered everyone through into a small conference room across the other side of the entrance hall, leaving the wives and girl friends to natter among themselves in the lounge bar which became fairly quiet apart from the clinking of glasses as the bar-staff gathered up scores of empties at the tables and on the bar top.

The room was crowded and noisy, as well as being warm and uncomfortable, so the film began almost immediately without the usual commercial introduction. After a few minutes, above the noise of the projector and the low buzz of conversation amongst the bored audience, I could hear a series of scuffling noises, bumps and whispered curses. In the flickering gloom I could see two shadowy figures crawling on their hands and knees around the large table which had been piled high with samples before the meeting started. When the

143

film had finished the lights went on just as O'Malley and Dougan were going through the door with their brief-cases bulging with samples and little bars of toilet soap. The table had been stripped clean.

"Ah, there you are Mr.... er ... dat's a fine fillum, very very good fillum, is dat. Well now, Sean and myself will have to excuse ourselves now because we have a couple of emergencies to see to, so good night to you now Mr.... er ... to be sure it's a pity we can't stay for something to eat." Dougan gave a cheerful wave and they both ducked out of the door, leaving Vic Unsworth speechless. The stunned silence was broken by someone who stood up at the front and made his way to the heavily-laden buffet table.

"Well, I don't know what anybody else is doing," he said, "but I'm going to grab something to eat now before those two buggers change their minds and come back for the buffet!" There was a wave of relieved laughter at his words and the evening degenerated once more as the elbow and knee brigade stampeded for food and more drink.

A little later, as I was telling Tanya about the Dougan and O'Malley rip-off, a short, balding figure in a sports jacket with trifle down both lapels swayed up to us, sweating profusely.

"Couldn't help hearing you talking about that. Very distasteful business." He took an unco-ordinated swig of beer and shook his head. Tanya began to laugh.

"Oh, it's all right you laughing, my dear, but it's not dignified and it gives all us doctors a bad name. Sheer greed — that's what it is." As he staggered off in the direction of the toilet Tanya was laughing her head off.

"What's so funny?" I said.

"Him. Talking all that pious clap-trap. Did you see what was in his pockets?"

"No, I didn't."

"They were absolutely stuffed with Dairylea Cheese slices and sausage rolls from the table!" We both laughed all the way to the car-park.

We stopped at the car and Tanya threw back her head,

flicking her hair from her shoulders. She drew in a deep breath.

"Won't it be good to get away for a couple of weeks? I'm looking forward to that."

"You can say that again," I murmured. "After tonight I've had my fill of doctors, never mind patients. I got this great idea today. Hang on..." I opened the car doors and we got inside. Tanya shivered.

"What about getting away to the borders, Dumfries and Galloway? Someone was talking about Scotland today and it reminded me of one or two good places." My voice became more animated at the thought of it.

"I thought we were going to London" said Tanya, mildly surprised.

"Oh hell, no. I couldn't put up with all that crap — traffic, people, you know the kind of thing I mean. I think we need space for ourselves. And time. There are some good hotels, beaches..."

"You sound like a brochure," laughed Tanya. "But that's fine with me. We all need a change of scenery, God knows."

I looked at my watch. "I thought it was later than that. What do you say to calling at the Norbury for a quick one on the way home? There's just time. Maybe we could talk..."

She shook her head slowly and smiled.

"No. I've got a better idea." She squeezed my arm. "Let's go home."

I looked across at her and read her eyes, and knew she was right. It was a much better idea.

# 15

Out of my head I would never have been able to pronounce Mrs. Puz's surname, let alone ever attempt to spell it. It was one of those long Polish names which seemed to have no vowels in it to relieve the strain to palate and tongue as they struggled over the scramble of harsh consonants. So we always referred to her as Mrs. Puz. Her husband had died fighting during the last war and she herself had been sent to the concentration camp at Treblinka which somehow she had survived. She came to England soon after the war but her physical appearance had not changed much since those days, according to her close relatives. Her wizened grey skin wrapped itself loosely round her small frame and her dark eyes blazed out of their sunken sockets like two beacons of accusation still burning from the memory of her barbaric incarceration. She had survived up until now by swallowing sodium amytal each night to give her a dreamless sleep, and she came regularly to the surgery for a repeat prescription, each time clutching a bag of "chucky eggs" from her hens for Ian or myself in exchange for her nightly oblivion. Over the years both of us had gone through the regular ritual of sympathy, but as I looked at her records which I had taken to the house, I could see that we had not noted very carefully just how many of these capsules she had been taking.

I pulled back the bed-clothes to reveal her tiny cold grey body. The grubby nightdress and bed were strewn with blue capsules of sodium amatyl, and I couldn't help thinking how ironic it was that we had, albeit innocently, probably contributed to her death. Through lack of attention to detail, we had succeeded where the efforts of the Third Reich had failed. I pulled the sheet to cover her up and looked across at her niece who stood at the other side of the bed, her round, shiny pink face radiating a healthy glow which seemed almost indecent in that damp grey room with its lifeless occupant. I saw the question on her face.

"An accident, probably," I said.

"You don't think she...?"

"Not necessarily, no. These elderly people, they ... get confused sometimes. You know – forget they've taken their night dose, wake up and take more. How did you find her, I mean what made you...?"

"Oh well, I was passing the yard on the way to the shops and saw the hens hadn't been seen to. I've got a key for the house, so I – "

"I see. You haven't seen her for a bit, then?"

"Day before yesterday. She was fine then." The woman took a large man's handkerchief from her bulging handbag, shook it unhygienically all over the place then blew her nose noisily. She pulled the handkerchief away from her face and examined the contents.

"Catarrh," she said brightly. "Always get it this time of year, before winter. I don't suppose while you're here you could give me a prescription – "

"I'm going downstairs to use the phone," I replied, gritting my teeth and ignoring her.

"...Only it would save me coming to see you, like," she continued.

"No. I haven't got my prescription pad with me," I lied. "Anyway, forget your catarrh. I have to inform the coroner and the police will call soon."

"The police? What are they...?"

"It's usual in these cases. Routine. Where's the phone?" I felt too tired to explain anything more to her at this stage, and I went down the stairs without listening to her as she told me where the phone was. I found it anyway and dialled the coroner's office. As the phone rang on and on at the other end I began to yawn. Thank God this was the last day before we went on holiday for two weeks. Two whole weeks away from women who scrutinised their own diabolical nasal discharge; away from depressing death.

147

The last ten days since our evening at the North Towers had not been enjoyable. I had hardly got a single uninterrupted night's sleep because of a flurry of calls to the police station. And I couldn't get out of my mind what Bill Snowden had said. It looked as if we were heading for a showdown either with the Area Health Authority or the Town Hall, or both, unless we could get delayed Matco's planning permission to demolish our surgery. At the moment, though, I was simply too exhausted to care. It would have to wait.

I stood by the phone and pulled a record card out of my pocket and looked at the name. It was my next call. Norman Parker. The message about his wife, Emily Parker, had come this morning. She had had her ovarian cyst removed. Everything had gone satisfactorily and the cyst was benign. Then she had a cardiac arrest post-operatively and died without regaining consciousness. While I was thinking about what I was going to say to Mr. Parker the coroner's officer answered and I filled him in about Mrs. Puz. I put the phone down and turned to the niece who was looking out of the back window, sniffing loudly.

"I've arranged everything," I said, the drone of my own voice nearly sending me to sleep standing right there. "There's nothing for you to do now. Just wait until someone comes to sort it out." She wasn't listening so I turned to go. As I did so the niece spoke.

"I should think we'll have to wring their necks and sell them off as broilers," she said, sniffing again. I stopped at the door leading to the hall.

"What?"

"Broilers. They're no use for anything else at their age and we can't be expected to keep them. Too much mess everywhere. Personally I think they're disgusting creatures." She pulled a face and for a moment I thought that she had become demented. An abscess on her brain due to her catarrh and frontal sinusitis perhaps. What the hell was she talking about?

"Me auntie's chickens, I mean," she said.

I stared at her. "Chickens? Ah yes, of course. The chickens.

Well, that's certainly an appallingly serious problem. I'm glad to say I can't help you there."

I walked out into the street to my car and was immediately stopped by a woman who had run from a house further down the street. She had her hand on her throat and greeted me breathlessly.

"Just caught you, doctor. I saw you calling down the road as I was cleaning me windows – " she spluttered. I carried on putting my bag into the back of the car, trying to quell my growing anger, for I knew what she wanted. " – So I thought, while you're here, can I have a repeat prescription for some of that cream I use for my rash?"

I cringed as I trapped my fingers in the handle of my case and slammed the boot lid down angrily.

"No, I regret to say I cannot do that," I said. "I cannot give you a prescription for your cream, nor a prescription for a bottle for your children's runny noses, shampoo for your husband's dandruff or cotton wool for your Christmas tree. Jesus Christ, Mrs. Seddon, I am not the stop-me-and-buy-one Rissotti's Ice Cream man!" I jumped into my car and slammed the door hard. Fortunately the car started first time, saving me the anti-climactic indignity of shoving it down the road, which would have made my outburst more ridiculous than it otherwise was. I derived considerable satisfaction from seeing her reaction in the driving mirror as she gaped down the road after me, but I slowed down as I saw her suddenly step forward, pick something up from the road and wave it in the air. I had no idea what she was up to. I finally drew up outside Norman Parker's house, and as I reached down to grab the door handle my heart sank. My stethoscope, which I had not put in my bag, had slipped out of my side pocket when I got into the car, and had jammed in the door. I opened the door and the stethoscope fell out onto the road. When I had slammed the door in the face of Mrs. Seddon I had neatly amputated the thin plastic tube three inches from the bell. That's what she had been waving about as I drove off from Mrs. Puz's house. I cursed under my breath.

I tried to concentrate my thoughts a little as I walked up the path, but trying to use my brain at that moment was as futile as trying to squeeze a bathroom sponge into a complex shape and make it stay that way. Mrs. Puz's unfortunate death had bothered me ever since the message came into the surgery earlier that morning, and in some perverse kind of way I couldn't help feeling that the two casual but thoughtless requests for prescriptions a few minutes ago, which provoked my irrational angry response, vaguely arose from the same grey uneasy area of the present day health service – medical care by proxy. The business of leaving prescriptions at the surgery to be collected by the patients or their relatives whilst on their way to buy the groceries or to have their hair done, made life easier for everyone, but it was an absurd end-result of years of research and expenditure which went into the production of drugs, that such prescriptions were treated with as much significance as a sliced loaf or a packet of cornflakes. And as though the Mrs. Puz episode were not enough I now had to face Emily Parker's family ...

"Don't stand there, doctor. Come in." Mr. Parker's daughter stood in the doorway and beckoned me inside. I wondered how long I had stood there without noticing her. She closed the door quietly behind me and I could see that she was very calm and in full control of the situation, which was a relief.

"I did all my crying yesterday, doctor," she said, smiling slightly. "So for me the worst is over. It's Dad I've sent for you to see. He's taken it very badly ... he didn't get a chance to see mum after her operation because of his chest, and it was too far for him to travel even door to door in a car. He's in bed. Been there since yesterday, complaining of his chest." She was silent for a second, and fidgeted with her wedding-ring which she kept slipping up and down her finger. I said nothing but waited for her to say something else that she seemed to be holding back.

"Doctor ..." She hesitated and dropped her eyes to her hands to avoid looking at me. I could tell what she was going to say next. "... D'you think that mum would have been better off ... I mean, I know you were keen for the operation to be done, and that ... well, I mean to say you were very kind and I don't mean to imply it was your fault in any way, of course, but perhaps it would have been best for her not to have the operation..."

"I know what you mean," I said. "Let's put it this way. The operation would have been necessary sooner or later and I felt sure that this was malignant..."

"But it wasn't, was it?" She smiled her little smile again but continued to look at her hands. I nodded grimly.

"No, but even the gynaecologist thought it was until he actually operated. This is the problem..."

"Yes, doctor, I realise that. It's easy to say after the event. I'm sure everyone did for the best. It always seems to happen to those who deserve it least, though, doesn't it? When I think of all those my mum helped over the years it seems ... well ... anyway, I'll take you up to see Dad. We can't stand here all day. I expect you're rushed off your feet."

She led the way upstairs and went into the main bedroom and stood at the side of the bed. Mr. Parker opened his eyes, which were bloated, watery and red. As he sat up against a pile of pillows he heaved his chest and coughed his rasping, gargling bronchitic cough which brought a dusky purple colour to his normally plethoric features. He took one look at me and began to cry, turning his head at the same time to look out of the window in the hope that we wouldn't see the tears overflow and run down his cheeks from his swollen, sagging lids. I couldn't think of anything to say that wouldn't sound hopelessly inadequate and so I kept quiet for a few seconds. Perhaps because I did not offer any comment, Mr. Parker settled down quickly, wiping his face with a quick circular movement of his hand. He turned to look at me.

"I'm sorry, doctor – it's just that it's fair knocked me sick, some road. When the missus went into hospital it was the first time we'd been apart for over forty years." He sat back and sank into the pillows behind him, looking exhausted.

"Yes. It must have been quite a blow..." I said, and winced as the words limped out of my mouth and died in front of my face. Mr. Parker closed his eyes.

151

"There's neither rhyme nor reason for it, to me. She never ailed in her life. By rights it should've been me, what with my chest... I just wish she hadn't..." He opened his eyes and looked at me through his tears. His daughter came round the other side of the bed and began fussing with the sheets.

"Don't upset yourself, Dad. Your chest is bad again and I'm sure the doctor wants you to rest. Will you sound his chest, doctor?"

I nodded and opened my bag. "There's not a lot I can say, Mr. Parker. I'm really sorry about your wife. Especially since it was I who advised her to have an operation. It's one of those things we don't have any control over – about heart attacks. It's not possible to predict these things." I took the pulse and pulled out my stethoscope to listen to Mr. Parker's chest, then suddenly remembered the chopped-off end and put it quickly away in my case. I examined him as well as I could by listening with my ear directly against the chest wall, and was quite surprised how effective this was. I did everything in slow motion, taking a long time, and while I palpated and percussed the old man's chest and abdomen I wondered whether I should go and collect the bell of my stethoscope from that Seddon woman, or wait until she arrived with it in triumph at the surgery. She would probably send a message round by one of her children, written on the back of an old used envelope which would read: "Will Dr. Rushton come and collect his instrument and while he's at it could he bring a prescription for some cream, and oblige H. Seddon (Mrs.)."

I finished examining Mr. Parker and closed my bag after getting out a couple of mild sedative tablets.

"Your chest isn't too bad, Mr. Parker. I've seen it a lot worse," I said. The patient nodded but showed no interest whatsoever, which was not surprising. "Anyway, I've left you a couple of tablets to help you get some rest tonight. I'll call in a couple of days if you like..."

Mr. Parker smiled grimly, leaning forward in the bed. "If you do call, doctor, you won't find me here. I'll be in the cemetery." It sounded like a plain statement of fact.

"Oh don't take it personal. There's nowt worth going on

152

for now. My chest is tight and I'm tired of struggling with all this phlegm..." He coughed as if to emphasise his point – a deep, rattling cough which squeezed tears out of his bloated eye-lids as he screwed his face up. "I just haven't the energy or the will to fight it any more. I doubt whether I'll need your tablets, doctor. Thanks anyway, it's nowt of your doing. I'm just buggered, and with the missus gone there doesn't seem much point in going on, that's all." He closed his eyes again and sank back into the pile of soft pillows which seemed almost to engulf his head and neck; it was almost like a half-dead survivor of a shipwreck who allows his weary body to slip over the side of the life-raft, the waves bringing an icy curtain across his pain.

"That's not your usual fighting talk, Mr. Parker," I said. "Maybe you'll feel different when you've had a decent night's rest. I'll see you in a couple of days."

"Goodbye, doctor." Mr. Parker pulled the covers up to his chin and lay there breathing regularly and noisily. I glanced at the daughter and she shook her head in a sort of apology. We went downstairs and I made sure she had my phone number.

"What do you think, doctor? I've never heard him like that before," she said anxiously.

"Nor have I. On the other hand he hasn't been faced with something like this before, either. He's lost the will to survive, it seems," I said.

"Can't you give him a tonic or something?" she asked. I shook my head.

"I don't think there's anything I can do to alter his state of mind. If he's decided to let go there's nothing you or I can do to alter it. Let me know if there is any change." She thanked me and I left.

It was about eleven o'clock that same evening that Mr. Parker's daughter rang to say that he had just died. I went round and confirmed the fact of death. On the death certificate I put "cardiac failure secondary to chronic bronchitis and emphysema" for the benefit of the Registrar-General. I could hardly put down on the certificate that the old man had simply switched off, but that was what it

153

amounted to. His prediction that he would die even before he needed to take the tablets I had left him had a chilling accuracy which was impossible to explain.

Driving home I couldn't help but think of May O'Reilly, one of the last of the great old school of nursing sisters at Wishton General, who was in charge of the male medical ward when I was a raw house physician. I was not sure what it was about the events of that day which brought her to mind, except perhaps something she had once said. She was an enormous, waddling, slow-moving Irish woman with a great sense of humour. She had a bemused tolerance for the housemen who disturbed her bedpans and bedbaths as they rushed round with defibrillators, cardiac monitors and the like, for she was more at home with the flower-arrangements and the patients' lockers being kept tidy than she was with electrolytes and fluid balance.

"Fluid balance, doctor?" she would say slowly as she scanned a droopy eye over the patient's chart, "fluid balance? Isn't that the amount of Guinness a patient can drink before he falls over?" Many was the time a couple of us would sprint to a cardiac arrest only to find that she had summoned the priest long ago, and he would be already there, giving the last rites. This happened so often that I was convinced she kept him in the bottom drawer of the resuscitation trolley. I remembered one occasion, when we *did* get there before Father O'Hara; we dragged the moribund patient to the floor, pumped his chest and gave mouth to mouth while a pupil nurse unravelled wires from the trolley. As I paused momentarily to draw my breath during the exhausting procedure, I glanced sideways to see the generous lower limbs of Sister O'Reilly, like two very old, wise tree-trunks sticking out from the lower reaches of her huge, tent-like uniform. I looked up and felt perspiration run down my cheek. She was shaking her head slowly and smiling.

"Ah doctor," she said, "when the good Lord puts your name on the little thrombus comin' down the coronary arteries there's nothin' you or I can do about it at all, at all." She turned to the pupil nurse, and said, "Now come along, my

154

dear. All you're doing is getting your stockings in a divil of a mess. Get yourself up off the floor and tidy up this place. Go and put the flowers nice for the relatives of the poor man when they arrive. 'Tis not the drama you have just seen that is important, 'tis the drama to follow when the relatives are given the news which matters now." The pupil nurse scurried off with a vase to sort out some flowers, giving a flushed apologetic glance at myself and the other houseman as we got up slowly from the floor, brushing ourselves down. May O'Reilly opened the door and waved us out. "Come along now, doctors, let's have a cup of tea. Remember that there's nothing so inevitable as birth and death, no matter what your wonderful machines tell you. All the scientific contraptions on earth won't make any difference. Yes, birth and death, no problem there at all, at all. It's the tirrible mess in between birth an' death where all the problems are, take it from me."

And now May O'Reilly was dead as well. She had died a few weeks ago in a car-crash. To be accurate, she did not die instantly but sustained severe head injuries and died, without regaining consciousness, a few days later. Had she woken up and found herself with half a brain and surrounded by all the life-support equipment of the intensive care unit, no doubt she would have switched herself off like Norman Parker. She always said she had a printed card pinned to her vest which read: "In case of accident do not take to Wishton Casualty." To which I was sure she had added another: "If found half-dead do not resuscitate – send for the priest. Half a life is not enough!"

# 16

The next couple of weeks away from the practice seemed all too brief: the relaxing, unplanned days with Tanya and the children came and went like a puff of smoke in a stiff breeze, their very transcience making them all the more precious.

Then, shortly after I returned from holiday, with dignity and without fuss, Miss Cope left. Her replacement – a kind, hardworking woman called Mrs. Hilda Penny – was no match at all against the insatiable demands of the patients and, watching her greet each incoming telephone call as if it were news of a Martian invasion, I realised what I had known all along; that Miss Cope had been remarkable and was irreplaceable.

Later that autumn, we found a new partner. By a stroke of good fortune, I heard that Molly Kirkham, who was a contemporary of mine in the early sixties in Edinburgh, was doing a general practice traineeship a few miles away. I remembered Molly well from those days. She was a tall blonde who came from a farm somewhere near Formby, and was one of the few students who never fell over at a dance or a party after consuming umpteen pints of McEwan's Export, when everybody else who wasn't actually horizontal had double vision or numbness of the lower part of the face or legs. She was a volatile mixture of energy, aggression, stamina and extroversion with an outrageous sense of humour, and she obviously impressed Ian with her no-nonsense approach. She was an almost perfect foil to his unobtrusive, conservative and dignified manner and, much to my relief, she added another dimension to the choice of doctors available to our patients. She worked with a breezy confidence which terrified old ladies and cowed strong men hoping for an easy touch for a sick note.

Amongst all these good qualities however, she had some outstandingly unfortunate ones. In her case her abrasive approach was combined with a lightning assessment of a situation which led at times to her jumping totally to the wrong conclusion. A couple of weeks after she joined the practice, we were sitting in our respective rooms writing out prescriptions before going out on our visits. Molly was waiting for a patient who had rung up earlier from his place of work to say that he had just developed a hernia, and would she look at it because it had suddenly become very painful. As I checked the last few prescriptions, I heard the sound of footsteps approaching Molly's room and a timid male voice called "Hellooo...? Is anybody there?" I remembered that Mrs. Penny had gone out for some stamps so I got up to see who it was. At the same moment, Molly flung open her door and I could see a diminutive figure in the doorway. Molly, without hesitating, grabbed him by the arm and pulled him into her room. Through the still-open door I could hear and see pretty well everything.

"Oh good morning, doctor ... are you the new lady doctor?"

"Well I'm certainly not Dr Rushton dressed in drag!" Molly said briskly. "Now come on, I've got to get cracking with my visits. You really should ring a bit earlier with these things you know – "

"I beg your..." began the bewildered man.

"Surgery finished a long time ago. How long have you been a patient here?"

"Oh, about fifteen years..."

"Then there's no excuse. You should know the surgery times by now."

"But I only – "

"Never mind, never mind," said Molly, flapping her hands impatiently. "Now come on – slip your pants down and let's be having a look at this thing of yours."

The patient went pale.

"What thing's that, doctor...?"

"Oh come on, don't be shy. I *am* a doctor, you know! I mean – it won't be the first time I've seen one of these things."

"Well I don't know..." He undid his belt in what seemed like shock and amazement and his trousers slipped down to his knees.

"Underpants as well!" bellowed Molly. His jaw sagged.

"Dr Rushton doesn't ask me to do this when I see him – "

"Look, Mr. O'Farrell," said Molly, her voice rising in pitch and volume, her flared spectacle frames jiggling on the bridge of her nose, "are we or are we not going to see this hernia of yours?" She folded her arms abruptly and tapped her foot in exasperation on the frayed carpet. The man looked bewildered for a moment, then pulled his pants up quickly.

"O'Farrell? Hernia? there's been a misunderstanding, doctor, my name's Perrin – William Perrin. I'm the window cleaner. I've come to collect my money – I always do that on the last Thursday in the month."

# 17

One Friday morning in November, after a light surgery, Molly, Ian and I sat in Ian's consulting room taking stock of our position regarding the health centre and our threatened eviction. The situation was still not clear: the planning department at the Town Hall had written saying that, while Matco had applied for planning permission to kick us out and knock down our surgery, the permission would only be granted subject to the health centre being completed or, failing that, the Area Health Authority finding us alternative accommodation in which to see our patients. The AHA, on the other hand, were not saying much at all, except to point out that they had no powers to delay Matco's planning permission, even though the health centre was going to take another two years to complete and in spite of the fact that we had been unable to find suitable alternative accommodation ourselves. Ian remained confident that the authorities would not allow such an injustice to take place in the face of the adverse public opinion which was building up. Molly and I did not share this optimism and continued to look at property in between running round after the patients.

"I have a feeling it will all turn out OK," said Ian, swivelling round in his chair. "I think we'll be able to stick it out here, you know."

I grunted. "I hope you're right, because the alternative doesn't bear thinking about. Can you imagine the lunacy of renting a temporary place, spending a fortune to make it decent – then moving again after two years into the health centre. Think of the inconvenience and the expense. Effort and money down the drain. I'm sorry, Ian, but I have a feeling it'll be a real shambles in the end, with us picking up the pieces. And all because of a supermarket which no one wants, and an Area Health Authority which doesn't give a shit."

I was still feeling angry later that day when I started my evening surgery. I picked up the first card and saw that it was Eric Birtles, a big wheel in Overton Town Hall, no less. He might prove to be our great white hope.

I rang the bell and in came Birtles. He was a small shambling man whose mottled, tired complexion reminded me of a faded tapestry. He had a long, narrow head with neatly parted silver hair partially overhanging his large ears which moved alarmingly whenever he opened his mouth to speak. As he rarely had anything worthwhile to say, this constituted a mildly irritating phenomenon rather than a major distraction to the onlooker.

Birtles sat down with his knees tight together and tucked his outsize overcoat underneath his backside. "Well now, doctor, it's like this," he said cosily, shifting round to face me but shutting his eyes and fluttering the upper lids. He wants a sick note, I thought. "I wonder if you could see your way to giving me a note for a week or two." He looked down at his hands which flapped about on his lap like fish out of water.

"It's ... well, I've been under a lot of pressure at the Town Hall, you know."

"Pressure? At the Town Hall?" I smiled. "No, I didn't know. What's the reason for that?"

Birtles hitched closer to the desk and I got a brief glimpse of the whites of his eyes as they disappeared like a couple of quail's eggs beneath his upper eye-lids.

"Oh well, personal problems ... you know how it is." He paused and I remained silent, waiting for him to continue. "To tell you the truth, Doctor Rushton, it's one particular problem actually. I've had a new assistant allotted to me and ... ah ... it's not worked out very satisfactorily. He's very aggressive and if I might say so, downright discourteous ... if you know what I mean. I don't like his attitude and it's having a very bad effect on my nerves. The worst thing is, I mean the most difficult part is..." He stuck his flapping hands under his armpits and squirmed in the chair "... the worst part is – and this makes it difficult for me to say anything – is that he's *coloured*." He screwed his eyes up and pursed his lips, nodding his head disapprovingly. "I mean – don't get me wrong, doctor – I've nothing personal against these lads but in practice it just doesn't work very well and the strain is beginning to tell on me. So I wondered if you could..."

Without replying I reached out and filled out a sick note, putting the reason for incapacity for work as "Ethnic Reverberations". I handed it to him and sat back. As he read it, a puzzled frown spread across his face.

"What does this mean, doctor, if you'll pardon me for asking? It's just so as I can tell them in my department."

"Oh ... well, it's sort of like a nervous debility, really," I said with a more or less straight face. Birtles nodded and put the note in his wallet.

"I've got a friend who lives in the Wirral and who's asked me to stay with him for a few days. That should help to settle me down. Thanks very much, I'm obliged to you, doctor." He got up from the chair.

"Just before you go, there is just one thing about which I'd like your opinion," I said, inviting him to sit down again. "You have something to do with Overton Town Hall, don't you?"

Birtles ran his index-finger round the inside of his collar, screwed his neck round and fumbled with the knot in his tie.

"I most certainly do, doctor, yes."

"You are aware, are you, that the Matco supermarket chain has bought this building and plans to demolish it to build another supermarket as soon as planning permission is granted?"

"I was aware of – "

"Which will leave us up the creek. We have no alternative accommodation at the moment. Which is going to make life very difficult for us and the patients. You can see that, can't you?"

"Dr. Rushton, this matter has been under discussion many times in council meetings and you can rest assured that at this moment in time the interests of the town are being taken care of – and if I may say so, your patients and yourselves. No sir, there will be no question of you being moved out until your health centre is ready. You have my word on that."

"That sounds encouraging," I said. "I hope we can count on that."

"Oh, I think you can. One or two of us have a certain amount of influence, you know. As a matter of fact the next planning committee meets next week and it is anticipated that a final decision will be reached then." He stood up and we shook hands awkwardly. "Well, doctor, thanks for the note. I hope I've managed to alleviate your anxieties over the other matter. Just leave it with me, and tell Dr. McDonald not to have any worries on that score. He and I have known each other for a long time. Give him my regards, won't you? How is he, by the way? I haven't seen him for a long time."

"He's very well, and he'll feel better still when this problem has been taken out of our hair," I replied grimly. Birtles smiled, waved and turned to go.

"Not to worry at all. Leave it with me, I'll not let you down. At the end of the day we've all got our jobs to do." He went out and I sat doodling on the desk blotter for a minute. I wasn't convinced by Birtles' performance at all.

By a curious coincidence the last patient of the day, whose name I hadn't noticed until the very last minute because his record card was right at the bottom of the pile on the desk, was Bernard Thornley. This really was a stroke of luck. Thornley was not only an aspiring local politician but was a lay member of the local Environmental Health Committee, a remarkable achievement for a man with such poverty of ability. Unlike Birtles, who was drifting comfortably towards the evening of his career with its inflation-proof pension, Bernard Thornley threshed and sweated in the merciless mid-day sun of his own endeavours like a salmon on its way to the spawning grounds, creating splashes and ripples but apparently making no headway. His out-of-hours activities on his various committees and political involvements, together with his job as assistant Personnel Officer at a large local factory, put such an enormous stress on him that he became a frequent attender at the surgery with such symptoms as tightness of the chest, dyspepsia, headaches and tiredness – all of which were due to the fact that he could not see that the gap between ambition and ability in his case was far too wide. He was not taken too seriously by either his colleagues at work or those at the Town Hall – a fact which he interpreted as being due to lack of sufficient effort on his part, rather than lack of sufficient competence. This interpretation sadly reflected his own profound lack of insight.

He strode in briskly, stood to attention, and gave me a tight-elbowed salute as used by American military personnel.

"It's the old duodenal playing up again, doctor. My stomach nerves have been taking a bit of stick of late which is not surprising really, seeing as how I've been rushing about." He sat down but twitched restlessly in the chair, looking across at me with a lop-sided clownish grin, his thick red hair flopping onto his forehead. His eyes were like little shiny mirrors reflecting the intellectual wilderness which lay behind them. It was frightening to realise that Bernard Thornley shared in the sort of decision-making which could affect a great number of people and involve vast amounts of money.

"I'm sure I'll be OK with the white medicine you gave me a month ago. By the way – how's the health centre coming on?"

"You probably know more about that than I do," I replied: "They've dug a few holes, put a few builders' huts here and there but not much else. What I want to know is – are we going to be thrown out of the building we now occupy before the centre is ready?"

"Not while I've got anything to do with it. After all, apart from anything else, I am a patient as well, aren't I?"

"Yes. We're aware of that." I passed him his prescription. "But I believe you have a planning meeting next week, haven't you?"

Thornley gathered up the prescription and stood up, brushing the hair off his forehead.

"Well ... yes. But of course – "

"And you have some influence on the AHA."

"I've never stopped talking about this particular – "

"I'd hate the thought of us getting thrown out of here and

having to find somewhere else until they decide to finish the health centre. It will make life very unpleasant for both doctor and patient, you know."

Thornley started to walk backwards towards the door, and stuck both thumbs in the air, nodding his head and turning down the corners of his mouth, as if he were giving me a certainty on the Derby.

"Don't give it another thought, doctor. That won't happen, not while I'm around. You'll see. I must dash now – I've got a meeting tonight. Anyway – you'll see."

We did see. About ten days later we heard that the town hall had passed planning permission for the surgery to be demolished and a final notice to quit the premises arrived the next day.

# 18

"Thirty years! Think of it – thirty bloody years I've run around wiping the noses of this town, and look how I'm being treated. It's a scandal. A bloody disgrace. Turned out of my own surgery. It's unbelievable."

Ian sat back in his chair, his hands clasped behind his head and his chin on his chest. We sat in his consulting room, Molly twirling a lock of her hair round and round in her fingers, which she usually did when she was angry or engrossed in thought. I stared blankly at the pile of letters which had once again been dug out of the file and now lay in a heap on Ian's desk – an untidy chronicle of procrastination and double-talk over the last ten years.

The phone buzzed. I picked it up and heard Mrs Penny's voice at the other end.

"Your call to the Area Administrator, doctor."

"Right, thanks..."

"Before you, er ... can I just mention there's a man at reception who looks very worried – "

"He's not the only one," I replied impatiently. "Who is it?"

"A Mr. McNair. He says you saw his father yesterday and he's much worse today – "

"Oh yes. Tell him to go back home. I'll call later when I've finished here. Put the other call through."

There was a click, then a girl's voice crooned in a bored voice: "Doctor Rushton? Major Dunning for you. One moment."

I stuck the receiver out at arm's length towards Ian who shook his head and turned to look out of the window.

"You speak to him. If I do I'm liable to lose my temper. No, go ahead."

At the other end of the phone I could hear someone talking

a distance away. There was some laughter, then more conversation which I couldn't quite hear. While I waited, I wondered what the trouble was with old man McNair. His son and daughter-in-law had him to stay with them from Glasgow from time to time. I had been called yesterday and was pretty sure the old man had had a coronary. He was in poor shape. I had ordered complete bed rest, all the usual things, and said I would call in forty-eight hours. Probably gone into congestive cardiac failure. Jimmy McNair's father was a prize candidate – chronic bronchitis, smoked like a chimney, drank like a fish. Not unlike Jimmy, really.

"Hello, Dunning here. Is that Doctor Rushton?" When I heard his clipped military tone I knew that we were doomed, for in his voice was the sound of total inflexibility.

"That's right," I answered coldly.

"Believe you wanted a word. Know how damn busy you GPs are, so fire away."

"As a matter of fact something has cropped up, yes. You know that Matco bought our surgery last year and have just been granted planning permission to demolish it? We have notice to quit as they want to start work on it in May."

"Yes I had heard, Doctor Rushton," he said brightly. "I was talking to your Mr Nately from the Family Practitioner Committee only yesterday, as a matter of fact. Such a damnable business for you."

"Damnable? It's a bit more than that. We've spent a whole lot of time looking round for another place, but there simply isn't anywhere suitable in this town, you know. What about this assurance from the planning department that they wouldn't kick us out until the AHA had come up with alternative arrangements?"

His voice took on a more defensive quality. "Come, come, doctor. I really do doubt that we'd *ever* give such an assurance."

"Wait a minute – I've got a letter in front of me from the Town Hall which says you did – "

"Oh no, no, no, my *dear* chap," he laughed. "You must know by now that you shouldn't believe *everything* people tell you, now should you – what?"

I could feel the hair on the back of my neck standing up and my palms began to sweat. "Then what's the point of sending a letter like this? I mean – who is responsible for this double-talk? This has really put us in a difficult position. There simply isn't the time to go chasing round finding accommodation as well as to look after the patients, and if we do find a place it's going to cost a small fortune unless we practise in a dump for the next couple of years, until you people – "

"Ah, Doctor Rushton," he said, his voice becoming a good deal harder. "Now I know your own good conscience won't allow you to practise from sub-standard accommodation. As far as the cost goes, I'm sure you'll find a way."

"A couple of thousand – " I blurted.

"A couple of thousand? Well, now that's not exactly a fortune is it?"

"It damn well is when you consider it wouldn't have been necessary if the health centre had been completed on time."

"Well now, that's beyond our control, I'm afraid. Anyway, I must remind you that you have a contract to look after your patients and it is your duty to provide adequate accommodation. It really is your problem, you know. You must work it out for yourselves. Stand on your own feet – that sort of thing."

"What you're saying is that the AHA is not – "

"What I am saying is that as general practitioners you must sort this out yourselves. The AHA cannot be responsible in any way for your misfortune. Now I really must go. Please give my kind regards to Doctor McDonald. Goodbye."

I heard the click and put down the receiver, staring at it for a moment before looking up to see Ian shaking his head.

"Don't tell me," he said wearily. "I gathered that the AHA doesn't want to know. My God..."

"That's about it," I said. "Major Sodding Dunning gave us the kiss of death. Politely of course."

"Of course," said Ian quietly. He sat quite still and stared at the desk. He suddenly looked old and grey. Molly compressed her lips and tapped her fingers on the desk.

"Right!" she said abruptly. "Sod it. Sod the AHA and sod the health centre. I'm all for buying our own place. What about that place we saw last week?"

"Whitehead's?" I said. "Sixteen thousand. Needs a few more thousand spending on it. Big, though. Lots of possibilities for a surgery."

Ian shook his head. "The bank won't lend us that kind of money. And the building societies won't lend for business, so where's the money coming from?"

"General Practice Finance Corporation," I said, feeling slightly hysterical at the daftness of it all. "Either way, if we bought a place, we would be in a good position. We could sell it after two years and recoup the capital – "

"Or stay in it and tell them to stuff the health centre," said Molly.

Ian nodded. "That's the only idea which appeals to me at the moment. I'm sick of the mention of the health centre and all the bureaucracy which goes with it."

We discussed the idea at some length and all the time I watched Ian's face. He was angry about the whole thing, and I could tell he was thinking that this was a hell of a time for him to be getting tied up in huge loans with the risks and pitfalls of selling his share to an incoming partner when he retired. As Molly and I tilted at windmills, he said very little to reflect his true feelings. He would think quietly about it for a long time before he made what would be carefully measured observations.

While Molly sorted out the paperwork for the loan, I went off to see Jimmy McNair's father. I opened the gate at the end of the small front garden and it came off its single hinge, falling off onto the path in front of my feet. I stumbled over it as Mrs. McNair came out of the front door to greet me.

"Ah, ah'm sorry about that, doctor. Jimmy's bin meanin' tae fix that for months," she said, with her broad Glaswegian accent.

"That's OK Mrs. McNair," I mumbled. "I'm getting used

to things falling apart at the moment. It's kind of symbolic, really."

She looked at me and laughed a little uncertainly, at the same time pushing the little gate off the path and onto a flower-bed with her foot.

"Is that right?" she said brightly. "Well that's fine, then. Come away in, doctor."

I went in and Jimmy beckoned to me from the narrow staircase. On the landing a small window with coloured leaded lights shone a greenish glow onto his face as he turned and spoke. He looked haggard and unshaven as usual.

"He seemed to get a bit brighter, y'ken, last night, but he's been in a sort of coma this mornin' – never touched his breakfast. He's a funny colour too – aw hell, see for yersel'. Through here, doctor. It's the same room as when ye saw'm yesterday – we havnae moved him, y'ken."

I walked over to the window and opened the curtains to let some light into the darkened room. On the chair by the bed was a tray with a couple of slices of bread and butter, an uneaten boiled egg and a mug of tea, now cold and with a skin on top. I looked at the old man's face and realised that he had been dead for hours. I drew back the covers a little. The body was quite cool with colour changes in the skin which indicated that he had been dead since about midnight. I turned to Jimmy and his wife who were standing at the other side of the room.

"Who brought his breakfast up?"

Jimmy shambled forward, frowning, and looking first at me and then at the corpse on the bed.

"I did, doctor. Is there somethin' wrong?"

"Well, he's been dead for hours. Probably not long after midnight, I should think."

To my amazement Jimmy suddenly looked relieved. He turned to his wife.

"Nae wonder he wouldnae eat his breakfast, hen!" He turned back again and shook his head in wonder. "Christ, ye must think wirra coupla real stupid buggers, doctor. Ah mean – we've both been up here a coupla times this mornin' before ah come tae fetch ye."

"Aye, that's right enough," Mrs. McNair nodded. "So we have. My God, I thought he was asleep or in a coma or something." She sat down heavily on a small chair by the wall and stared blankly in front of her. Jimmy shuffled about and lit a cigarette as I examined the old man as quickly as I could. I was reasonably sure that he had had another coronary during the night, so I closed my bag and told Jimmy that he could call at the surgery to pick up the death certificate.

"That's fine. Right y'are, doctor." He began to smile, though his eyes were a little moist. "Christ, just think of it! There's me shovin' his breakfast on his lap and goin' on and on about him eatin' his wee bloody egg that it'll do him good an all tha'." He sniffed loudly. "Still, he went the best way, eh, doctor? In his sleep. Aye, peaceful. That's the way tae go. Well, thanks, doctor, for comin' and doin' what ye could — " His big bony hand grasped mine and he shook it solemnly. We exchanged a few pleasantries downstairs and then I left. As I drove off I couldn't help smiling at the thought of Jimmy standing by the bedside imploring the poor old man to eat his "wee bloody egg". To be fair to Jimmy and his wife, though, it was a fact that, because of years of poor diet and excessive booze, the physical appearance of Jimmy's father in life was not, in recent years anyway, much different from what it was in death.

# 19

We wasted no time sending the loan application form off to the local family practitioner committee for its mandatory approval, but we were not hopeful. In the fine print it had said that we might not get the grant approved if a health centre was being planned in the area. This looked very much like being the big catch, making approval in our case very unlikely. We awaited the reply with gloom and despondancy. A few days later Nately, the chief administrator, was on the phone.

"Just had sight of your application for a GPF company loan. What's this all about? You're not contemplating buying a place, are you?" His voice was patronising.

"It's a possibility," I replied flatly. "We have to get round this mess without losing too much money if we can avoid it."

"Hmm, I see. You realise that Area will not look kindly on an application like this," Nately replied peevishly.

"Since when did they give a damn about how we did things unless it put a spanner in their particular works?" I replied. Nately coughed.

"Well . . . you can see our . . . I mean their point of view. You're committed to the health centre now, and the implication here is that you might want to back out if you own your own premises. You do see the difficulty, don't you?"

I remembered what Bill Snowden had said when we met at the North Towers a few months ago. It began to look as if he was right.

"It's not a legal commitment though, is it?" I asked. "I mean . . ."

"Not exactly, no," said Nately carefully. "But there are some problems. Even if we did approve your application in principle, we would then have to approve the suitability of the property as a surgery and there might be difficulties there. Then again, I don't think you have a cat in hell's chance of getting planning permission for this place as a surgery with the health centre under construction."

"Why not? The decision for approving planning permission doesn't depend on there being a health centre in the offing, surely?"

Nately sighed audibly. "Not directly, no. But Area have ways of influencing these things, and as a result other objections may – "

"Bloody hell – you mean they can put the screws on *our* application and yet they can't do a damn thing about a supermarket chain demolishing our surgery. That's unbelievable."

"That's the way it is, I'm afraid. Anyway I'd like to meet you tomorrow at the surgery. Some property has come up for let and we could perhaps have a look at it together if that would help. I may be able to make suggestions..."

"We don't have much option do we? Where is this place?" I asked.

"Bentley Street," Nately replied. "It's part of the old Burgoyne Factory offices. It's old property, but – "

"Are you serious?" I said incredulously. "It's a pig-sty – a real shambles. It'll cost us a fortune to make it fit for human beings after all these years!"

"Let's see it first," said Nately patiently. "You never know, it may be quite suitable for a short time. About eleven o'clock be all right?"

"Yes, eleven. We'll be there, though God knows what for."

"Right then. Eleven. Goodbye, doctor."

I went round with Molly the next day. It was bitterly cold and icy rain whipped our faces as we approached the place, each of us gloomily silent at the thought of another wasted journey. Nately stood outside in a long grey overcoat, stamping his feet and hunching his narrow shoulders to push the upturned collar further up his long thin neck. He smiled and waved us inside the dilapidated building. It was much worse than I had imagined it would be. There was rubble and broken glass all over the floor, and the light which came through the filthy windows had a yellow tinge which gave the building an indescribably depressing atmosphere. Radiator pipes, cement, plaster, bits of wood and cardboard were everywhere. On the stair landing leading to the upper floor someone had urinated into a dish which had since been overturned, spilling the urine down the stairs where it had dried into the wood, staining it like a miniature frozen waterfall in an ornamental garden. The whole place stank like a badly kept public lavatory.

Nately, presumably to keep himself warm and to avoid Molly's withering looks, loped around with a large tape measure, muttering about where we could put the reception area, waiting room, and so on. Molly protested that it was an insult to all her years of hard work and study to have to see patients in a dump like that. I wasn't even listening. I was too cold, and the whole place was so utterly desolate that I could not imagine what would have to be done, irrespective of expense, to make it tolerable for seeing patients.

Nately made it clear that by accepting this property we would be making life easier for everyone, which made me want to burst out laughing. His selective perception was working on overdrive: what he meant was that if we lay down and shut up we would be out of his hair, and the AHA could keep its files nice and tidy. It gave us a breathtaking insight into the administrators' low regard for us and our patients.

We decided, therefore, that the best plan of action was to do precisely nothing. We wrote to the directors of Matco and told them that under the circumstances they would literally have to throw us out on the street before they could demolish the surgery. The effect was immediate, but in a way an anti-climax. Matco's directors converged on the surgery a few days later, armed with note-books, drawing boards and pocket calculators, to make us a deal. It was very simple: they would close down one of their small retail outlets in the town and convert it into a surgery to our own design and specification. All we had to do (apart from paying the rent and the cost of all the alterations), was draw some sketch-plans, and their builders and architects would do the rest. In return, we were required to move out into the prepared premises by their deadline of July the first. If we didn't move out by then, they told us, they would have to pay a large development tax on the supermarket they planned to put in the place of our surgery, and in the end we would have to move out because we didn't have a legal leg to stand on. So everyone would lose.

Put like this, it was an offer we couldn't turn down, for after the frustration of dealing with the local council and the AHA, this seemed like a triumph of private enterprise. My own initial disappointment at failing to buy our own place in the face of crushing bureaucracy turned to relief, because I was sick of the whole business. We could now leave the construction of a temporary surgery to someone else while we concentrated on more important matters. Increasing tension in the surgery, frayed tempers and the like, had already resulted in the first casualty – Mrs. Penny. Her surges of adrenaline, hot flushes and panic attacks became more frequent, and she left. We replaced her with two experienced girls who, by the following spring, had the surgery running so smoothly that Ian, Molly and I were able to relax a little and put our minds to things which for the past few months had appeared to have become secondary – looking after the patients.

# 20

During the following few months the practice increased in size and so did the work-load; so much so that I finally decided to resign from my police-surgeon duties, much to Tanya's relief. After five years of interrupted sleep it would be a novel experience to wake up refreshed and full of energy for the next day, for once again I had begun to enjoy the work which I had wanted to do for as long as I could remember. General practice, someone once said, is like a sewer: you only get out of it what you put in to it. And given the limitless variation in the patients, their illnesses, their backgrounds and their attitudes, it was impossible to predict the outcome of treatment with one hundred percent certainty, so that each day presented a different crop of problems and challenges. Each day something new was learned. It was a lifetime of surprises.

At the same time I had tried to spend more time with Tanya and our three children. I watched with fascination and pride as the boys' intellectual development and individuality seemed to grow and flower each month, but as the work encroached on either end of the waking day, the time we spent together was never enough. It was impossible not to feel a little guilty about all the interrupted stories and postponed games which were the consequence of being called out to see a patient, or to the police station.

I could still feel Carl and Stacey's disappointment as I drove to the surgery one damp drizzling Sunday morning in June. I had promised them a trip to the lake to feed the ducks, but a call had come from Stallbrook which I couldn't put off. They had put their hands deep in their pockets and said nothing, but it was a broken promise all the same, and their faces let me know it. This kind of overdraft was going to need a lot of paying off.

The rain snaked in greasy rivulets down the side windows of the car and the tyres hissed on the empty road. The only other vehicle in sight was an Express Dairy float jerking its way along on the other side. It stopped now and again and the driver jumped out, tossed bottles into a crate and trotted, with head bent against the rain, to the doorsteps of the few terraced houses which still stood on this particular stretch of road. His ports of call were fewer than they had once been, for in the last couple of years this end of the town had been reduced to a waste-land by the Ministry of Transport whose by-pass road had sliced through the belly of this small community like a surgeon's knife, spilling its guts out for all to see. The rows of small houses, with their neat donkey-stoned doorsteps and lace-curtained windows framing pottery alsatians or ferns in large vases, were nearly all gone. Instead, there was a rubble-strewn area which stretched back thirty yards from the road, exposing the backs of the terraces behind. They now showed their untidy shirt-tails as if caught with their pants down: row upon row of ramshackle back yards with leaking lean-to's and outside toilets, ginnels strewn with rusty bicycle-frames, old tyres, dustbins, and washing hanging limp on sagging lines strung across moss-damp gutters.

As I passed I saw an old woman in a large faded pinafore come out of a back door, carrying an aluminium tea-pot. She was going across a small flagged back yard to empty the dregs of the previous night down the toilet before taking the first ritual drink of the day.

I picked up a few things from the surgery that I knew I would need at Stallbrook and as I turned to climb into the car I noticed that the contractors had made a flying start clearing the land and outbuilding behind the surgery itself. They had only begun a few days before, but they had already torn down a few walls and nearly half of an adjacent disused warehouse. Two bulldozers and a mechanical shovel lay massive and silent amongst great heaps of brick and timber in the shell of the half-demolished building, like giant prehistoric predators

176

slumbering amongst the bones and empty carcasses of their prey.

When I arrived at Stallbrook police station Detective Inspector Early greeted me with a solemn handshake.

"Good morning doctor. I'm sorry to hear that you're ringing down the curtain on your short but spectacular career as Area Police Surgeon. Won't be quite the same in here. Still, it's a mug's game really, isn't it? I bet your good lady's glad you're packing up, eh?'

I took my coat off and nodded. "It does tend to be a bit disruptive to family life, yes," I said and yawned. "What's the problem you've got here at the moment?" The room was airless, thick with pipe-smoke and the clammy smell of rain-soaked overcoats. Early turned to a vacant-looking constable who stood nearby, and handed a foolscap sheet to him.

"Here you go, sunbeam. You wrote this lot down, so perhaps you'd be good enough to read it out in your own inimitable style. Reading it aloud the way you do gives it another dimension altogether."

The PC flushed then cleared his throat. As he read it I wanted to burst out laughing. His clear pedestrian pronunciation was better than music-hall.

"I was proceeding down Viaduct Street at seven forty-three pee hemm and I turned off onto some waste ground where there was a series of lock-up garages. As I went to the back of these garages it was there that I saw the accused, whom I now know to be one Cyril Leslie Tutton of no fixed abode, lying naked on the ground. When I approached him he waved at me and said: 'Good evening, officer'. Whereupon I asked: 'Would you mind telling me why you are lying down, naked?' and he replied 'So as I can get closer to the ground,' to which I replied, 'I hope you're not taking the – '"

"Right!" interrupted Early, passing his hand over his forehead. He screwed up his eyes and shook his head. "Right, son, that's enough for now. You've given us the picture nicely."

"Ok, sir... Er... Can I go upstairs now for bacon butties? I'm due about now."

Early closed his eyes and nodded. "Oh aye, son. Go and get your ... butties." The PC turned and went out, and Early looked up at me despairingly.

"Butties! Bloody hell, what sort of a word is that from a grown man? Come to think of it, what sort of a word is that from *anyone*? We're recruiting all sorts of shit these days, doctor, that's a fact, and I always seem to get saddled with it. Just like I seem to get saddled with a case like this."

"He doesn't appear to have committed much of a crime though, does he?" I murmured.

"Depends how you look at it. Indecent exposure, behaviour likely to cause a breach of the peace, that sort of thing. Could have given an old lady a nasty turn had she stumbled across him, if you see what I mean, doctor. He may be a dangerous lunatic for all I know."

"OK. I'll have a look at him," I said and went down to the cell with one of the station officers. The officer opened the cell door and ushered me in apprehensively.

"Just give us a shout, doc, if there's any trouble. I'll be right outside." He rolled his eyes and left me along with the prisoner.

The neon strip light on the ceiling of the cell shone its hard shadowless glare onto a pathetic looking character who sat on his bunk with his hands clasped loosely on his lap. He was clean-shaven, about fifty, and looked as though he was wearing someone else's discarded clothes except for a pair of open-toed sandals which looked almost new. His hair style gave the game away: it was done in the cruel basin-cut style beloved of mental institutions of years ago – fiercely shaved in a neat line from the nape of the neck to a point half an inch above the uppermost point of the ears, and above that was a matted thick hatch of hair resembling a coarse wig which had been casually thrown on. He looked across and smiled benignly as I spoke.

"Hello ... er, Cyril. It is Cyril, isn't it?"

"That's right."

"I'm the doctor."

"Oh yes. They said you would be coming." He continued

178

to smile but his eyes were cautious.

"What's brought you here?" I asked. "They tell me you were found lying with nothing on, on some waste ground somewhere."

The prisoner nodded and looked serious. He glanced round the empty cell as if checking for the presence of someone else, and I found myself looking round too.

"It's a long story and I've never – " he leaned forward very earnestly, lowering his voice to a near-whisper, " – I've never actually told anyone this before. You see, during the last war I used to work on Boeing bombers. I was a riveter."

"A riveter. On Boeing bombers." I nodded and sat down, stunned by this bizarre opening.

"That's right – you've got it. Only, not just an ordinary riveter. I was a *master* riveter. The best there was at the time. In fact, I would go so far as to say that I was the best riveter the world had ever seen in any war." His eyes began to widen and shine as he continued. "Well, there was one day when we were working on a new aircraft, and just as I was putting in the last rivet I suddenly felt my spirit – my soul if you like – come out of my body, shoot down my right arm, through the riveting gun into the rivet and then into the aircraft itself. So you see, my own spirit and the aircraft were as one." He leaned back and smiled sadly, then was silent.

"I see. Is that it, or . . . ?" I asked. I had already decided that the prisoner was probably schizophrenic, but I was keen to hear the rest of his story.

"No, that's not the end of it. You see, shortly afterwards that aircraft was shot down over Cologne, so you can see what that meant, can't you?"

I nodded blankly. "Well, no . . . I can't, really."

Cyril leaned forward again and made a wide sweeping movement with his arms.

"My soul was spread out to all corners of the skies, and so whenever an aircraft passes overhead it acts like a magnet on my physical body, trying to suck it up to join my soul-being in the sky. This means, of course, that I have to lie down close to the ground to help the gravity keep me from being sucked up.

Recently the spirit-force has been getting stronger, and to counteract this I have had to take my clothes off so that there is no resistance to the gravity force which keeps me on the ground. Which is very inconvenient at times, doctor, as you can appreciate," he said, nodding gravely.

"Yes I can quite see that. Tell me, Cyril, what do you think is going to happen now?" I asked. He sat back and winked, putting his finger on his lip.

"I've got some very important contacts, don't worry. Since I was pensioned out of the RAF I've had letters of praise for my work – riveting and that – from Ike and Lord Tedder and people like that. They won't let me down, if only because of who my mother was."

"How do you mean, Cyril?"

"My mother?"

"Mm, yes."

"Well ... I don't quite know how to tell you this, doctor. I mean it was quite a shock when I found out, you understand."

"Found out what?"

"The Virgin Mary. My mother was the Virgin Mary."

"How did you find that out?"

"About eight years ago, on News at Ten. That's how I found out, and it's very humiliating to find out things like that second-hand, so to speak." He didn't appear angry, merely tearful and utterly desolate.

"You realise, Cyril, if your mother was the Virgin Mary, who that makes you?" I said, standing up and feeling mentally drained. Cyril stood up too, shaking his head thoughtfully and very seriously.

"Yes, doctor, I do realise who that makes me, and let me tell you, it's a terrible responsibility."

I stared at him for a moment and could think of nothing to say. It was all very sad. Cyril Tutton might just as well have been on another planet surrounded by alien beings for all the help and sympathy he was going to get in this place, he was so out of touch with reality. Before leaving the cell I established that he had no GP in the area and that the only hospital he had ever attended was one in the South of England some years ago. This was bad news because it meant that short of leaving him where he was I would have to try and get a bed in the local psychiatric unit which would be no mean feat. I went back through into the office where Early sat reading an old copy of *Exchange and Mart*. He looked up.

"What d'you think, doc? Not so good, eh?"

"No. He's really disorganised."

"Crackers, you mean?"

"He's a bad schizophrenic. You weren't thinking of charging him were you? He doesn't know what day it is, you know."

Early sighed. "That's as may be..."

"Oh come on – he needs sorting out. What's to be gained by charging him? He'll have to have psychiatric reports, social reports, God knows what. You know that."

"Well..."

"I'll get him in somewhere. Give me that list of numbers." He passed me a list of hospital phone-numbers which were clipped on a board near the phone, then closed his eyes.

"I suppose you're right. It'd be a whole lot less trouble. More tidy. Less paperwork for me. Aye, go ahead doctor. I'll take your advice."

After a futile argument with one of the residents I finally managed to get Cyril admitted. I put the phone down with relief. Early stared at the floor.

"Did you manage it then, doctor?"

"Just about. He's going to Millersfield for a spell."

"Very good. Nice and neat. A few chats and then the magic pills and he'll be as right as rain, eh?"

"I doubt it," I replied. I phoned for the ambulance while Early lit his pipe.

'You don't sound so sure, doc. Not getting cynical in your old age, are you?"

I shook my head. "Oh they'll keep him in there for a bit, then discharge him to the care of the social services to keep an eye on – which they won't – then the whole thing will happen again somewhere else. The old story of CRF."

181

"What's that?" asked Early.

"Chronic Recurring Futility. Somebody somewhere will see him behaving a bit oddly, albeit harmlessly, see it as a threat to the neighbourhood and ring the appropriate authorities to take action. I mean, let's face it – have we really done any favours to him as a result of all this? Admittedly, sending him to Millersfield is marginally less useless than charging him and sending him to prison, but who have we really helped apart from ourselves in that we have got him out of our hair?"

"Oh aye, if you look at it like that ..." Early said thoughtfully. He stood up, yawned and stretched his arms full length above his head. "Still I'm very grateful to you, doc, for wrapping it all up like that – CRF or no bloody CRF."

"That's quite all right," I said. "Out of your sight, out of his mind, eh? Expediency is the name of the game." I laughed harshly, thinking that I sounded no better than all those administrators whom I had castigated in the past.

"Oh aye – I nearly forgot. Your missus phoned while you were examining Cyril in there, doctor," said Early apologetically, handing me a piece of paper. "You've a call to do on the way home, it seems."

I winced and looked at the name and address. Mrs. Percy, Stock Street. Number thirty-eight or fifty-eight, I couldn't tell which. Early laughed softly.

"My word, doctor, people up and down the country must envy a bloke like you – dashing about all over the place at eight o'clock on a Sunday morning, snatching people from the jaws of death and so forth. I mean, what else might you be doing instead? Lying in your bed sipping a cup of tea and reading the *Sunday Times*? Very decadent. Makes you go blind, that does. Anyway, cheerio doctor. I'm sure we'll be seeing you before you finally take your leave of us altogether." We shook hands with mock solemnity once more, then I left.

Stock Street was not very far from the surgery – in fact it was just off the main Manchester Road near to where I had passed earlier that morning. It had stopped raining but the

182

roofs of the houses glistened against the slate-grey sky. Sporadic clearance of the area around Stock Street had left groups of terraced houses sticking up like bad teeth in an old jaw, while on one side of the street a newly-built, clean, rectangular building which was a working men's club, stood incongruously amongst this mess like a gold filling in a mouthful of decay. On the other side of the street the demolition had stopped, for no apparent reason, half way along a row of houses, so that the last remaining side wall to be left untouched was covered with peeling wallpaper stained with the rain and the soot from the fireplaces which gaped black and empty like a corpse's mouth. Broken roof-slates, bricks and rubble spilled over from the waste ground onto the pavement and into the narrow roadway. As I stopped the car I disturbed two small dogs who were bickering over a bag of chips left in the gutter from the night before. They stuck their heads in the air and barked peevishly before running off up the street.

The door of number thirty-eight had been painted bright blue and the old woodwork underneath gave the one-coat gloss a wrinkled, pitted surface. As I stepped up close to it I noticed that it was slightly open and I pushed it gently, at the same time pulling out a scrap of paper from my coat pocket. Glancing at the number on the paper I still couldn't make up my mind whether it was thirty-eight or fifty-eight.

I stepped into the short narrow hall and immediately found myself at the foot of the steep stairs which led to the first floor. My eyes followed the scuffed bannister rail which was loosely screwed into the wall. The faded patterned wall paper at the level of the rail was marked with a grey, greasy film about two feet wide, dense in the centre and becoming fainter at the edges where hands and clothes had brushed the paper countless times as their owners had gone up and down the stairs. At the top of the stairs on a small landing, not more than three feet square, I heard a small grunting noise and in the dim light from a partly boarded window on the landing I saw a three year-old boy in his pyjamas squatting and peering intently down at me. He was chewing on a large thick slice of bread smeared heavily with jam. As he chewed on the centre of the slice the two sides curled round until they almost touched his ears. He put the bread down slowly on the top of the landing by his feet, and with a piece of bread and jam still sticking out of his half-opened mouth he stood up very slowly and quietly, never taking his eyes off me. I took one step forward and the child suddenly burst into tears, shuffling off into one of the bedrooms.

"Anybody home?" I called. "It's the doctor." This didn't seem right. I was fairly sure that this was not the house, though it was possible that Mrs. Percy's relatives might have arrived. Then I heard a woman's muffled voice call from one of the rooms upstairs: "Hello, doctor! Come on in, we're all at home!"

I climbed the stairs and went into one of the bedrooms, realising at once that it was, of course, the wrong address. In the large double bed sat Mrs. Veronica Taylor, drinking a mug of tea and smiling brightly as if this was a completely normal event for her on a Sunday morning. Underneath her hair-net her blonde hair had been furiously back-combed and lacquered the previous night and was like a heap of highly inflammable Shredded Wheat on top of her head.

"Well, doctor, this is a surprise. Fancy seeing you again!"

I nodded and took a deep breath. If Mrs. Taylor and her family had been given Green Shield stamps for each surgery attendance they would have been able to furnish the house from top to bottom on the proceeds. I was annoyed with myself for not guessing it was the wrong house right away – God knows I was familiar enough with the family as it was.

"How did you get in? Had I left the door open when I brought the milk in?"

"Yes, I suppose you must have," I replied. She dug her elbows into a large mound next to her and it stirred slowly. A great hairy arm came over the top of the bedclothes and pushed them out of the way to reveal the bloated face of Eric Taylor. He screwed his eyes up against the light, and squinted at his watch.

"Look, Eric, it's the doctor. Popped in to see us," said Mrs.

Taylor, looking quite pleased. He looked over at me very briefly.

"How do," he said thickly, pulling the sheets over his head and turning over. Mrs. Taylor dug him in the back again with her elbows. His muffled voice rose indignantly from beneath the bedclothes.

"Wassemarra? Somebody ill or summat?"

"No – well, I don't think so," said Mrs. Taylor, looking at me questioningly.

"Thank Christ for that," her husband mumbled. "Some of us have been working, you know. And it is a bloody Sunday, when all's said and done."

"Ooh, Eric! What a thing to say to the doctor!" Mrs. Taylor said, punching him in the back. She turned to me with an apologetic smile. "He's always like that when he's on late shifts. I think it must be the fumes."

I couldn't help smiling at this, although for one brief moment I felt like throwing my bag at him. The fumes, my eye. Eric Taylor worked in a brewery and drank as though prohibition was going to be declared within the hour. I glanced under the bed and saw a couple of half-empty crates of beer.

"Bringing his work home as well, I see," I said. Mrs. Taylor rolled her eyes and shrugged. "Anyway, as you may have guessed by now, I have been given the wrong address – "

"I was wondering about that," she said, nodding thoughtfully. She leaned forward and picked up her little boy and put him on the side of the bed. He spat out of his mouth a large well-chewed bolus of bread and jam. It landed on my shoe and stuck to it like a giant mauve amoeba. Pretending not to notice, I flicked it off and it thudded against a beer crate.

"Yes – actually, I'm looking for Mrs. Percy. Is she . . . ?"

"Oh you want number *fifty*-eight" said Mrs. Taylor. "Oh yes, Mrs. Percy. There's been some trouble about the gas. Funny woman . . ."

"OK. I'll get along, then," I muttered. "Sorry to have disturbed your . . ."

"Oh that's quite all right, doctor. You could have had a cup of tea, really. Shall I make you one? There's some in – "

"No thanks. I'd better be off." I had caught sight of Mrs. Taylor's young son relentlessly preparing another glutinous projectile inside his mouth, so I left without delay.

The door of number fifty-eight did not look as if it had been painted since the house was originally built, and the brown varnish had perished into a fine mosaic like the surface of an old oil painting. I knocked and the door was opened almost immediately by a middle-aged grey-haired man with rimless spectacles. The skin of his pinched face was thin and translucent and clung to the facial bones like a pre-packed frozen chicken. He wore an immaculate grey overcoat and black leather gloves.

"Doctor?"

"Yes."

"Oh good. Come in. It was me who called you. It's auntie, actually, of course." His tone was quiet, friendly, educated. He sounded like a solicitor or a headmaster.

"A word before we go in," he said in a near-whisper, as we both stood in the cold, dark hallway. His breath smelled strongly of mints. "Have the social services been in touch with you at all?" He glanced to see if the door to the living room was closed.

"No. Should they have?" I asked, automatically dropping my voice as well, although I had no idea why we were whispering like this.

"Well... she's been behaving strangely of late – I'm her nephew by the way – I mean, she's always been a bit of a recluse and never has had much to do with doctors and so forth."

I nodded. I couldn't remember the last time I had seen her.

"Anyway," continued the nephew, "I think she's ... she's going a bit, er – I hesitate to say this of course – but I think she's going a bit senile." He pointed his finger at his own temple and waved it round in circles as if he thought I couldn't comprehend the spoken word.

"How old is Mrs. Percy?" I asked.

186

"Eighty-seven."

"Eighty-seven? And you say she's getting a bit senile?"

"Yes. I'm afraid so, doctor."

"She's, er, in the right age group for it, isn't she?"

"Correct, doctor. That's so very true." He nodded and frowned and stared at his shoes. "The thing is . . . she's taken to wandering about a bit, knocking on neighbours' doors – that sort of thing. And of course there's the gas." He stared hard at me with pale, unblinking eyes.

"The gas?"

"Yes, the gas. She's convinced there's a gas leak. She's had the Gas Board here several times but they can't find anything. It was them who actually contacted the social services. I gather they were getting a bit fed up with being repeatedly called out."

I nodded and pointed to the living room door. The nephew nodded.

"Yes, she's in there. I must warn you, doctor, it's a bit of a tip. She tends to hoard things. I suppose that goes along with her condition, does it?"

I didn't answer but opened the door and went through. The sight was incredible. In the small dark room I could just about make out a piano in one corner, a couple of battered easy chairs and an old commode. They were not instantly recognisable because piled high on every available surface – on the floor, the chairs, the piano top, the piano keys, in the hearth, in fact everywhere – were stacks of old newspapers and magazines wrapped in brown paper and tied with string into flat parcels, each about four inches thick. Some of these piles were chest high, and where the lower levels had collapsed new stacks had been precariously laid on top of the uneven base. In the midst of all this sat Mrs. Percy. Her beady eyes darted from one to the other of us as we entered, and as she opened her concave mouth to smile apprehensively the creases spread radially from the surrounding skin. She wore a thick woollen skirt and had several loose garments over her body which defied description. Slung loosely over her shoulder was a coarse green blanket.

"It's the doctor come to see you, auntie," said the nephew loudly. She nodded and shoved her hands up the sleeves of her jumper.

"I see," she said, as if she had just had an obscure mathematical problem explained to her. She screwed up her eyes and pursed her lips. "But it's not a doctor I need. What I need – "

"Auntie, just let the doctor – " began the nephew, holding out his arms in my direction like a master of ceremonies introducing a stage act.

"What I need," continued the old lady doggedly, emphasising her words with nodding movements of her head, "is someone to inspect the gas, I keep saying there's a leak – can't either of you smell it?"

I sniffed and could smell only old newsprint, stale food and above all, stale urine. I glanced at the nephew who shrugged, pulled down the corners of his mouth and wrinkled his nose which sent his glasses bobbing up and down in front of his eyes. I turned to the old lady, and, leaning against the piano, went through a fairly standardised set of questions to establish what her general health was like and to get some idea of her mental state. She answered in a dull monotone, but I could tell that apart from being forgetful she seemed to be in reasonable health – at least she had remarkably few symptoms for someone of her age. She was certainly not deranged.

"Look, Mrs. Percy" I said, leaning towards her and getting a powerful whiff of sweat and urine, "I think it would be a good idea if I was to give you a quick examination just to see that ... everything's OK. Won't take a minute."

She shook her head indifferently. Her earlier apprehension seemed to have gone and had been replaced by sullen resignation. As I struggled to help her peel off the first of many layers of cardigans that she was wearing I looked over at the nephew who had turned away. He was staring at the tiny one-bar electric fire which stood in the empty fire-place.

"Can you give me a hand?" I asked. The nephew looked round and pushed his gloved hands deep into his overcoat

188

pockets, then looked away in embarrassment and distaste.

"Er, well, I just want to get something from the car ... I've left it in the ... I think I've left the ignition keys in. I won't be a minute." He edged rapidly towards the door and went out into the hallway. I heard him go out of the front door, and knew that he would make himself scarce until the examination had been completed. I didn't blame him, for the old lady was a sorry picture of self-neglect. I pulled off the innermost garment, which was a filthy grey woollen vest, and a shower of skin scales scattered in all directions from her dry, unwashed body. I examined her as best I could and found nothing very remarkable apart from the fact that she was emaciated and anaemic, probably due to lack of proper nutrition, and that she also had stress incontinence which accounted for the strong smell of urine. When I had finished, Mrs. Percy insisted on dressing herself and I picked my way through the piles of papers and other debris into the back kitchen to wash my hands. The kitchen was very small, with a cracked white porcelain sink underneath the window on one side. A single cold water tap snaked its way up from somewhere below to where it hooked over the top of the sink and pointed down into the bowl. It was wrapped along its length with dirty rags and looked like the long scraggy neck and head of a bird of prey looking down at its victim. On the other side of the room was an old gas cooker with four rings, three of which were layered with grease and dirt, and on the fourth was an old kettle. At the side was a small collapsible table on which were a couple of cups containing cold tea, a half-opened packet of sliced bread with the top slices curling up at the corners, and a piece of cheese so old and dry that it looked as if it would crumble like an old brick if it was touched.

I washed my hands in a trickle of cold water from the tap and used a large piece of gritty green soap which was on the draining board amongst some bacon-rind and a few old clothes. I found a damp grey towel hanging on the inside of the back door, and as I dried my hands the nephew came in from the living room, closing the adjoining door quietly behind him. Because of the size of the room we had to stand quite close together, and at close range I noticed that his left eye twitched nervously.

"How these old folk are allowed to get into a state like this is beyond me," he muttered. "I thought you people were supposed to visit elderly people on your list every month to prevent this sort of thing?"

Here it comes, I thought. The hoary old chestnut borne out of guilt, fear of the unfamiliar.

"That's an interesting problem," I replied. "We have got nine thousand patients to look after – over one thousand of whom are in this age group. If you would like to devise a way in which I could do one thousand visits a month without cancelling my surgeries and all the visits for acute illnesses I would be glad to hear about it." I looked straight at the nephew who flushed slightly.

"There must be some way of doing it – keeping an eye on them, I mean," he said, almost to himself.

"Well," I said slowly, "as things stand at the moment there are one or two possibilities..."

"Can you not get auntie in hospital today?" he interrupted impatiently.

"That was not one of the possibilities I had in mind," I replied.

"Oh? That surprises me, doctor," he said, a little taken aback.

"Well, look – she isn't a medical emergency by any stretch of the imagination. The hospital quite simply isn't for this sort of case. She needs a good bath and a few good meals inside her, and someone to look after her for a short while. Do you live far away?"

Mrs. Percy's nephew looked at me in amazement. "I hope you're not asking..."

"I'm only asking – "

"We live in Egerton."

"Egerton. About seven miles away. When did you last see your aunt?"

The nephew turned his eyes away quickly and stared at a

couple of flies which were copulating on the bacon rind. "It must be over a year ago," he said. "But really, we couldn't possibly take her, you know. We have a fairly big house with no children, but in my business we have to entertain a lot and ... well really ..." his voice trailed off as he looked round at the kitchen.

"She's no other relatives?"

"No ... we are the only ones who come. Surely you can get her away today? Something ought to be done!"

I stared at him coldly: he made it sound like a job for a pest control agency.

"There's no one in social services until tomorrow morning. I'll contact them in the morning and see if we can get her in an emergency bed in an old people's home locally."

"Tomorrow! But I can't stay here all day. I've got to get back later. I've got an early train to catch to London tomorrow." He began to look agitated and wrinkled his nose a lot. He took off his glasses and began to wipe the lenses nervously.

"Don't worry," I said, side-stepping toward the sitting room door. "She's gone for a long time with nobody to look after her. I'm sure that one more day won't make a great deal of difference. We'll have it all sorted out tomorrow."

The nephew turned and followed me to the door. "I sincerely hope you are right, doctor," he said with tight-lipped resignation. As we went through the door I sniffed the air.

"That's funny. I thought I could smell gas as I came through there." I looked at the nephew who stopped and sniffed too.

"Well I can't smell it," he said impatiently. He looked at his watch. "I shall be leaving here after lunch, I'm afraid. I simply can't stay any longer. Anyway I'm glad you've seen auntie, because it at least shifts the responsibility away from me..."

"Yes, of course." I smiled, trying to hide the sarcasm from my voice. "What time you leave here is entirely up to you ... I'll leave a mild sedative for her just in case she gets agitated."

I went through and explained to Mrs. Percy that I wanted

to get her away for a few days' convalescence and to correct her anaemia and so on. She nodded indifferently.

"That'll be all right with me, if that's what's best," she said. "Then they can fix the gas, eh?"

I nodded. "We'll get someone round tomorrow and get it seen to, don't worry." I walked to the front door and the nephew followed, clearing his throat noisily as I stepped onto the pavement.

"Well I must say I'm a bit disappointed you couldn't find your way to getting her in hospital, doctor," he said bitterly. "I would have thought at least you could get someone to stay with her tonight. After all, this is what the community services are for, isn't it? I sometimes wonder where all the taxes and national insurance contributions go to that we pay. I mean, I realise that my wife and I are next of kin, but we do have our own..." His voice trailed off as he saw my face. I felt like throwing up.

"Something wrong, doctor?"

"No. I just felt a wave of nausea coming over me. I think it must be the fumes."

"The fumes?"

"Yes. You could say that." I walked off down the road to the car and drove home.

I parked the car in the drive and was greeted by Carl, our eldest boy. He was leaning on his bike.

"Want to give me a hand cleaning the car?" I said. He shook his head and frowned.

"You can't? Why not?"

"We're playing at doctors. I've just been called out."

He grinned, jumped on his bike and rode off.

# 21

It was about ten-thirty the next morning, in the middle of a heavy surgery, that I managed to get through to the social services. The social worker was unimpressed with my suggestion that Mrs. Percy needed tender loving care, not hospitalisation. She couldn't agree: Mrs. Percy was demented and couldn't be cared for in an old people's home, she said — would we arrange for the geriatrician to admit her to hospital? It was pointless pursuing the conversation, so I rang off and spoke to the geriatricians at Wishton. They were sympathetic but they had no beds — had I tried the medical side? I thought they were joking and rang off. I saw a few more patients, then phoned David Neale, the psychiatrist. I put him in the picture and he readily agreed to go and see her but held no real hope of getting her a bed. They were even more short of beds than the medical department.

I had barely finished the surgery, around mid-day, when David rang back. It seemed only a moment ago that I had asked him to visit and I thought at first that he was ringing to say that he could not go, or that he had been delayed on account of another bizarre crisis involving one of his patients.

"My God — that was quick," I said. "Something wrong?"

"No, no," he began breathlessly, starting to giggle at the same time. "Actually I had an acute emergency quite nearby so I thought I might as well call. You really have got some oddballs in Overton haven't you?"

"A few. What did you make of Mrs. Percy?"

"Ah, yes. You were quite right about her — she's perfectly *compos mentis*. I mean — she's getting on and of course the old cerebral arteries are a bit choked up, but she's not too bad. The living conditions are really incredible though, aren't they? How bloody sad. She's got close relatives and all that but the place is a complete shambles. It looks like a newsagent's warehouse."

"Yes. I'm sorry that I had to involve you in this..."

"Oh don't worry about that." He started to giggle again. "You've got a strong case now for getting her admitted to social services accommodation anyway. No question of that."

"What makes you so certain? They seemed very —"

"Oh, balls to that. This old lady's quite correct about that gas leak, for one thing."

"How do you know?"

"Because when I got there the Gas Board were digging up half the flaming street and they've traced it to Mrs. Percy's house. They've already started to tear up the floor to trace some pipe or other — the whole area looks as if it's taking part in a civil defence exercise. Some neighbour raised the alarm in the early hours of this morning, apparently."

I laughed quietly to myself. As often happened, some outside event had precipitated a solution. The relevant authority (in this case the social services) would now jolt itself out of its inertia and somehow, from somewhere, shelter would be found for this pathetic old lady. She would be saved from the inevitable consequences of isolation and self-neglect.

"So much for the social worker's assessment," I said grimly.

"Oh you don't have to tell me," David said with an uncharacteristic groan. "The more case conferences I attend to hear duffle-coated girls with social science degrees talking about compassion, the more I yearn for the old days. At least the old mental welfare officer knew what he was talking about and offered real help, even if most of our wards *did* stink to high heaven of piss and paraldehyde. What we get now is a load of fine theory scrubbed clean of any practical application whatsoever. I mean, you only have to look at the recent growth of self-help organisations to realise that we've screwed it up somewhere."

"Well thanks for seeing this old lady, anyway," I said. "I'd better get cracking and get something sorted out for her." I glanced at my watch. Molly had just come into the room with the visit book, and it was late. David rang off. I put the phone down and stared at it for a few seconds.

"Things seem to be going from bad to worse around here," I said, turning to Molly. She sat down, crossed her legs, took a small handkerchief from her bag and blew her nose loudly.

"You can say that again," she spluttered nasally from behind the handkerchief. "One of these calls this morning is some fellow you sent down to the outpatients at the Royal about six weeks ago with what you thought was gout."

"Oh yes? I seem to remember . . . What's his name?"

"Hayter, twenty-nine Fields Road."

"That's right. Big red swelling, right hand. No trauma, vague history of gout. As far as I recall I've never seen him since. I haven't received any correspondence about him either. That's funny."

"His wife rang to say that they kept him in for five weeks and he very nearly died," said Molly. "He's out now, full of bedsores, and she's no idea what's been wrong with him. There's no discharge letter, of course."

"Of course," I said in disgust. "I mean – why should there be? Everyone knows we've got ESP. That means I'll have to ring round the wards and everywhere else to find someone who remembers what he was in for – if they remember him at all. I could have done without that this morning." I told her about Mrs. Percy. She nodded sympathetically and looked at her watch.

"If you're going to ring social services you'd better do it now before they knock off for lunch," she said.

"Or disappear without trace in one of those interminable case conferences," I replied, reaching for the phone. I got through and let the duty officer know about Mrs. Percy. It wasn't the one I had spoken to earlier and she didn't know much about it. She would pass the message on. She seemed a bit put out when I insisted that the problem be resolved that afternoon. They would ring me back and let me know. Good. Right. Cheerio.

"You haven't forgotten that we're going round to the

temporary surgery this afternoon to arrange the electrical installation, phones and what have you?" said Molly when I had put the phone down. I groaned.

"No. Shouldn't take long though, should it? I hope not, anyway. These visits will take nearly all day." I glanced down the longish list, noticing all the familiar names. It was amazing that, when there was an epidemic of 'flu or food poisoning, the same families seemed to get it every time. Or perhaps they were the only families who bothered to call when they did get something like that.

We sorted out the visits, dividing them into two approximately equal groups. I had the bigger of the two because Molly had a few things to arrange for the temporary surgery that afternoon. She had done a lot of chasing about arranging the removal, the fitting of carpets and all manner of mind-bending trivia which would help to make the move go more smoothly and our stay at our new quarters less unpleasant. I had passed the site of the new health centre the other day, and there had been no activity at all. Just a few wooden huts, a few holes and a few piles of rubble, but little else. It looked as if we would be in the temporary place about two years.

"Isn't it this Saturday we are actually moving?" I asked vaguely, knowing that asking in this way would irritate Molly no end. She had been organising the transition with an almost military precision down to the last detail, and the mercurial energy with which she pursued and dealt with each problem, no matter how mundane, arising from this whole dismal episode, made me go limp with admiration. The mere thought of spending the next two years in a cold, cramped, neon-lit converted shoe-shop induced a curious sense of detachment in me whenever I was forced to think about it – which, I suppose, was some form of mechanism for preventing me from blowing my lid at what should have been avoidable in the first place. Apathy began to creep out of every pore.

"What d'you mean – is it this Saturday when we actually move?" cried Molly in an outraged voice. She rose to the bait superbly as I knew she would. She saw me smiling and burst out laughing.

"You know damn well it is! You are doing the surgery, don't forget. I've got to be round at the other place to sort things out as they move the stuff in. Have you put the notice up about – ?"

"Oh yes. I'm surprised you didn't see it on the outside door. It's a damn great poster in fluorescent colours which asks patients not to come on Saturday morning unless it's a dire emergency, on account of the fact that we won't be here. Words to that effect, anyway." I yawned. "They won't take a blind bit of notice, as per usual, though, I can guarantee that. The people of Overton are great creatures of habit, you know. Once they've got a seat in the surgery it'll take an earthquake to shift them."

"Well, the removal men are arriving dead on ten am," said Molly, standing up. "They've got another job to go to, so I hope the surgery is clear by then. Right, then – see you later at Mary Street, about two o'clock."

"Mary Street? Where's that?" I asked, trying not to smile.

"Mary Street. Where the new surgery – oh bugger off!" Molly swept out, laughing loudly as she went down the short corridor to the front door.

I made a futile attempt to get some details on Mr Hayter's stay in the Royal before I went to visit him, and I was on the phone for nearly a quarter of an hour. The ward sister and the departmental secretaries were at lunch, the consultant was at a staff-patient liaison committee meeting (the breath-taking irony of this did not go unnoticed) and only one resident vaguely recalled the name. The other residents I spoke to had never heard of the patient and one even asked if we had got the right hospital. At this point I gave up. Poor Mr. Hayter: hospitalised for five weeks and nearly died at one point according to his wife. He probably had all kinds of diabolical tests done, was the subject of much discussion, collected a fat wad of case-notes containing path lab reports, X-rays and the like, and yet two days after his discharge no one could remember him.

When I got to the house Mr. Hayter was sitting in an

197

armchair with his right leg up on a stool. His foot and ankle were swathed in a neatly wrapped crêpe bandage at the end of which poked the pink, waxy skin of his toes. He looked up as I came in behind his wife and a huge smile broke out on his tiny old face.

"How do, doctor, how are you?"

"Not bad – how's yourself?"

He laughed and shrugged his shoulders. "Not too bad, not too bad. Well, I mean, I'm all right of meself, like, but they've put me on these 'ere pills and I'm not sure as they suit me."

"How's that?"

"Well, when I tek 'em they make me go mazy."

"Mazy..." I repeated, half to myself, listening to the sound of the word. Although it could not be found in any medical dictionary, it had a precise meaning when used by local people, for it was an endemic condition in Overton.

"Aye. Mazy, you know, it's like – "

"I know," I said. "You feel you're going over, the ground rushes up to meet you, your legs seem to go from under you. Like that."

Mr. Hayter sat up and shook his head in amazement. "That's exactly how it is. You've hit the nail right on the head, there. How did you know that?"

I smiled at the sight of the patient's wide eyes and good-natured face. "Because it's my job. I'm paid to know these things."

Mr. Hayter sat back, winked one eye and stuck up a thumb. "That's right, doctor. Every man to his trade, is what I always say, every man to his trade." He turned to his wife. "Where's them pills, Edith? Show the doctor." She leaned over his bandaged foot and took a small brown bottle which had been placed on the mantelpiece behind a little blue jug with white embossed letters on it, which said, "A present From Scarborough". She passed the bottle over and I read the label. Allopurinol. So it *was* gout after all.

"Gout," I said.

"Pardon, doctor?" said Mrs. Hayter.

"These tablets. They're for gout."

198

"Oh, gout." She knitted her brow and let out a sigh of exasperation. "That's what you said it was before he went in. But haven't they written to you about him? I mean, he was in there for five weeks, all those tests..."

"Not a word I'm afraid, Mrs. Hayter," I said.

"Well I don't know, it's a right rum how d'you do, this is," she said. She didn't appear to be angry, just disappointed, somehow. "D'you know doctor – we went three times to out-patients after the time you originally sent him down, and we saw a different doctor each time. They kept X-raying and taking blood tests, and each time we went back to see about the results the doctor didn't seem to know why we were there. And they couldn't find the results of his tests, either. The last time we went down they couldn't even find his notes."

I got a sinking feeling. It was not exactly a *déjà-vu*: more like the feeling you get with the sudden recurrence of an unpleasant illness of which you thought you had been cured. I sat down.

"So what happened then?" I asked dully.

"Well, they decided to admit him to the ward..."

"I had all the students and everybody round me the first day," broke in Mr. Hayter. "Never had so much attention. Then I never saw a doctor come near me for a fortnight."

"Well that's not quite true," said Mrs. Hayter. "There was a doctor come every day to take blood samples – "

"Regular as clockwork, dead on nine o'clock in the morning. Never used to say owt, mind you. Neither did yon feller that took samples of t'other."

"Samples of ... what?" I sank lower into the chair.

"Me motions," said Mr. Hayter cheerfully. "Every day. Wouldn't let me go to the toilet. Had to use them ... under me..." He made little thrusting movements with his outstretched hands as if he was tucking a bedspread under a mattress.

"Then there was the urine collections," said Mrs. Hayter. "Every single day, so far as I could tell, and we've still no idea what it was all for. Nobody told us a thing."

"Oh come now," I said with disbelief. "I can hardly

credit – "

"It's true as I stand here," Mrs. Hayter replied. Mr. Hayter nodded vigorously in agreement. "I went to visit him one day and there were screens all round his bed. I found out from one of the other patients that he'd had a sort of stroke and was unconscious, so I had to wait in the corridor for quite a while and I could hear the sister discussing his case with the doctor. I popped my head round the door to ask what was wrong with him and they said it was none of my business." She looked up and shook her head sadly. "Well, I would have thought it was, really. After all, he *is* my husband..."

I nodded quickly and turned away from her questioning look. I slowly unwrapped the bandage from Mr. Hayter's foot, thinking that there was not much I could say to put matters right. When I got the last few inches of the bandage off, a piece of lint fell off his heel to reveal a large, crusty bedsore. I examined the rest of him and found that he had bedsores on the other heel, both elbows and his buttocks. He had no residual signs at all of a stroke, but he had obviously been kept in bed for a long time. What a shambles. He went with a swollen hand because of gout, and came out five weeks later with a crop of bedsores with no one being any the wiser at the end of it. These people deserved better than this.

"I'll get the district nurse to see to these sores," I said, "then I'll ring again and try and find out what all this was about. I'm sure that there is some simple straightforward explanation."

Mrs. Hayter sniffed. "All the more reason, in that case, why they could have said something to me. All they said at the end that he was ready for going home. And fancy not letting you know either..."

"Oh that sometimes happens. Not to worry," I said.

"Well you might not worry, but I do. I mean ... Mr. Hayter and me, well, I know we're nothing special or anything like that, and I know they've lots of worse cases to deal with, but we've always had a lot of faith in hospitals and doctors and we've always worked hard all us lives ... we've never claimed half the things we're entitled to ... well ... I just think that it were a bit shabby some road, the way we weren't told anything. I mean, we're not stupid."

"Oh give over, love," said Mr. Hayter. "Doctor's not got time to listen to all that. Main thing is, I'm all right now."

"Aye, but it's as if they don't treat you like human beings any more. Seem to resent you asking questions as if you've no right, some road. Oh, I know I should be grateful that he's better and all that, but I can't help feeling a bit angry because I feel in a way we've been mucked about. Can you understand how I mean, doctor?"

I nodded. "Yes, I think so," I said. I could think of very little to say. I was angry and frustrated over the absence of communication from the hospital and resentful in a way that I should have to listen to all this. And yet I sympathised with Mrs. Hayter: it seemed to me that she was right. Whatever good had been done was almost completey wiped out by the way they had been left in the dark.


When I got to Mary Street later that day the front door of the building was open and I went inside. A couple of handymen were putting the finishing touches to the small reception-counter and another was slapping emulsion paint over the walls of the short entrance corridor as fast as his huge dripping brush would allow. I edged past and went through to what was to be the waiting room where Molly and Ian were standing thoughtfully gazing round. Ian looked up and nodded a greeting.

"What do you think?" he asked. I stood in the middle of the waiting room and looked round. It was barely fifteen feet square, a tiny dungeon-like room with no windows and illuminated entirely by neon strip. It looked depressing and claustrophobic, but most important of all was that I had forgotten how tiny it was.

"It's really small," I said and laughed at the moronic obviousness of what I had just said.

"Mmmm..." Ian replied non-committally.

"Can you imagine what it's going to be like on Monday mornings?"

Ian smiled slowly. "Yes. I can see that some of our

menopausal ladies will faint from lack of air."

"Well, if they do," I said, "there's no danger of them hurting themselves. There just won't be enough room for them to fall down."

Molly burst out laughing, but Ian began to look serious again. "You're right. It is too small. Far too small. Still – it does look fairly bright and new and clean, what with all the new paintwork and everything. I think it'll be OK for a while, don't you?"

I didn't answer but wandered through into the two consulting rooms. They were also very, very small. In fact one of them was hardly big enough to put a desk and couch in. Seeing a hundred patients a day in this place was going to be no joke over the next two years, in spite of its clean plaster walls and neat paintwork. I felt intensely disappointed and angry with myself for being carried away by the architect's drawings which we had looked at a few months ago. They had made the place look a lot better than it actually was: those neat, clean plans which told us nothing about the scale of the place and the problems that would arise. We should have known better. Well, it was too late now.

We hung around for a short while discussing where various bits of equipment should go, before Ian had to leave to do a few home visits.

When I got back to the surgery there was a message on my desk to ring social services. I did so and spoke to a Miss Kerfoot. She was a tired, grey, middle-aged woman whose dead-pan voice seemed to indicate that she had seen it all. There was nothing that would shock, thrill, inspire or move her in any way.

"Just to let you know that we've sorted Mrs. Percy out," she said in her curiously detached voice. She sounded as if her mind was on something else. Maybe she was filling in a footballs pools coupon or checking through a shopping list.

"Really?" I said, surprised at the speed at which they had acted. "How did you manage that?"

"We've put her into Smallwood House. The emergency bed there … it's … for this sort of thing. Did you know about the money, doctor?"

"Money? What money?"

"In the carrier bags."

"In the *what*?"

"The carrier bags. They were in the pantry, doctor. Several thousand pounds, by the look of it."

"That's fantastic. I wonder how ..."

"Well of course she did run a business earlier on in her life. A newsagent's shop, actually. I suppose she must have saved a fair bit over the years."

"Carrier bags, though. Bloody hell."

"It takes all sorts doesn't it, doctor?" she said in a weary voice, "I wonder what Doctor Neale would have made of that?"

I couldn't miss the sarcasm in her voice. There wasn't much of it but it was easily detectable, like sour milk in a cup of weak tea.

"He'd have put it down to a touch of eccentricity, I should think," I said. "Did you let the nephew in Egerton know about it?"

She sighed. "Oh yes, he knows. He's coming up to see her tonight when he gets back from London, according to his wife. She said that they would drop in every day to see how she was getting on. I should think they'll be coming a lot more to see her now that they know about the money."

I laughed. "Yes, I can imagine. They'll be there like flies round a midden."

"I expect they will, doctor. Will you be going to see her? She'll be all cleaned up – I don't suppose you will recognise her."

"No I don't suppose I will."

I called into Smallwood House on the way home after evening surgery and found her sitting on an easy chair in the bright clean lounge amongst the other residents. The transformation was startling. Her hair, which before was lank and matted, was now very white and clean, and each well-rinsed strand gleamed like glass-fibre in the light of the sun which streamed in through the large windows. The skin of her face was pink and shiny and glowed from the unaccustomed abrasive action of soap and water. She wore neat, clean borrowed clothes, and yet as she sat there brooding amongst that silent group, I could see that her eyes were looking not outwards, but inwards down the years, beating a resentful retreat from the defeat of her independence. Beneath her scrubbed and respectable exterior, which smelled of Pears soap and Vosene, a subtle change was already taking place which was impossible to define exactly. The slightly bowed head, the slump of the shoulders, the empty fidgeting hands, all seemed to herald an irreversible mental and physical disintegration which I had seen so often before. It would not matter how much care and attention was lavished now.

"He's done well for himself, you know," she said softly. I had no idea what she meant.

"Who's done well for himself, Mrs. Percy?"

"Our Maurice. My nephew. He's got a very good job, you know. I'm very pleased about that, anyway. Being as I brought him up like, more or less, on account of his mother dying early on." Her voice sounded far away as if she was talking to herself, which I suppose she was. "Funny how things turn out ... still, he'll be relieved to know that you managed to get me away somewhere. That'll be a load off his mind."

"You'll be well looked after here, you know," I said. My words, though they were meant to be cheerful and encouraging, sounded instead like a noisy intrusion. She nodded slowly and smiled.

"Aye. It's funny really, when you think about it. It's true what they say. Help often comes from where you least expect it, but it's best appreciated when it comes from them as matters. Any road, I expect he'll come and see me now and again ..." Her eyes misted over as she looked past me to gaze across the room and out of the window, but she did not see the red tiled roofs of the overspill estate reflecting the bright evening sun. Her mind was in another place, in another time.

# 22

On the Saturday morning I was awakened by a finger of sunlight which poked through a chink in the curtains of the bedroom window, pointing into my eyes and making me turn my head to one side as I got out of bed. It was very early and I shaved slowly and deliberately, listening to the subdued, wakening murmurs of the two eldest boys as they lay talking to each other. Their voices had a hoarse, nasal quality because of the dry warm air of that June. Carl and Stacey stirred when they heard the tap-water running and, while the baby still slept, they came into the bathroom, staggering and yawning, screwing their eyes up in the bright morning light. Even though the summer had hardly begun, they were deeply tanned and their brown hair was beginning to bleach slightly as it did every summer. Their conversation became more animated and they dressed quickly, for like creatures of nature they were wakened by the sun and were impatient to get outside.

I made some tea and took two cups back to the bedroom. Tanya had not stirred and she lay on her stomach with her head to one side, each breath gently stirring a wisp of hair which trailed close to her lips before coiling lazily on the pillow. I drew back the sheets a few inches to reveal her beautifully tanned shoulders and back, and slightly scratched the skin between her shoulder blades. She woke like a child, without stretching or grimacing.

"Mmm, mmm. Thanks, Steve," she murmured sleepily.

"For what? The tea or the scratch?" I sat on the bed and she turned over and looked at me a long time before speaking.

"Big day today. Last day at the old mausoleum."

I grunted. "Hm. Well, it'll be a bit messy, I suppose. But we'll get over it."

205

Tanya sat up. "You've really let it get to you these last few months, haven't you?"

"Oh, I don't know. I thought I'd switched off from it, myself. It has dampened my vocational fervour though, as they say in academic circles." I kicked off my shoes and slid onto the bed, leaned on one elbow and looked at her.

She gently touched my chin. "You've cut yourself shaving again. Thank God you didn't make surgery your career."

"Surgery my career?" I burst out laughing. "It was written that I wasn't going to, don't you remember?"

"Shall I ever forget? Writing a profane, libellous letter about the Professor of Surgery and his department to our best friends, at the same time as applying for a registrar post..."

"And putting them in the wrong envelopes..."

"And then going to the Regional Board to ask for your letter back. My God, it's a wonder I didn't go into premature labour." She began to laugh.

"Sir Fergus McArd."

"What?"

"McArd. Professor of Surgery. His idea of advising you on your career was to remind you that suffering is good for the soul, like a good old fashioned hymn. What a prick. And then of course the dog becoming doubly incontinent in the main corridor at the Royal on Christmas Day put the final nail in my surgical coffin."

Tanya was giggling uncontrollably by this time and I found myself doing the same. After a while we became silent, breathing rapidly with the exertion of laughing. Then Tanya asked:

"What did you say about your vocational fervour?"

"Limp. As in flaccid." I replied.

"Oh come on, Steve, that's being defeatist. You're doing what you wanted to do, you know that."

"I know. It's all this political stuff that gets me. Inept people running inept committees. I'm thinking of writing an anthem and dedicating it to these people. It'll be called 'Piss in the Path of Progress', to the tune of 'The British Grenadiers'."

"Cynicism is not going to..."

206

"I know, I know," I growled, and got off the bed. I stared at the tea on the dressing-table. It had gone cold.

"Still, it shouldn't have gone as far as this. Not with the surgery and the health centre fiasco."

Tanya shook her head. "Maybe not. But what does it amount to? It's your heart and your head which count, that's all. Concrete and glass and all that stuff doesn't matter. You have to rise above it, not get buried underneath it."

I turned and stared at her. "You know, of all the many reasons why I married you – and I thank Christ I did – one of them is that I think you help me keep my sanity. But above all else I love you, you . . ."

I dived full length onto the sheets and we rolled about laughing and tangling over the mattress like a couple from a post-war French bedroom farce. My carotid pulse felt as if it was going to blow the top off my skull as I tried to tear off my tie, and I turned my head to one side to get some air, in time to see our eldest son standing wide eyed at the doorway, his hands and face smeared dark with soot.

"Oh God," I groaned. My whole body sagged and my head dropped onto Tanya's breasts.

"What is it, son?" I mumbled from that soft, warm, wonderful place. "Tell Daddy."

Tanya turned, pushed me to one side and looked towards Carl who shifted from one foot to another, glancing every now and again out onto the landing.

"Our Stacey's found a big box."

"What has he done with it, sunshine?" asked Tanya apprehensively.

"He set fire to it with the magnifying glass by an accident." His eyes were wide and he kept glancing out of the door. I rolled off the bed and straightened my tie.

"Cardboard box, was it?" I asked.

"Mmm," he nodded nervously. "That one by the fence . . ."

Tanya jumped out of bed and I raced downstairs four at a time. I got outside in time to see a section of the fence alight and Stacey standing a long way off sobbing with fright. I soon put out the fire and consoled him, then we went indoors to comfort and talk to them. They listened in shocked silence.

I looked at the railway-station clock which hung in the kitchen, and hurriedly kissed Tanya. She smiled and we hugged tightly by the door.

"Great start to the day," I said.

"Nothing's perfect," she replied, straightening my tie. "See you later."

"Mmm. Not half."

As I drove to the surgery I wondered grimly if the patients would take any notice of the "Emergencies Only" request which had been pinned up on the entrance door. Probably not.

When I arrived my worst fears were realised. It was eight forty-five and the waiting room already contained about twenty people, most of whom were familiar faces and in the pink of condition.

I smiled grimly as I picked up the pile of case-notes on my desk, and looked at the time. I would have to work fast, very fast. The removal men were due in just over an hour and they would want to shift everything as quickly as possible.

I summoned in the first patient and for the next hour I went flat out. I looked into ears and down throats, examined abdomens, calmed harrassed women, reassured old ladies, listened to infants' chests, removed sutures and gave injections. Then at ten o'clock Anne, the senior receptionist, came in with another stack of record cards, signifying that the waiting room was still packed out. Just after ten a large vehicle drew up to the surgery and out climbed two burly figures in overalls, flat caps and large boots. They made their way through the waiting room and into the reception office. I got up and introduced myself.

"There may be a bit of a delay, I'm afraid," I said apologetically. "I've still got quite a few patients to attend to yet." The two men grinned and lit up cigarettes.

"You mean that crowd in there, doc?" one of them said, stuffing his cigarettes and matches into the top pocket of his overalls. He screwed his eyes up and coughed until the veins stood out on his neck and forehead. "They look all right to me. Thought they were all waiting for a coach to take 'em to the seaside. Anyway, don't worry about that, squire. You just carry on, you know, snatchin' 'em from the jaws of death, so to speak – and Tommy and me'll just shift a few things quietly like so as not to disturb anybody." He winked at his mate. I shrugged and told them to carry on. I went back into the consulting room, but a few moments later the waiting room erupted into a cacophony of bangs, crashes, scraping chairs and shuffling feet, interspersed with the loud, ebullient voices of the removal men. And then, there was silence.

Anne walked into the consulting room, shaking her head and smiling quietly. She picked up the record cards from his desk.

"You won't be needing these any more. Not this morning, anyway," she said, and turned to go.

"Why is that?" I asked. "You don't mean to say that those two – "

She nodded. "Yes. They've not only cleared the furniture out of the waiting room – they've cleared the patients out as well. See for yourself."

I went down the short corridor and opened the door to the waiting room. I couldn't help laughing, for the room was completely empty. I stepped through the outer doorway expecting to see a resentful huddle of patients in the drive outside, but the only people around were the two removal men who were bundling furniture and equipment into their large truck. One of them spotted me and jumped off the tailboard. He wiped his hands on his overalls and grinned.

"Done yer a good turn there, doctor," he said, taking his cap off and wiping his brow. His hair was matted with perspiration.

"Yes," I said smiling. "You certainly did. You must come more often."

The man carefully removed a bent cigarette end from the lining of his cap and lit it with difficulty.

"Makes yer think, though, dunnit?" he said, shaking his head slowly. "I say, it makes yer think – makes yer wonder why they come in the first place seein' as 'ow they all buggered off sharpish the minute we started tekkin' them chairs away. Can't have bin much wrong with any of 'em really, doctor."

I shrugged. "We'll never know now, will we?"

The other man sniffed. "I think they only come because you're 'ere. Same as mountaineers, like," he said thoughtfully.

I stared at him. "I'm not sure I follow..."

"Well," he said, lighting up another cigarette, "mountaineers climb mountains because they're *there*. And these people – yer patients, like – come to see you because you're *'ere*. Well, I mean, it's the same *thing*, innit?"

The opaque logic of the man's argument was beyond me. "I suppose you've got a point there – somewhere," I said slowly. I looked at my watch. "Well, I expect you'll be wanting to clear the rest of the premises now, won't you? We have to set it all up again in the other place when you've taken it across." I turned and walked slowly back through the waiting room and into my consulting room to sort out a few things ready to put into the truck. I told Anne to go across and join Molly so that they could receive all the stuff and start setting up shop in the temporary surgery. I was glad to get away from the surgery now that it was being dismantled from the inside, for as all the worn, friendly bits of furniture were being removed, the interior of the old Victorian building was gradually exposed as it really was – a dry carcass smelling of dust and decaying linoleum.

I went back to the car and noticed a young woman in her early twenties hovering nearby. She was dressed in crumpled, dirty jeans and wore a torn anorak which was several sizes too large. On her feet she had a pair of frayed grey tennis shoes. The whole appearance suggested that she had clothed herself from a local jumble-sale. She kept looking furtively over her shoulder as if she was being followed and it wasn't until she turned and looked towards me that I recognised her face. My heart sank, for it was Maureen Bailey. Maureen was an unmarried twenty-two year-old who attended the surgery at least once a fortnight, and in all the countless times she had attended with tiredness, no interest in things, aches and pains and so on, the only thing I had managed to establish was that she lived with her father who was very strict and rarely let her out on her own for more than a few hours at a time. Each time I had tried to probe further she had shrugged her narrow shoulders and stared at the floor in silence. Very early on in the series of consultations I gathered that she was suffering from depression. I had diagnosed this, not in a conventional way, but from the simple fact that as soon as she entered the consulting-room she made me feel profoundly depressed. In fact the girl seemed to radiate depression, affecting everything around her. Whenever she came in I felt a heavy weight press on the back of my head, my shoulders sagged and my blood seemed to congeal, turning my limbs to lead. Even the room seemed to go darker. In spite of my many offers of help she persisted in pressing me for simple tonics to "give her energy".

Today, I noticed a significant change in her facial appearance. Instead of the usual heavy-lidded, dead-pan expressionless features, she had an animated, fearful look and her eyes were wide with terror. I put my bag in the car and asked her what the trouble was. She swallowed and looked at me with a pleading, desperate expression.

"It's me dad, doctor. He's cracked up, definitely. He's..." She stammered and burst into tears. "He'll kill me if he finds I've come to see you."

"Now hang on a minute, Maureen," I said calmly. "What...?"

"He's gone berserk!" she blurted. "Something'll have to be done now. He's breaking the house up. Has been for weeks. The floor boards, doors – you name it. He's using them for firewood. I – I can't go on like this. And he's talking funny as well, and very violent, he is."

"Violent?"

"Oh yes," said Maureen, her voice quavering hysterically. "He threatened me with an axe this morning. How I got away I'll never know, doctor – can you go round and send him away? I can't go back there – not now."

I took a deep breath. "It sounds as if your dad's got a problem, all right. I'll see what I can do. An *axe*, you say? Hmm ... tell you what. You go to the police station – you've no relatives round here have you? No – well, go to the police station. Tell them I sent you. I'll ring them up and explain what's happened. I'm sure they'll make you a cup of tea while I sort things out. I'll probably have to ask them for a helping hand anyway. If he's running amok with an axe and I go on my own it would put him at a slight advantage, wouldn't it?"

She nodded balefully. "All right, doctor. I'll go to the police station. You will get him away, won't you?"

I nodded confidently, but felt uneasy. An axe! I wondered if she was kidding, but a last look at her terrified gaunt face convinced me that she wasn't. I went back to the surgery and rang the duty social worker. Fortunately the one on duty lived locally so it would be only a few minutes before he got to the house. I didn't know him at all. He sounded young, enthusiastic and inexperienced which seemed a deadly mixture for this particular job. However, he seemed to know about the Mental Health Act and would remember to bring the relevant forms to be signed if – as seemed very likely – the patient would not agree to go into hospital voluntarily. We arranged to meet at the patient's house in ten minutes. I rang up the police and the ambulance station to warn them that I was going to have a quick preliminary look round at the house before I started all the emergency services screaming into action.

The busy streets were thronging with people. Mothers hurried in and out of the shops buying in food for the weekend as fast as they could, so that they could spend as much time as possible, later, lounging in the warm sun in their back gardens. Fathers scowled with boredom and displeasure as they pushed trolleys containing hot, restless infants, while older little boys sulked irritably as they were dragged in and out of shops to be measured for sandals and tee-shirts and all the other things which seemed suddenly to be necessary when the days were hot and sunny. As always at this time on a Saturday morning, the traffic was dense, and where the four roads met at the traffic lights the air was heavy with exhaust fumes and the smell of warm tar on the road.

I weaved my way through the junction and down Hiley Road, then, about a quarter of a mile further on, took a right turn into Bents Road just in time to see two figures grappling with each other outside number forty-eight. The larger of the two, a great bear of a man with shoulder-length hair and a thick tangle of beard, picked his opponent up by the lapels and the crotch and threw him bodily over the low garden wall. He landed heavily on the pavement. As I drew up alongside, the victor mouthed a few obscenities through his beard before disappearing inside the house.

I got out of the car and helped the trembling, white-faced figure up off the pavement.

"Thanks. Thanks very much. Are, er, you Doctor Rushton?" he said in a hoarse high-pitched voice. He picked up his brief-case and as his breath panted in and out of his mouth little white flecks of foam formed in the corners.

I nodded. "You'll be...?"

"Marcus Grills. Social Worker." We shook hands and Grills brushed the dust off his trousers.

"Ah yes," I said, smiling. "Just having a meaningful one to one confrontation situation with a client, I see."

Grills laughed grimly. "My client just so happens to be your patient, Maurice Bailey."

"Yes, I gathered that."

"You were quite a time arriving," said Grills. He mopped a spot of blood from his upper lip and looked at his handkerchief apprehensively. "So I thought I'd, er, have a chat with him before you came."

"I don't think he's amenable to a chat at the moment," I muttered. "He's got an axe for one thing – or so his daughter says. Personally I would be inclined to believe her after what I've just seen."

Grills went even paler. "An axe? Good grief. Shouldn't we...?"

"Get some reinforcements? Yes. I should get in your car, if I were you, and drive round the corner out of sight. I'll get a couple of policemen, the ambulance and that sort of thing, then I'll come back."

"I hope you've got something in your bag to put him out," said Grills, glancing back at the house apprehensively.

"Well, I haven't got any tear gas but there's a couple of things in my bag that'll settle him down a bit. That's if we manage to get near enough without being sliced down the middle with a cleaver." I got back in my car and went to the police-station. The desk sergeant nodded but said nothing as I outlined my requirements. He painstakingly continued putting a large poster on the wall above the counter. On the poster were the words "Have You Seen This Man?" in bold type, which underneath was the usual identikit portrait of something only vaguely humanoid, with wire brush hair, bat-ears, slit eyes about one centimetre apart and a thin, cruel mouth about half a centimetre from the point of a ridiculously long chin. It looked for all the world like the sort of portrait drawn by a seven-year-old when asked by his school teacher to draw a picture of "daddy".

"Martians landed, have they?" I said, nodding at the poster. The sergeant grinned.

"Aye. Summat like that... Now then, doctor, about your patient – the one with the axe. His daughter's through here with a WPC having a cup of tea. Did you want a word with her?"

I shook my head "No – not until I've sorted something out. What can you spare to give me some back-up?"

"Only got two available. They're good lads, though. Plenty of beef on em."

"Good. We'll need it." I lifted the phone and ordered an ambulance round to the house, to be parked round the corner out of sight and in position in ten minutes. Then I rang Millersdale and told them I was sending the patient. I wasn't going to take any drivel about them having no beds and I put the phone down as soon as I had told them the patient's name.

"Right, doctor," said the sergeant, yawning and stretching his arms above his head. "I'll send these two lads in straight away. They'll be there by the time you get back to the house."

I drove round to Mary Street where Molly was supervising the arrival of the equipment in the temporary surgery. She was dashing around amongst a pile of cabinets and chairs, orchestrating a messy gaggle of joiners, plumbers and removal men while Anne was quietly sorting a lot of loose papers and forms which were blowing about. Molly's slacks and sweater were dusty and grimy and, by her flushed appearance and the light film of perspiration on her forehead, it looked as if she had been mandhandling some of the heavy furniture herself. I felt guilty that I wasn't able to help, but when I explained why Molly shrugged and waved me off.

I got to Maurice Bailey's house and took my bag from the back seat, found a syringe and some large needles and drew up two hundred milligrams of Largactil as well as fifteen milligrams of Serenace. That should do for a start. I got out of the car and was joined by two young, heavy policemen with the inevitable cackling two-way radios. I briefly explained what I wanted them to do, and as I walked to the door with the loaded syringe behind my back I caught sight of Grills lurking about up the street. I signalled him to join us and then knocked on the door.

For a moment there was silence and I knocked again. From inside there was a scuffling and scraping noise, then a gruff voice snarled, "Oo izzit?"

"It's the doctor, Mr. Bailey."

"Don't need no bleedin' doctor," said the voice within.

"It's about your Maureen. I want to see you about your Maureen," I lied. I held my breath. A bolt slid noisily away from the door and the two policemen and Grills stepped sideways out of sight. I suddenly felt extremely vulnerable, thinking that even with a syringe full of Largactil and Serenace I would be no match for Maurice Bailey if he got nasty with his axe. Maybe he had a sawn off shotgun, too. I had a sudden vivid picture of Tanya sitting with the children who were all tearful as she said: "Daddy won't be coming home from the surgery ever again." I wanted to run. When the door opened I gaped inside and for a moment my fear was replaced by astonishment. I thought at first that Maurice

215

Bailey was a four-foot dwarf – either that or the man was on his knees – for his grotesque bearded face only came up to my chest. And then I realised that all the floor boards and spans in the hallway were missing and that Bailey was actually standing in the rubble and dust of the sub-floor two and a half feet below.

"Maureen?" Bailey snarled, glowering menacingly at me. I stepped back half a pace and took a tighter grip of the syringe behind my back. "Maureen's *gone*. And for that, she'll have to be *sacrificed*!" As he said the last word I caught a glimpse of atrocious yellow teeth and smelled putrid breath.

"Look, Mr. Bailey – "

"Don't 'look' me!" shouted Bailey. His eyes glared maniacally and saliva dribbled over his lower lip onto his grey, nicotine-stained beard. "You'll all have to be eliminated eventually!" He put up his hand and pointed at my head. The sudden movement made me flinch. "God has given me the power of jurisdiction over – " He stopped dead in his tracks as one of the officer's two way radios squawked with an incoming message. The officer, who was pressed against the wall of the house out of sight of Bailey, opened his eyes wide and his lower jaw dropped in dismay. He threw both hands onto his top pocket to smother the noise, looking as if he had been shot in the chest. Bailey poked his head round the door and saw them. He roared an animal roar, then turned to pick up a lump of rubble at his feet. On the assumption that he was about to throw a rock at someone rather than set about tidying up his house, I stepped smartly to one side and the two policemen dived through the door, plumeting into the sub-floor on top of the snarling Maurice Bailey. I climbed in after them while Grills stood, transfixed, near the garden wall.

Holding the syringe in my outstretched arm I crawled gingerly on all fours to the mauling, grappling mass of arms and legs that was Bailey and the two police officers, nearly being kicked in the head as they rolled from side to side like a harpooned octopus. A movement at the open door made me turn my head back just in time to see an ambulance attendant dive full length towards us and I couldn't move fast enough to prevent most of his weight landing on me and flattening me on the concrete floor, knocking the breath out of my lungs. I raised my head just long enough to see three pairs of dark-flannelled thighs spinning towards me and I shut my eyes and plunged the needle home, emptying the syringe through the trousers and into the thigh muscle. There was a shriek and in the corner of my vision I saw Bailey's head jerk back suddenly and hit the concrete floor with a dull thud. He lay still, and the rest of us rolled away slowly and picked ourselves up. The air was full of panting noises and the smell of sweat.

"Nice uppercut that was, Norman," gasped one officer.

"Aye," said the other, rubbing his left buttock vigorously and at the same time glancing at the rubble-strewn floor. "Tell you what, though – I must have rolled onto a bloody big nail round here. Stings like buggery."

I stared at him as he lowered his pants. I glanced at Bailey who lay quite still, breathing heavily and mumbling snatches of the Old Testament, then I looked back at the officer's left buttock. There was a nice, neat, blood-stained puncture mark whose appearance was quite unmistakable. I looked down at the empty syringe in my hand, and my mouth went dry.

"Oh, shit," I said slowly. The officer pulled his pants up and blinked.

"What's up doctor? You don't look very happy."

"No, I'm not. Neither will you in a few minutes. While you were dealing Maurice Bailey an uppercut, I ... in the confusion of the ... I emptied the syringe into your backside instead of his."

He went pale and leaned against the wall. "Oh great. Thanks, doc. What does that stuff do? I'm supposed to be going to a dinner dance tonight."

Well, he wasn't going to any dinner dance, that was for sure. Two hundred milligrams of Largactil and he'd be groggy for hours. He sat down and was blinking and shaking his head even then at the thought of it. There was nothing I could do about it now, so I asked the ambulance attendant to contact his HQ on the radio in order to get another vehicle. He would have to go to Wishton for observation. They took

Maurice Bailey away, still mumbling and groaning and with a large bump on his head. Grills followed them in his own car to Millersfield with all the necessary paperwork. By the time the other ambulance arrived the officer was slumped against one of the interior walls, snoring his head off. My God, what a shambles.

After they had all gone I had a quick look round. The place was incredible. All the wallpaper had been torn off the walls right down to the plaster, the bannister rails had been torn out and even some of the stair panels were missing. Through the door into the kitchen I could see that most of the floor boards were still intact but the carpets and linoleum had been rolled back and cut up into small pieces and scattered into corners. There was very little in the way of furniture. Just a couple of small chairs and a table. In the fireplace a huge pile of wood ash, cigarette ends, tin-cans and spent matches spilled over the brown-tiled hearth onto the floor. Most of the floor boards by the look of it had ended up there, on the fire. I shook my head in amazement. How could Maureen Bailey have lived amongst all this? What was more to the point – how could it be that she had never given the slightest clue, during all her many sullen consultations with me, that she lived like this? Or maybe she *had* given me clues but I had not picked them up.

# 23

I drove off back through the centre of the town and it was, if anything, busier than when I had passed through earlier. The strangeness of the Bailey episode contrasted sharply with the bustling, purposeful normality of the people of Overton as they scurried around from shop to shop buying sliced loaves and frozen chickens, but the thought of that demented man, his appalling house and his pathetic, unhappy daughter, hung around me like a shroud, leaving me in a curious way detached from the sounds of the busy streets and crowded pavements. Looking out of the car window was like watching the picture on a silent TV screen in the corner of a crowded, noisy room: the images were flickering, transient, incomprehensible, dream-like. I laughed to myself. Maybe it *was* a dream world, for surely only in a dream world could the outrageous behaviour of Maurice Bailey go so long unnoticed by anyone – including his neighbours!

I cleared my mind as I turned into Mary Street and pulled up the car with the near-side wheels running onto the narrow flagged kerb. The wooden-framed doorway of the surgery was wide open, and although all the furniture and filing cabinets had been taken inside and the removal truck had gone, I could see plenty of movement within. I got out of the car slowly and placed my bag on the bonnet. As I did so I heard from close by a sound that was as familiar and evocative as it was unexpected and I turned round to locate it. From the back window of a high attic bedroom in an adjacent building, came the thin, metallic sound of an alto saxophone running up a few minor scales and diminished thirds. It was not well played: the tone was wobbly, with a reedy edge, and the articulation was halting, but it had the uncomplicated innocence of a clean, fresh stream and it made me smile. I leaned against the car as the notes came floating down from the window and across an untidy back yard, and I thought of student days in Edinburgh. I thought of the Roost, at the east end of Prince's Street — that dark crowded place where we had played every week until fire regulations had closed it down. And Ainslie Place where we had played more or less non-stop for two days before falling over from booze and exhaustion. I thought about those rare moments when, on a good night, each had played to the very limits of his ability and in doing so had catalysed the other, creating a collective exhilaration, like being on a roller coaster. And those other times: the disastrous Mickey Mouse gigs, such as the McVitie's Biscuit Factory Annual Knees-up where Pitkiethlie had played half a dozen ferocious choruses on the chords of "I Got Rhythm" before throwing up into one of the potted palms on the stand. It was one of the many places where we were never asked to play again. I thought of Stuart Robertson: a shy, talented individual who never cursed, even when faced with the most appalling pianos to play, and who, when he played, winced and drew his hands away from the keys as if he were playing a bed of thorns. Mike — sizzling and crackling like a slow-burning fuse behind his drums and Avedis Zildjan cymbals which he cared for more than anything else in the world. Max: his hair over his eyes as he stooped over his bass, occasionally throwing his head back and guffawing with pleasure but never missing a beat. And Dave — whose dry, muscular tenor sax playing held us together with its discipline and authority.

Things were simpler in those days, all right. I laughed quietly to myself as the hidden alto player in the attic bedroom across the yard falteringly began to play the first few bars of "Body and Soul". Just wait until he gets to the middle eight...

"Are you going to join us, or what?"

I turned quickly round out and saw Molly standing nearby humping an armful of empty cardboard boxes onto the pavement.

"Yes, sure," I mumbled. I followed her inside. The place

220

seemed to have shrunk by half now that it was full of our equipment and furniture. I stepped over piles of books, reagent bottles and loose wires to enter the larger of the two consulting rooms off the entrance corridor. Molly had already got the room well laid out – in fact it was all ready for action. The sphygmomanoter, tendon hammer, anriscope and telephone were all within reach, and she had even dug out and arranged a box of multi-coloured Kleenex tissues on the corner of the heavy oak desk. I looked round enviously.

"Nice. You're all set up, I see."

Molly pulled a whisp of sweat-damp hair away from her forehead. "Well we haven't exactly been standing around doing nothing while you've been roaming round the town," she said grinning. "We left your room. We weren't sure how you wanted it arranged. It's a funny shape."

I went through into the other consulting room and looked round. It was an impractical L-shaped room and much smaller than Molly's. It's only saving grace was a large window admitting daylight on one wall. A basin had been plumbed into one corner, and my desk, examination couch and other equipment were heaped in the middle of the carpeted floor, making it impossible to move.

I began to shove some of the larger articles around, trying various combinations in order to make it possible for me to get up from my desk without climbing over the chair; then I put down a stack of books on the desk top but they toppled over, spilling over the desk onto the floor. There was no room to put a shelf up for the books without danger of lacerating my scalp on it. They would have to stay in their cardboard boxes, probably until the time came to move out of this place. I picked up a couple of larger text-books and ran my hands over the covers. They still had the durable green dust-cover which had been so fastidiously sellotaped over in that funereal place where I had bought them fifteen years before – from off the dark shelves of Donald Ferrier, Teviot Place, Edinburgh: the chapel of rest of many a soporific tome. I gently brushed the turned-up ends of the book shop's white adhesive sticker on the cover with my fingers and murmured,

"That's lovely, serrr..." in a passable Edinburgh accent. That's what they always said at Ferrier's when you handed them a book over the counter that you had picked out. And as the money came reluctantly out of the back pocket the assistant would flutter his eyes, put his hands together and smile an undertaker's smile and breath softly, "Ooooh. That's really lovely, serrr," once more. All the same, I loved those books. I felt ashamed that they should now be relegated to a torn cardboard box which had previously contained one gross of Farley's Rusks or whatever, and that they should be shoved ignominiously beneath the examination couch to gather dust for the next year or so. I only hoped that the clean, oppressive walls of this new dungeon in which we now found ourselves would not have the same effect on my brain. The space and the facilities which we were able to offer the patients were now so paltry that it was going to need a tremendous amount of will-power and self-discipline in order to avoid sinking into a pre-comatose sloth, anaesthetised by disillusionment and by the breath of bureaucracy.

While I was staring round the room the phone began to ring. The rest of the building was silent and I realised that Anne and Molly must have gone out, so I rummaged under a pile of boxes and equipment and picked up the extension. It was Wishton Ambulance Control. They'd heard about the police officer whom I'd accidentally injected with Largactil: they thought they'd make my day and let me know that Millersdale would not let Maurice Bailey out of the ambulance until they had received the section 29 papers from Grills – and he'd been half an hour late because he'd got lost somewhere this side of Warrington. Meanwhile Maurice had come round and in the scuffle which followed, one of the ambulance crew had injured his leg, suspected fracture of the tibia; didn't you wish you'd never got out of bed today, doctor?

I put down the phone and my stomach turned over. I made a mental note to have a word with Maureen Bailey and get the social services to help her out, and also to check on the police officer whom I'd shot full of Largactil. I was so wrapped in thought that I was at first unaware that a woman was standing at the door of the consulting room, wagging her finger at me and carping furiously about not being able to get her repeat prescription for her sleeping pills. I stared at her and vaguely recognised her as someone I had known from my schooldays. She had looked middle-aged even in her teens, as I recall. She jerked her shoulders sharply upwards and gave a harsh bovine cough, then turned to go out. I heard her mutter something about reporting me to the BMA. I couldn't help smiling. What she imagined would happen then, I could not guess. Maybe a posse of distinguished grey-haired physicians would arrive from Tavistock Square and beat me senseless with rolled-up copies of the *British Medical Journal*. Who knows.

"I sorry to bother you, dogtor."

I looked up at the sound of the heavily accented voice of Mrs. Ludnika Wilcinska. She stood in the doorway smiling apologetically and with her trunk tilted back slightly to balance the weight of the surviving twin baby that she held in her arms. I calculated that it was about ten months since she had given birth to her twins and since then I had not seen her very much at all. I apologised for the mess and asked her to come in. She picked her way carefully over the books and journals, looking down at the floor as she came into the room. She hesitated for a moment.

"You have too many problems – maybe I go now, I come back another time," she said, smiling brightly. Too brightly.

"Well, things are a bit of a mess at the moment ... What's the trouble?"

"The baby. She got pretty bad nappy rash. I don't know – I pretty careful wid everything. Anyway ... you see, dogtor." She looked round for somewhere to put the baby. I stepped forward and moved a mound of books and prescription pads from the couch onto the floor. She put the baby down and began to peel off layer after layer of delicately-sewn cotton garments, eventually undoing the nappy. The baby made tiny sounds and looked all round the ceiling, unconcerned with what was going on. I examined the child and found a very modest nappy rash. I grovelled around for a prescription pad and sat down at my desk, but instead of writing out a prescription I watched Mrs. Wilcinska slowly dressing the baby. Her mouth twitched and her eyes were moist with tears. She sniffed and lowered her head so that I could not see her face, and I knew that she had not come about her baby's nappy rash. It would have taken a lobotomised gorilla not to have gathered that.

"Why don't you sit down when you've finished dressing the baby?" I asked in a matter of fact voice. She looked up briefly, showing a grey face with red, hollow eyes. She sucked in her cheeks and nodded quickly, then bent her head again.

After she had finished, she picked up the baby very gently and whispered in its ear, brushing the soft down of the ear lobes with her lips. She turned and stepped gingerly over the cluttered floor towards the only other chair in the room and I jumped up again to clear the surface of the chair of specimen bottles, disposable gloves and syringes, stumbling over a copy of Davidson's *Medicine* as I climbed back into my own chair. We sat face to face across the small untidy room, but as I looked at her, the room and its randomly-strewn contents did not seem to matter very much. In fact they did not seem to matter at all.

"I should have had two babies here now. One baby in each arm, hey, dogtor? What you say?" She looked down at the surviving twin and smiled, the tears running down her face and dropping onto the back of her hand as she fidgeted with the baby's smock. I pushed a few books under the desk to make room for my feet and shifted about in the chair. I leaned back and made myself more comfortable, for I knew that I would be sitting there for quite a while.